WILLING

Connal slid his arms around her at that and pulled her closer, kissing her deeply, letting his tongue and hers slide together in slow passion.

This was heaven and hell in one neat little package called Bethany Doyle Delaney. Surely he would lose himself, his mind, his soul, everything, in the pursuit of loving her as completely as his body cried out for him to do.

But it was the little moan she gave as he edged her lips with his tongue, that unbidden sound that thrust him over the edge.

He drew her back into his arms to feel the whole length of her against him. Bare skin to bare skin. Luscious softness to hardened muscle.

"Dear God I want you."

BOOK YOUR PLACE ON OUR WEBSITE AND MAKE THE READING CONNECTION!

We've created a customized website just for our very special readers, where you can get the inside scoop on everything that's going on with Zebra, Pinnacle and Kensington books.

When you come online, you'll have the exciting opportunity to:

- View covers of upcoming books
- Read sample chapters
- Learn about our future publishing schedule (listed by publication month *and author*)
- Find out when your favorite authors will be visiting a city near you
- Search for and order backlist books from our online catalog
- Check out author bios and background information
- Send e-mail to your favorite authors
- Meet the Kensington staff online
- Join us in weekly chats with authors, readers and other guests
- Get writing guidelines
- AND MUCH MORE!

Visit our website at
http://www.kensingtonbooks.com

The Wicked One

ELIZABETH KEYS

ZEBRA BOOKS
Kensington Publishing Corp.
www.kensingtonbooks.com

*To all hearts who yearn
for the isle of magic and myth . . .*
Go mbeannaí Dia duit!

Prologue

County Kildare, Ireland
1844

"You have killed your cousin."

Killed? The word pierced the pain-filled haze suffocating Connal Delaney.

No. Connal struggled to deny the charge despite the fiery weight pushing against his chest. He could not force out so much as a peep. It took all his strength just to draw breath, pitifully shallow and harsh as the effort turned out to be.

"Now, what's to be done with you?" Uncle Brennan's disgust sounded far away.

Connal's thoughts swirled. Bile lay bitter against his tongue. Damnation, if only he could force his eyes open. His struggles led to naught save exhaustion.

He was cold, so very cold, despite the weight of the coverlets atop him. What had happened? What was happening?

One certainty sluiced through him, colder than reality. The taste in his mouth wasn't bile.

It was blood.

Footsteps crossed to the bed, boot heels clicking on floorboards to join Uncle Brennan's vigil.

Connal tried again to open his eyes, to twitch or utter a sound and let them know he was still with them. Nothing stirred save the faint rattle of death in his chest.

"He was mad with anger—"

Finn.

"—looking to lay events at my feet as he always does."

True to his nature, the man he'd considered more brother than cousin tried to slither out from under his father's condemnation by shifting the blame.

"What were you thinking in the first place, dueling with Connal?" Uncle Brennan's rough tone cut through his son's excuses. "It was madness to agree. He is a far better shot than you, Finn, angry or not. Now I have lost you both to this folly."

Folly? Folly. The duel. *Rosleen.*

Icy memories froze Connal's heart as fragmented events clicked into place. Rose was dead. Betrayed by her innocence. Betrayed by her trust in her betrothed.

He'd failed her in life and in vengeance. The realization pushed him farther into the darkness.

"It was an accident," Finn protested. "His grief made him lose count. My pistol misfired—"

"Liar." The sound of Jack's voice warmed Connal the tiniest bit as he cut Finn off. One friend in the room.

"Enough!" Uncle Brennan barked. "We must make the best of this sorrowful muddle. Jack, go down and see if that was Dr. Ryan's horse on the drive. If saving Connal is out of the question, he must do everything he can to at least prolong the lad's life."

"He was shot in the back." Jack's voice shook with rage.

Never one to back away from a brawl, *Black* Jack Branigan could only be spoiling to start one after this evening's work. "Family standing will not allow you to sweep away what Finn's done this time, Brennan Delaney. There is more than one family involved. Little Rosie's—"

"We can argue this out later. Connal needs the doctor now." Uncle Brennan's urgency broke through Jack's tirade. "Get Ryan up here and see he has all he needs."

Any other time, Connal would have tried to step in the middle of the argument brewing between his mother's brother and his father's. But at this point he could barely feel his limbs; barely feel anything save searing regret and surging pain. His days of intervening between them were done.

"This isn't over." Jack stomped across the floor and slammed the door with a bang almost loud enough to rouse the dead.

Almost.

"Da—" Finn sounded closer, tense and hesitant.

Connal could practically taste his cousin's panic. Mixed with the blood coating his tongue, it made a bitter elixir.

"There is no time for your pretenses." The hard edge in Uncle Brennan's voice cut his son off. "I will deal with the Careys. And Jack Branigan, too. You must get far from here. And quickly. The Lord alone knows how long your cousin will last. Despite everything, I will not have my son swing for murder."

Connal willed himself to snatch his hand away as Finn's sweat-soaked fingers clasped his. Nothing moved, as if rigor mortis had set in already.

"Rosleen's death. Her child. Now Connal."

Finn's tone was hushed, choked—the one he used whenever he sought to expiate guilt. No doubt his head was bowed, his shoulders slumped as he knelt by the bed holding the hand of the man he'd slain—the very picture of abject contrition.

Another contrite face floated in Connal's thoughts. Poor, sweet Rose. How different things might be if he'd recognized the depth of her desperation. If he'd given her the comfort she sought, the protection she deserved when she'd finally summoned the courage to make her confession. Guilt savaged him, it was too late for all of them.

"Connal will shoulder your share of the blame. I will see to that." Uncle Brennan's hand brushed Connal's, impersonal and quick, as he pried Finn away. "At least he'll be spared the shame of living in disgrace.

"Take this purse, Finn. You must be on your way while Jack and the doctor are busy here. Leave on the first ship outbound from Dublin. Get yourself to America. I have included the direction of an old friend who will help you there. No one here must know where you are until I contact you and tell you it is safe to return."

"I'm sorry, Connal I am truly sorry." The words Finn spoke so many times during their childhood would now follow Connal to his grave.

The chamber door clicked shut, leaving him utterly alone as he surrendered himself to icy darkness and the welcome embrace of death.

Chapter One

County Kildare, Ireland
1855

The Wicked One.

The reputation he'd been saddled with for the past decade clawed at Connal Delaney with fresh bitterness as he watched the sun fade behind the indigo and green of Kildare's distant hills.

He took a deep breath. *The Wicked One, and now, the Only One.*

His lips twisted over both labels. The scattered pages behind him on his desk delivered neither the enlightenment nor the satisfaction he had anticipated when he began his enquiries so many years ago. Instead, they contained only the barest of facts, a few tattered news clippings and a surprising sense of loss.

He took another swallow from the glass he'd kept filled since his solicitor's boy delivered the packet from Boston, and continued to stare across the paddocks and meadows of Glenmeade Stables. His home. His future.

His alone.

The heavy tread of boots in the hall reminded him he was not quite alone. A moment later, Jack flung open the study door and strode into the office without knocking.

"How went things with the farrier?" Connal asked, not turning away from the window casement and the soothing colors in the distance. He was not ready to face the last remaining relative he possessed in this world. Not yet.

"Well enough, though I expected ye ta be through with the accounts and down ta see fer yerself at some point before he departed."

The chink of crystal on glass signaled Jack's pouring his own dram from the decanter. Connal smiled, though his lips felt stiff. Jack had never been one to stand on social niceties like knocking or waiting to be offered refreshment. Honesty, brashness, those were the trademark characteristics Connal counted on from his mother's brother. And loyalty, that most of all. A rare familial commodity in his experience.

"I can see ye've yet to finish the accounts to any aegree," Jack observed tartly.

The ledgers Connal had been so eager to reconcile were still spread on the broad desk behind him. They had long ago left his thoughts. He shook his head. He felt like a year had passed since he'd risen this morning.

"What's this about big news from yer solicitor?" his uncle continued in a falsely jovial tone after a few moments of joint silence. "It couldn't be too big, I said to Jenna O'Toole, else ye'd have sent fer me down in the stables."

Connal took another sip from the tumbler he clutched and continued staring into the distant shadows of his homeland. The crosscuts in the glass dug into his fingers as the burn of the whiskey registered through the numbness still encasing him. He doubted his housekeeper had any true idea of just how big the news he'd received had been. Questions answered at long last. Ambition realized. Where was the satisfaction he'd anticipated all these years?

"That letter's from America, lad?" Jack's question was less inquiry than statement of fact. "About Finn. *From* Finn?"

Connal nodded, but held his peace.

"I've more than a few words I'd like to say to him." Jack dropped all pretense of casual interest. "And a visit he'll not soon forget. Ye cannot allow him to assert his claims here. He gave them up the day he cuckolded ye and shot ye in the back. After hanging ye with the stench of his deeds all these years even he cannot possess the brass to try and rob ye of the fruits of yer labors."

"Nay," Connal shook his head, trying to clear some of the wool he'd gathered while perusing the paddocks and lawns. He turned and met his uncle's piercing gaze. More gray hairs than black covered Black Jack Branigan's temples these days, but a decade had not dimmed the fierce allegiance that shook his voice. "That is one offence he will never commit."

Connal ran a hand through his hair and blew out a long breath. There was no need to soften the news for Jack's sake. "Finn's claims are quit forever. He was shot dead by the husband of the woman whose bed he occupied. Several months ago. After all these years, Glenmeade is mine alone."

Silence held for the space of a dozen heartbeats.

"Praise be." Jack didn't bother to feign sorrow over the news as satisfaction glinted in his eyes. He took a long swallow of whiskey before raising it in an empty salute.

"May the Devil give his spit an extra turn fer every day ye've faced since he left ye ta shoulder the *prácás* he created." Jack sighed the words out with the reverence of a long-awaited prayer.

"It took more than one to create that mess," Connal reminded him before tossing back the dregs from his own glass. The whiskey did little to burn away the resentment and regrets still lashing him despite the passage of time.

"Stop—"

Connal waved a hand to still the hot protest forming on his uncle's lips. "I am not excusing Finn. But there were two of them trysting behind my back."

"There's plenty of blame to spread around, that's fer sure." Jack's voice tightened with indignation. "Brennan Delaney and his libelous misdealings, fer one. Heaping the blame on ye while helping his own son to escape the hangman and start a new life with a clean slate. Why ye've never so much as tried to clear yer name, I've yet to understand . . ."

"I will not fail Rosleen a second time." Connal closed his eyes and swallowed hard, leaning his head back against the casement. "Her death was an overpayment. Adultery does not need to be added to her sins."

Even after all this time, his emotions for the girl he had once planned to wed still created havoc. He could not forgive her. He could not abandon her again. He wouldn't blacken her name more to save his own. That final protection he owed her for his failures. Although the county might have the details of their story wrong, he deserved the reputation he'd been saddled with since Rose's death, if only for not protecting her from Finn's attentions.

"She made her choices, lad." Jack's voice gentled. "Ye cannot hold yerself responsible. Ye deserve better. If people knew the truth—"

"Enough, Jack. People believe what they choose." Connal cut off Jack's favorite litany. "I am the last Delaney of Glenmeade. The last there will ever be. Deserve it or not, at least my title here is finally clear. Once the papers are filed, I will be able to pursue the expansion of the Stables free of any possible impediment."

"Ye cannot mean ta take James Carey up on his offer to help ye refinance Brennan's loan? Not when ye're so nearly out from under." Jack peered at him through the thickening shadows in the study. Connal reached for the decanter and refilled both his and Jack's glasses.

"The Stables are mine to do with as I see fit, Uncle." He stoppered the decanter with a decisive clink and tipped his glass against Jack's. "The risks and the benefits will be mine to shoulder."

Jack nodded, his lips pressed in a thin line as he held his peace, then he downed the whiskey without further comment.

The weeks following the news of Finn's death passed with barely a ripple in the day-to-day routines at Glenmeade. Still, change was in the wind and Connal needed to blow away his doubts. The temptation to continue racing through the green hills and shallow valleys long into the night rose as Teagan, one of Glenmeade's finest stallions, stamped and pawed the ground beneath him.

Shadows lengthened on the dirt path ahead, matching Connal's darkened thoughts. His first meaningful act as sole owner of Glenmeade would be to sign away a good portion of it, even if it was only for a few years. A galling reality, but the payoff was too tempting to pass up. The stock he was purchasing, along with the added outbuildings to house them, would advance his breeding program several generations, and perhaps a decade sooner than he could afford on his own. The risk was surely worth the benefit. If only his misgivings did not sound so similar to the ones Jack had voiced before departing for England.

"Ye need ta be wary when something appears too easy, too good. There's a price ta be paid fer everything. Either before or after, the piper always gets his due." The old adage one of their nursery maids had lectured Finn with when he'd been caught in some mischief surfaced now from the depths. Also eerily similar to Jack's warnings.

He pulled his mount to a halt. James Carey's steadfast friendship through the years, especially after the tragedy forever linking their names, should have mitigated Jack's doubts about Connal accepting James's help in securing financial backing to expand Glenmeade's business. Still, now that he was committed, Connal found he could not quite escape a nagging feeling that the course he'd chosen held unseen pitfalls, or that events were about to spiral out of his control.

"Enough," he warned himself. The entire matter was a sensible arrangement between gentlemen. Advantageous to both Connal and the group of investors James had found to back him. The die had been cast the minute he'd accepted their offer, second-guessing himself at this juncture was fruitless. Jack was likely on his way back from England with the new herd even now.

Connal patted his mount and turned back toward Glenmeade Stables and the papers awaiting his signature.

He cantered up the lane and into the yard to find his neighbor's black mare tethered near the front entrance. "Best get this over."

Perhaps he would feel better once the deed was done. He slid from Teagan's back and tossed the reins to the stable lad who'd rushed forward to greet him. His commitment to advance Glenmeade Stables was all he had to hold on to.

A small collection of valises and trunks piled on the far side of the front portico caught his attention as he strode across the yard. Had James brought one of the principals to look over his investment? Connal slowed his steps long enough to peruse the mismatched collection of luggage. They were battered and covered with dust—not the sort of items any man of James Carey's acquaintance was likely to possess. So what were these doing here?

Jenna's earlier mutterings about mice and clearing out the storage room echoed back to Connal. Apparently she'd found lads to help her accomplish the task after all. Not surprising, considering his housekeeper's determination when she set her mind to something. These had likely moldered in some corner for too many years. He'd have to speak to her about airing such things in the front drive when she knew they were expecting a guest, even a guest she did not care for. But that could wait until after he'd dealt with James and their business.

Straightening his shoulders, Connal flung open the oak door to the Manor.

"James?" The gloom of the entrance hall swallowed his call.

The faint hum of voices coming from the drawing room opposite his study was his only answer. Good, Jenna was seeing to his guest's comfort. The difficulties of a bachelor managing both a thriving business and a household on his own needled him at times, but no decent woman would ever consent to wed him and take management of the Manor into her delicate hands. Actually, he and Jenna muddled along quite comfortably, she was more than capable of handling the few social niceties she was called upon to supply—rarely more than a full decanter and a dust-free room for him to conduct his business meetings in.

Stripping off his gloves and hat, he tossed them on the hall table he passed on his way to join them.

A dark blue velvet-trimmed cloak and traveling bonnet flung across the arm of the settee inside snagged his gaze before he cleared the drawing room doorway. Obviously not the sort of items James would wear. Traces of cinnamon and vanilla twined together to halt him just outside the entrance to what looked to be an empty room. He could have sworn the voices he'd heard had come from here.

"Thank you, sir—" A woman's voice as warm as sunlight on grass flowed through the vacant drawing room, confirming he was not imagining phantom conversations at least.

Just phantoms, it would seem, as the disembodied voice continued, "—I am quite certain I would have been unable to coax even the barest spark for another half hour at least."

Whoever was speaking was definitely not Jenna O'Toole. Her accent seemed oddly familiar, yet utterly alien at one and the same time. Smooth dips and hollows in tone and a flowing lilt gave her words softly rounded edges. Languid heat inexplicably curled through his middle.

"My pleasure entirely, I assure you." James Carey's reply confirmed their location, hidden behind a sofa on the far side of the drawing room by the fireplace. "Peat is not easily lit if one is unfamiliar with it."

Who in all Ireland did not know the difficulties lighting peat could present? And why had James brought her to today's meeting? He had not mentioned any guests when they had made their arrangements.

Caution kept Connal in the hall. He leaned forward far enough to catch sight of James straightening from a crouch by the hearth. Delicate fingers lingered in his grasp as his companion rose to stand beside him in a genteel rustle of skirts. James was not an overly tall man, but his guest barely cleared his shoulder. For a moment they were silhouetted against the fire's blaze, their features indistinguishable.

"We have little need of fires at home," she spoke

ruefully. "The whole process is something I never quite mastered. We would both be quite cold if the task were left to me."

Who was she?

Firelight danced in her auburn tresses bound in a simple chignon. Her plaid dress—blue crossed with black—though a little worse for wear, suited her nonetheless, showing off her attributes. Despite her diminutive stature, her figure proved alluring enough to warm the room without the aid of the fire. From the soft curve of her cheek to the pale skin of her throat, and across the regal set of slender shoulders he could almost feel beneath his hands, she made an attractive package.

"I am in your debt," she continued, looking up at James with a soft smile.

No gentle females had called at Glenmeade Manor in well over a decade—James was as aware of that harsh fact as he. Could she be his mistress? Connal rejected the thought out of hand. Beautiful as she might be, she hardly had the look of a plaything. There was an aura of decency, of honesty, about her he had not seen in a long time and certainly not in the kind of woman who allowed herself to be kept by any man other than her husband. So what then was she doing here with James Carey?

He'd tarried too long already pondering a mystery that would be solved as soon as introductions could be made. Whatever intentions either of them held behind this visit, whether James had lost a bet or she had accepted a dare to come and meet The Wicked One, it was time for him to greet his guests.

Connal stepped out of the shadowy hall and into

the drawing room. "Hullo, James. I see you were able to make yourself comfortable."

Damnation. Despite himself, his last word held more than a hint of censure. He'd spent too many years away from polite society to handle this with ease.

They both swiveled their heads in his direction. James lifted one brow as he released his companion's hand at last.

The gentle smile on the woman's lips for James and his gallantry died away as her gaze focused on Connal. Her mouth parted in surprise. Face-to-face with The Wicked One her shocked expression mirrored the standard response of women countywide. He might as easily have been sporting two horns and a devil's tail.

"Our host has arrived at last." James shifted his gaze from his companion to Connal and back. Awkward silence thickened the air.

"I hope I am not intruding." Connal dangled his brusque observation as more barb than apology for his lateness.

To her credit, his unknown guest did not flinch in the face of his rudeness, although her fair skin paled another shade. Her chin raised a fraction as she closed her lips. She took a deep breath and stepped forward across the figured Persian carpet, her shoulders set as though resolved to face a firing squad. "We simply were not aware of your arrival . . . Mister . . . Delaney."

Her pronunciation of his name came with a hesitance at odds with her determined advance. He was not sure if he should step back out of her way or forward to meet her. The scents of cinnamon and vanilla lanced him anew as he drew in a quick breath. He had never been so swiftly conflicted about any woman, attracted and leery at the same time.

She halted a few paces away from him and extended one small hand. She raised her gaze. "I'm . . . pleased to make your acquaintance, I—"

Her gaze met his full-on for the first time. Her eyes were a blue so pure and vivid, they robbed him of breath. Innocence, pain and fortitude mingled in their limpid depths—as though her very soul lay full open for the briefest of unguarded moments.

Shock registered in those depths, followed just as quickly by relief. Her lips quavered and she blew out a soft breath. "Your eyes are brown."

"How very observant of you, Miss—?"

He let his question dangle along with the hand she still extended.

"Missus." She pressed her lips into a fine, thin line and dropped her hand to her side. Her gaze fairly devoured his face, but she remained silent.

So, she was married.

Should he be surprised? A woman so beautiful would be a treasure any man would prize. Yet what kind of husband allowed his wife to call upon a man of Connal Delaney's reputation, even if escorted by someone of James Carey's impeccable character? His gut twisted, unless that husband was James.

"Shall I do the pretty?" A wry grin quirked James's mouth. When had he joined them on this side of the carpet?

With a small flourish James gestured toward

Connal. "I would like to introduce you to our host, Mr. Connal Delaney of Glenmeade Stables."

Turning to Connal he continued, "Connal, may I introduce you to Mrs. Delaney. Mrs. *Finn* Delaney come to visit you from America. Her hired coach deposited her fresh from Dublin just before I came up the drive."

Finn.

Mrs. Finn Delaney.

This mystery woman belonged to Finn? Blood roared at his temples. *Mrs. Finn Delaney come to visit you from America.*

Envy seared a path through the shallow remnants of the life he'd lived alone for over a decade—that he would live alone for the rest of his life, thanks to the scandal Finn created for him. There would be no wife for The Wicked One, no little Delaneys to fill Glenmeade Manor, no family to saddle with the ostracism he bore. He was condemned to a solitary life, thanks to Finn. And all the while his erstwhile cousin made a new life for himself with a beautiful wife by his side. The inequities struck like hammer blows.

Her azure gaze held steady, watching his reaction, awaiting his greeting. He should say something. Welcome her here. Welcome her to the family.

"Finn's . . . wife?" he managed, sounding daft even to his own ears. "From America."

"His widow."

Her correction held a brittle edge. She shivered and relinquished her scrutiny of him at last, turning on her heel to glide back the length of the room toward the hearth. She stood there, rubbing the arms of her cotton gown, her head bowed toward the flames.

Finn's wife. His *widow*. Still mourning his death it would seem, despite having cast off her widow's weeds far earlier than convention dictated. Unless American conventions were that much different.

Had he detected a hint of censure in her gaze as she looked away? What had she expected? What had Finn told her to expect? He needed a shot of whiskey to burn away the sudden dryness in his mouth. The dryness in his soul.

Finn's wife remained safely out of earshot as James lowered his voice and stepped closer to Connal. "This is rather unexpected, is it not? You never mentioned Finn leaving a widow. Nor the fact that she intended to visit."

"I did not know of her existence until this very moment." Connal shook his head. "The newspaper accounts of his death said nothing of a wife. At least, not *his* wife."

"Do you believe her?"

"Why would she lie?" *Could* she be lying? "What would compel a woman to travel alone all the way from America for a lie when a letter could do the same?"

"I am sure you are right." James shrugged, giving his affirmation of Connal's judgment just a tiny twist of doubt.

Another shiver shook the woman they were both studying, but she kept her rigid back to both men, ignoring them as if she wished she was anywhere but here. Why cross the ocean, then—just to introduce herself to her husband's remaining family and turn away from what she found? Had she come all this way looking for shared grief, to look for Finn in the home he had torn apart so long ago? Or could she be a bold liar, looking for some unknown gain?

"Perhaps I should leave you two to get better acquainted," James offered at a volume meant to reach her ears as well. He clapped Connal's shoulder. "Our business can be accomplished another day. The Stables are not going anywhere and the new stock has not even arrived."

Glenmeade.

James's not-so-subtle reminder struck Connal. Had she journeyed across the ocean to lay claim to Finn's portion of Glenmeade Stables? Anger flooded him. No greedy strumpet from a world away would find her fortune here at his expense. Married to his cousin or no.

"Stay." He put his hand on James's sleeve, but his gaze remained fixed on the woman by the fire. The woman who turned back to face them with a troubled look in her wide blue eyes at the mention of the Stables. Her lips parted, as if set to spill whatever tale she'd contrived. He had no desire to listen. Especially not alone. "I told Jenna you would be dining here tonight. She was planning your favorites and I would hate to disappoint her, too."

"Too?"

"Aye." Connal saw no reason to spare her by lowering his voice. "Finn's wife is about to discover she made this trip for naught. Only a male Delaney can lay claim to these lands."

Footsteps sounded in the hallway.

"Well, now. That's that. I'm ready fer some tea." A cheery voice called from the hallway behind them. "The nursery's just as I remembered, if a trifle dusty. That Jenna O'Toole and I have our lad settled in and sleeping as if he were born here. Her daughter is setting with him til one of us goes up."

Our lad? The staggering possibilities in that statement barely registered as a smiling woman, possessed of rampant red curls touched with gray, entered the drawing room. Recognition welled, followed by a flood of enough warmth to distract Connal momentarily from her simple statement, *our lad.*

"Bridget Doyle!"

Connal crossed to the doorway in two strides and scooped the buxom woman into his embrace with a whoop. "I never expected to see you again."

She squeezed him back full measure. "I'm right pleased ta see ye, too, Master Connal. Appears the news of yer demise was a tad premature when it reached us in the Carolinas."

"That's right. One of the Carolinas." Connal took a step back but kept his hands on the shoulders of the woman who had once been his salvation. "I had forgotten where you went. I only remembered that you deserted us."

Bridget had worked as nursery maid at Glenmeade the summer he had been five. During the awful months when his mother had been ill, only Bridget's cheery smile, fanciful games and stories had helped ease the gloom. Her father sent her to live with her brother in America shortly afterward, and with the rest of the local Doyles lost to the ravages of The Great Hunger, he'd all but forgotten about Bridget. Yet here she was with laugh lines around her eyes, looking a little plumper, but none the worse for wear despite the years.

"What are you doing at Glenmeade?" he asked. "And who is this lad you spoke of? Yours?"

That hope was fleeting, but he had to ask. The connection between this woman and the one by the fire seemed crystal clear as he noted the same brilliant blue gaze and the red casts to their hair. Bridget's was a brighter color, but Finn's wife—his widow's—held a fiery depth that threatened to scorch hotter.

"Nay, I never married." Bridget shook her head and for a second her gaze flew beyond him to Finn's wife by the fire. She received an almost imperceptible nod. "As for the lad, he's Master Ross Brennan Delaney. Named fer his two grandfathers. Yer uncle and my own brother, Ross Doyle. My brother's been gone from these parts fer quite some time and from this world some five years or more. But he lives on in the twinkle of his grandson's eyes, that's fer sure."

Connal's gut squeezed. Finn's son.

Dread settled like a rock in his chest. Ross Delaney, heir to his father's share of Glenmeade. Any hope that this visit was some horrid pretense, or even a bizarre social nicety, vanished with Bridget's cheerful revelation.

Finn's *son.*

Bridget winced as Connal's grip tightened while he fought to absorb the news and all its import. He released his hold of her.

"It is good to see you again, Bridget," he lied through his teeth. "It appears we have a great deal of catching up to do."

"Aye." Bridget flashed him a smile that lit the twinkle in her eyes, a twinkle he remembered from his faraway youth. At the moment he felt quite ancient. "I see ye've met my niece, Bethany."

"Bethany?" he repeated stupidly. He longed to be on Teagan's back right now, still racing through Kildare's hills unaware of what awaited him.

"We were just getting acquainted, Aunt."

Finn's wife spoke from just behind him. Connal nearly jumped. When had she moved from her stance by the hearth?

"Mr. Carey was kind enough to assist me with building a fire in here to ward off the chill while we awaited our host's welcome."

Her soft accent failed to dull the edge of condemnation in her tone as she stepped past him and put her arm protectively around her aunt's shoulders. "Why don't you have a seat by the fire and I will venture to the kitchen and see if I can find you some tea."

"Now, don't fret over me." Bridget shook her head. "Ye're every bit as travel-weary as I am. I left ye with strict orders ta sit and try to recoup yerself, as I recall." Bridget shook her head, but allowed herself to be guided past Connal as she favored her niece with an indulgent smile.

"I will go inquire about refreshments for you ladies," James offered. "That way you could both have a seat and a chance to get better acquainted with Connal here. I am quite sure you have any number of things to discuss *en familia*."

"I could use some refreshment a little more substantial than tea," Connal muttered to his friend, trying to gain a little time and equilibrium.

"That would be most kind, Mr. Carey." Bethany Delaney's soft smile for James disappeared as her gaze slid back toward Connal while she arranged her skirts and sank gracefully onto the threadbare settee.

"Thank ye anyway, sir, but that Jenna O'Toole already said she'd bring a tray in directly." Bridget halted James before he could even turn to the door. She joined her niece near the hearth and fixed her regard on James. "A Carey, are ye? Ye have the look of them."

"I beg your pardon, Aunt Bridget, I should have introduced you." Finn's wife's cheeks flushed over this lapse in manners and she squeezed the older woman's fingers in apology. "This is Mr. Carey. Mr. James Carey. A neighbor, I believe."

"And a lifelong friend to this family." James sketched a shallow bow. Connal fought an irrational urge to choke his friend for behaving as if this was an ordinary social call.

"I am pleased to meet ye, sir." Bridget narrowed her eyes as she gazed at James in frank assessment. "Now, would ye be that serious lad who came from over by the river ta visit every now and then? I spent a few months one summer tending ta Master Connal back in the day. What was the name of yer parents' property, Mr. Carey?"

"Oak Bend, Miss . . . Doyle."

James's eyes held a polite yet slightly uncomfortable glaze that Connal, shallow man that he was, found satisfying. Even as a lad, James had seldom wasted much attention on the servants or village folk. He appeared flummoxed at how to proceed in conversing with a former nursery maid who now appeared to be a member of his neighbor's family.

Shifting his regard to Bethany, James's eyes took

on an entirely different glitter. Connal's hackles raised at the exchange. Bethany Doyle was certainly attractive enough to garner appreciative stares from most men, especially since casting off her widow's black only months after her husband's death all but declared her eligibility for such attention. Protectiveness in the face of James's obvious attraction to Finn's widow clashed with unreasoning outrage at her flouting convention.

"Ah, yes, I remember now," Bridget said, forging on in the awkward silence. "The Careys of Oak Bend. You had that pretty little wisp of a sister."

That was the last straw. Connal strode to the small sideboard that held the decanter of whiskey he'd been craving since walking into the room.

"Rosleen died a number of years ago. I . . . We . . . still miss her terribly."

James's careful declaration of his family's loss stabbed Connal afresh with guilt over the part he had played. He splashed spirits into a tumbler and welcomed the burn, though the liquor did little to ease the conflicts raging inside him.

"If you will both excuse me—" Following the requisite murmurs of sympathy from the women on the settee, James managed his escape. "I believe I will join our host in his libation."

He accepted the glass Connal proffered him and downed a goodly portion of the contents before stopping to raise his glass. "To Finn's demise," he said quietly.

"Aye." Connal drained his glass. "Though he's still saddling me with his consequences."

James glanced over at the hearth and the two women. "I believe you have enough to deal with this evening. I will come back with the papers for us to go through in a day or two, once you have had a chance to untangle some of this."

He couldn't blame James for wanting to escape this uncomfortable encounter. Hell, he'd gladly go home to Oak Bend along with him if he could. Connal nodded his agreement and again unstoppered the decanter with another soft chink. Finn's widow turned her head at the noise. Her gaze fixed first on his hand, then flew to his face. He could read the wary calculation and censure in her eyes even across the room.

"Damnation." Mrs. Finn Delaney was sadly mistaken if she thought a mere look askance from her would change any of his intentions. This was still his home, no matter what claim she might try to advance on her son's behalf. He'd have a second drink if he chose.

And a third.

Chapter Two

Connal Delaney's entry into his parlor at Glen-meade Manor played and replayed itself in James Carey's mind as he made his way back to Oak Bend. His neighbor's shock and consternation had been well worth tangling all of his carefully laid plans, especially because he had been present to savor them.

Finn's widow seemed quite charming and lovely, somewhat naive, but more than a little intriguing. Up to this point, she had been almost boringly predictable and easy to manipulate. But then, she had been gullible enough to stay married to Finn for all those miserable years. And he'd made sure they were miserable indeed. He'd shrugged off any guilt in that regard long ago. She made her bed when she married Finn Delaney and birthed his spawn.

He'd never imagined the little doormat would actually be able to carry off escaping to Ireland with her whelp. Pity her hopes for a scandal-free fresh start were bound to be dashed.

The cool feel of her hand in his, her petite frame,

fair skin and fire-kissed hair slid alluringly through his thoughts. She had a figure that might prove interesting, but as tempting as exploring the Widow Delaney might seem, that wasn't where his concern over her unexpected arrival truly laid.

No, it was the transfixed look she'd given Connal that had inexplicably raised the hackles at the back of his neck. The way Connal had responded to her only confirmed the necessity of paying attention and shifting his plans into an accelerated pace.

James slid from his mare's back and released the animal to his groomsman. He pulled his collar up to his ears, as the evening mist had begun to dampen the air. Not that he would turn down the opportunity to exploit the Widow Delaney's years of being cowed into obedience by her husband, should such an encounter present itself, mind.

Picturing the fiery beauty trembling beneath his touch stirred him with surprising strength. His ability to indulge himself in the county was limited. He would have to schedule a trip to Dublin soon.

For now, he would focus his attention on altering his plans for the future of Glenmeade to fit the latest developments. How to turn the day's events to his advantage, that was the challenge. He loved a challenge.

He took the steps to the house in quick strides and stripped off his gloves as he entered the foyer, without even glancing at the butler waiting for his coat and hat.

"Sir—"

"What is it, Morrison?" He stopped to glare at the rotund servant. God save him from servants and their need for conversation when a man had things to work out in his mind. Especially ones who grew fat in his employ.

"I beg your pardon, sir." The balding man sketched a quick bow. "I thought you should know there's a lady in the front drawing room."

James lifted a brow. "Who is she?"

"I don't know, sir." Morrison bowed again, looking nervous. "She said she wanted to surprise you. She was very insistent on being admitted. She came with trunks."

The butler's nod drew James's attention toward a rather large pile of baggage in the corner of the foyer, polished leather and brass fittings with large bolts at the fastenings. Expensive, by the look.

"Interesting." He stopped to take a quick glance at himself in the mirror by the staircase. The mist had dampened his pale hair to a darker blond cast, slick against his scalp. He smoothed out the ring that came from his hat, then stroked his mustache. As always, the clear light blue of his eyes gave away none of his thoughts. "The drawing room, you say?"

"Aye, sir."

"Thank you, Morrison. Take these to my study." He handed the butler the packet of papers he had taken to Glenmeade to seal Connal's fate. Whoever was waiting for him had better be worth this distraction. "I will ring should I have further need of you."

"Very well, sir." The butler bowed once more and turned gratefully away. James watched the incompetent fool waddle off toward the study. What had the man been thinking—allowing some unknown woman to ensconce herself in the drawing room without even determining her name. Still . . .

James's gaze moved to the brass fittings and leather straps.

He opened the drawing room's pocket doors. They rolled smoothly out of the way. He stepped inside and shut the doors just as soundlessly as he'd opened them.

He ran his gaze over the woman standing before the fireplace holding a cut-crystal glass. Thick dark hair glistened in an elegant chignon atop her slender neck. Lush, expensive black velvet in the latest fashion covered her to the floor. Cinnamon and jasmine scented the air.

"Vivian, how appropriate."

Her chin rose at his quiet observation. She was definitely more than worth the distraction she would provide.

"Two widows in one evening."

She glanced over her shoulder, her dark eyes asparkle, then placed her tumbler on the mantel and turned to face him fully. The cut of her dress accentuated her lush breasts and narrow waist. Her cool, ivory skin, offset by her widow's black, glowed more ethereal than ever. With her black eyes, aristocratic cheekbones and full red lips she looked ripe indeed.

"Is that the only greeting you have for me?" Her lips curved upward, invitingly. "I have been quite pining for you for what seems an age."

As always with her, his desire stirred easily.

He crossed the room and took her in his arms without preamble. Her breath caught as he tipped her chin and took her luscious mouth, his tongue delving between her lips to lave hers. She tasted of his finest whiskey. Trust Vivian to make herself at home, with or without invitation.

She sighed into his mouth and wrapped her arms around his shoulders, molding her lush body against him in patent invitation. He bit her lower lip and released her.

"That was better." Her words came low and husky as she looked at him through her lashes. Her passions were easy to ignite. They always had been. Theirs was a relationship borne of desire and danger. They both liked it that way.

"What are you doing here, Vivian? Is it the slow season in Boston already?"

"Darling." Reproach marked her tone as she slowly smoothed her hands down the front of her gown, letting them caress the curves of her breasts under the guise of straightening the fabric.

His groin tightened, lust surging to the fore, as she knew it would. He fully intended to trace the path she blazed with his own hands.

But, not just yet.

He pinched her chin between his thumb and forefinger. "Answer my question, Vivian. I was not expecting you. Why are you here?"

"Are you so displeased ? You did not seem to be just a moment ago. I needed to see you."

Her lips tilted in an enticing smile. His thoughts splintered into fantasies of exactly what he'd like her to do with those lips. He shook off the pictures with an effort. She was good at this. Almost as good as he.

"I want answers first." He brushed his thumb across her mouth with just the right amount of pressure. "Then we can talk about your . . . needs."

Her eyelids drooped over her brilliant black eyes and she shuddered. Desire pinched again. Oh, yes, he would see to her needs tonight, several times. And enjoy each more than the last.

But he would have his answers first. She knew better than to resist him much longer. He gripped her by the shoulders and gave her a little shake. "Vivian."

"Very well." She pouted ever so slightly. "I am here because I have lost everything. All that I had when Sherman was alive has been taken from me by his loathsome offspring."

"What do you mean?"

"Nathan and Frederick, who do you think I mean?" A touch of irritation colored her tone. "You know they never approved of me. They certainly made that plain enough whenever they extended themselves to show any respect to their father. Poor Sherman, he never understood. I am not sure when they arranged things or how I managed to miss the entire plot."

"Explain yourself, Vivian. But with brevity."

She paced away from him, trailing her long, elegant fingers along his marble mantelpiece. "Sherman left his money, his businesses and the house, *my* house, to his sons in equal measure. He left me nothing but the clothes on my back and the jewelry he bought for me over the years, along with the wish that I would be able to make some other man as happy as I made him."

She turned back to him, a hard edge lurking in her gaze. "I believe if those two jackals had been able to come up with a reason to have my jewelry taken from me they would have stripped the very rings off my fingers without so much as a second thought. I earned that house. I took it from drab to fabulous."

"Indeed." So the old goat and his brats had the last laugh after all. This really was a day for surprises.

She straightened her shoulders and lifted her chin with a haughty air. "Naturally I came straight to you, my love, even though I had to sell my emerald necklace to finance the trip from Boston. The only good thing that came out of this is that my marriage is no longer an impediment to our being together."

She traced her finger lightly along his jawline. "And you do owe me something in view of the . . . tasks . . . I carried out for you these past few years."

"Really? Need I remind you how much you enjoyed those . . . tasks? Almost as much, I daresay, as I enjoyed having you perform them for me."

A hint of color flowed over her high cheekbones. She stepped closer to him, enveloping him in her cinnamon and jasmine scent. "Do not toy with me further, James. I was desperate. You know how seasick I get. I came here, despite the miserable crossing, because I had no other choice."

"I know that." He cupped her cheek and brushed his fingers against the embarrassed heat of her silken skin. "I am truly sorry for your loss, Vivian. Sherman's death was never part of the plan."

A sparkle of tears lit those dark, enticing eyes, whether for the dear departed Sherman or for herself he couldn't tell. One could never be truly sure of Vivian's motives. That was part of what made her so interesting.

"Come now, you are here and the past is the

past." He dipped his head to cover her mouth with a more affectionate kiss.

She moved into his arms, leaning into him. The affection he offered turned more ardent in a heartbeat. Her mouth opened beneath his. For the flash of an instant he considered enjoying her favors here in the drawing room, imagining the shock on his butler's florid face if he walked in on his master and the unnamed woman in the throes of passion. Another day, perhaps.

He lifted his head and savored the desire tightening her lovely features. She wanted him as much as he wanted her.

"Take me." Her whispered plea was husky and oh so low. There was an urgent tightness in her stance. How many months had she gone without a lover?

"I intend to, my dear."

He kissed her again, quickly, his mind already forming a use for her visit. "You are my family."

Another kiss.

"My . . . cousin." How apropos.

She molded herself to him.

He kissed her more slowly, tracing his tongue along her bottom lip. "Come from America."

He ran his hands over the bodice of her gown as he continued to nibble her lips, cupping the roundness of her breasts. "Although we will need to give you a different name."

"Mmmmm," she moaned as he increased the pressure of his caresses. "What are you saying? I don't understand."

She tilted her head back as he moved his lips to her neck, nibbling and licking. Her fingers dug into his arms, pulling him closer, encouraging his attentions.

"We need a reasonable explanation for you to stay here, darling. Living in my house without a chaperone."

Confusion darkened her features as she pushed back from him enough to see his face. "But I—"

"Shhh." He squeezed her breasts once more and watched her eyelids droop again. She might have come here eager to discuss marriage possibilities, but he had other plans for Vivian's loveliness. "I will explain it all to you. Just remember who you are."

"Your cousin." She purred in a low tone.

He drew her lip into his mouth and ran his tongue over the edges. "And we will have to get you out of those mourning rags."

"Then take me upstairs."

"Good things come to those who wait, my dear." He smiled, enjoying her easy acquiescence as he released his hold of her and guided her toward the door with his hand at the small of her back.

"Now, darling cousin, let us ring for my staff and get you situated in suitable quarters. After your long journey would you like a tray in your room? I believe I will be retiring early myself."

She giggled against his neck as he pulled the bell for Morrison.

Within the hour his servants had Vivian installed in a suite at the opposite end of the hall from his own. For propriety's sake, of course. His housekeeper, Mrs. Mulrooney, was as efficient as always.

He practically oozed sympathy as he explained Vivian's turn of bad fortune after her husband's death the previous year. And that she would like to be left alone for the rest of the evening, in fact perhaps for several days as she rested from the rigors of her trip.

His housekeeper had personally brought up a tray of tea and toast for the "poor thing." She'd thoughtfully provided a small decanter of sherry on the tray in case the widow needed something a little more bracing to help her sleep. Other than the valise that contained her night things, her trunks could be unpacked in the morning.

"Thank you, Mrs. Mulrooney. I will help my cousin settle in and then take a brandy in my study. Send along a cold tray, will you. That will be all for the evening."

Vivian played her part to the hilt, sitting on the settee clutching a lace handkerchief.

"Aye, sir. Madame." The woman bobbed a curtsey and bustled out with an air of satisfied benevolence. Vivian's accommodations included an outer sitting room that should soothe any qualms the old housekeeper might have. She could imagine her employer sitting quietly there with his cousin to discuss her situation without having to picture the bedchamber beyond. And that worked fine for him.

He waited a moment or two, then slid the latch on the door before following Vivian into the bedchamber and closing that door as well.

"Come here . . . Cousin."

She came toward him with a teasing smile.

He gripped her to him and plundered her mouth with his own, enjoying her moan, part pain, part pleasure, as she welcomed his urgent attentions. His fingers worked the fastenings of her velvet gown in rapid succession. The bodice came loose first, then her full skirt and petticoats fell to the floor. And all the while he took pleasure in delving deep inside her lush lips.

He released her long enough to step back and enjoy the sight of her panting and ready for him. Full breasts, straining against the confinements of her black silk corset, begged his attention. Ruffled pantalettes covering her long, sleek legs beckoned his explorations.

"Take your hair down."

No need to play the smooth lover with Vivian, they both knew she was his to command.

She sucked in a long breath, licked her lips and lifted her arms to remove the pins from her coiffure. Her breasts rose higher and fuller still with her movements, practically bursting free from their prison. The pins fell to the floor and her long dark tresses spilled free, reaching to her hips in lustrous waves.

"Come to me." He was practically bursting to take her, raw and hard. But drawing out the pleasure would only make it sweeter. And he so enjoyed drawing out the pleasure with this woman. Enjoyed bending her to his will.

She moved forward, lips wet, her eyes shining. He put his hand on her shoulders and pushed her down until she knelt before him, her fingers working the fastenings to his trousers. In moments she had freed his hot flesh. Her fingers caressed his length. She licked her lips and looked up at him, awaiting his permission to proceed.

"Show me just how much you have missed me, my dear."

She gave him a wicked smile, then her mouth

opened and she took him into her wet heat. He groaned, loving the feel of her tongue writhing against his rigid penis. He slid his fingers into her hair, cupping her head as she moved over his hot length. Back and forth, back and forth, sucking and laving him. God, she was so good at this.

"Vivian." All he could manage was her name. His thoughts ran together in a dazed kaleidoscope of plans and events. He had so much more to consider now that she was here as a new pawn in the game. But he could think of nothing beyond the feel of her suckling him.

He toyed briefly with the idea of letting her suckle him to completion and then reluctantly decided it would be better to give her pleasure as well. At least this first time. Compliance was often more readily achieved through self-denial.

He pushed her back with an effort, his breathing ragged, his entire body throbbing for release.

He reached down and pulled her up to stand before him. Her lips were swollen from the attentions she had showered on him. Her eyes were glazed with passion as she awaited his next command.

He kissed her long and hard, thrusting his tongue deep inside her mouth, enjoying her utter surrender to his will.

"Now, let's give you some of the attention you deserve, shall we? Bend over that table." He nodded toward the side table by the windows that Mrs. Mulrooney had thoughtfully cleared for Vivian's toiletries when she unpacked in the morning.

Vivian shivered and bit her lower lip. Her even, white teeth glistened against her lips. She turned to comply, offering an enticing sight as she crossed the room with the ruffles on her pantalettes hugging the roundness of her buttocks. He always enjoyed the sight of her in motion.

"Hurry, my love." She whispered her plea as she spread herself on the table.

He joined her, first skimming his hand over her silk-clad curves, then slapping her on the buttocks. Not too hard, just hard enough to offer a little sting to remind her just who was in charge.

She gulped a breath and moaned both at once. "Oh, James."

"You are a naughty girl, aren't you . . . Cousin? Arriving here without any notice." He slapped her again and then again, enjoying the firm roundness of her bottom beneath his hand and the sighing moans she emitted at his treatment.

"Is it time to give you what you came here looking for?"

"Oh, yes." She wriggled. "If you think it is."

Pleasure that she had learned her lesson so early made him benevolent. He undid the lacings of her pantalettes and tugged them so they dropped to the floor in a little whoosh of sliding silk. Her bottom glowed white in the lamplight. White with a rosy blush from his attentions.

He skimmed his hands over her soft flesh, enjoying the contrast between the cool and hot patches of her curves.

She sucked in a breath that was more a whimper of expectation.

He reached his fingers between her legs, finding the hot core of her, wet and eager for him. She moaned and pushed back against them.

"I know what you want." He thrust his fingers roughly up inside her wet sheath. "I always know."

"Yes." She moaned and wriggled against him, slick and eager.

He moved his fingers in and out of her, back and forth. She moaned deeply, and spread her legs wider. He reached with his thumb to find the nubbin of flesh at the apex of her thighs.

"Ahh, oh, James, yes." She groaned as he teased and rubbed her. Faster, slower, faster, slower. In moments, she was panting and arching her back.

"Tell me what you need."

"Oh, please, James, please take me."

"Give me what I want first." He commanded her release.

She shuddered and moaned and then a high, broken sound came from her as she crossed over the threshold of pleasure. Her body convulsed around his fingers as she climaxed.

He smiled, enjoying the total control she offered him.

He removed his fingers from her and spread her legs wider still. He drew her to the end of the table and drove his member fully into her hot, wet body with a satisfied grunt.

His groans mingled with hers as he began to move inside her. Pushing himself against the lush roundness of her bottom he showed her no mercy and she begged for none.

He wound his hand through the silken length of her hair and tugged slightly, pulling her up from the table as he rode her, pumping himself into her with long, hard strokes.

"Oh, yes." She groaned her pleasure as he

reached around and pulled one of her breasts from the confines of her corset. The silken mound filled his hand as he fondled her. Finding the rock-hard nipple, he pinched the sensitive tip.

"Yes." She shivered beneath him, pushing herself back to meet his thrusts, then forward to fill his hand.

He pinched and twisted and increased the rhythm of his strokes, pounding into her soft, yielding flesh, enjoying having her beautiful body completely in his power. She would lay herself open to his every desire before this night was through.

She cried out as he allowed himself to climax inside her, the two of them shuddering together in the tremors of pleasure.

Long, damp moments later it was over. His legs had grown weak and he felt more sated than he had in too long a time as he panted above her. Sated for the moment, at least. Vivian was always an exciting partner, eager for the next time, open to anything he wanted her to do.

He grinned, aware of the darkness outside and the lamplight spilling over both of them before the open curtains. If any of the staff was out for an evening stroll they'd just gotten quite an eyeful.

He pulled out of her body and squeezed her buttocks affectionately.

She turned to face him and stood, a thoroughly satisfied smile on her features. She untied her corset ribbons, releasing the garment to slide down to the floor. Her high, proud breasts gleamed in the light as her hair swirled around her naked form.

"That was a far better greeting than your first

one." She trailed her fingers over his chest. "Now, let's get you out of the rest of your clothes."

"I thought you might prefer my undivided attention." He couldn't keep the satisfaction out of his voice.

She laughed. And tugged his jacket off his arms. His cravat and shirt quickly joined it on the floor near her underpinnings.

"Speaking of divided attention." She kissed the pulse point at the base of his neck. "Who is this second widow you mentioned downstairs?"

"Later." He cupped her breasts and offered them each a healthy squeeze.

"Mmmmm." She twined her arms around his neck and tipped her head up for a kiss.

He smiled, loving the fact that she responded whenever he reached for her. He'd spend the entire night with her if he thought he could manage the gossip amongst his staff. A glimpse in a window was far different from openly defying all convention. Still he could manage at least another hour or two before he would need to leave Vivian's side.

He drew her close and lifted her in his arms.

"To bed, then?" She whispered the words against his neck. Her breath warmed his ear and he could hear the smile in her voice.

"Aye, I have a few ideas you might find . . . interesting."

"I especially love your more interesting ideas."

He spilled her onto the satin coverlet atop the massive four poster that dominated the room. Her hair fanned out across its deep green plushness. "I have several."

He followed her down onto the bed.

She turned into his arms and they shared a slow, deep kiss.

"Tell me all of them," she whispered against his mouth before nibbling gently at his lower lip.

He smiled, more than willing to comply with that request. "I will. One at a time."

And then, in the morning, the real work could begin.

Chapter Three

"Coming here was a horrendous mistake." *Like so much else in my life.*

Apprehension streaked through Bethany Delaney, chased by more disappointment than she'd ever wanted to face in her life again. How could she have thought that Ireland, that Glenmeade, would provide her with anything beyond disaster?

She clutched her woolen shawl closer around her shoulders as her gaze sought the small figure of her son sleeping under a soft quilt at the opposite end of the spacious nursery.

In a bed that once belonged to his father. Her breath caught in her throat, knotting with the false hope she was busy swallowing back.

Despite the hellish nightmare of her marriage, she could never count Ross among her mistakes. He was the only blessing from those bleak years. A wash of light from the lamp on the table beside him made him seem even smaller than his seven years, especially with the shadows cast around him.

She shivered, despite the peat fire in the hearth

nearby, recalling the look on Connal Delaney's face when he learned of his young cousin's existence. He had seemed so like Finn at that moment she'd struggled with herself not to rush to the nursery, snatch up her son and run straight out the door.

"What was I thinking, Aunt Bridget? Coming all this way without thinking through all the possible consequences?"

"Hush now, *isean.*"

Bridget had used Gaelic for "little bird" as a pet name for Bethany as long as she could remember. Her aunt reached across from the rocker by the hearth and rested her fingers over Bethany's. Bridget, her father's youngest sister, had been the one constant in Bethany's life, always there to love and support her.

"Ye fretted yer way across the whole Atlantic and up the Irish Sea. We've reached our new nesting grounds safely. Things will work out, ye'll see. We've come home."

Home.

Bethany sat back against the side of the window seat and sighed, wishing she could believe her aunt's reassurances. She drew her feet up onto the cushioned seat and tucked her toes under the hem of her gauzy cotton nightgown. The right weight for warm North Carolina nights, but not enough to keep away the Irish chill. The Irish countryside seemed so cold and forbidding. Not at all what she'd hoped for.

Leaning her head against the thick glass for a moment she could feel the rhythmic spattering of rain on the other side of the pane. Her visions of a fresh start—far from the infamy of her husband's death and the loss of the business he'd beaten into the ground—vanished with her first sight of the master of Glenmeade Stables striding into his study this afternoon.

Connal Delaney was as nearly a twin to her late husband as their fathers had been. Finn had never told her. But then, Finn had lied about so much, even telling her his cousin Connal had died a tragic death more than a decade ago. She rubbed her arms. Like a ghostly harbinger Connal Delaney had appeared, ramrod straight and silent, stealing her breath with his stomach-wrenching scowl. Every bit as alive as Finn was dead. If she had any sense at all she'd pile their bags on the nearest cart and leave Glenmeade Manor as soon as the sun kissed the horizon in the morning.

"I know you are happy to come home to County Kildare, Aunt. But all I have seen so far are gray skies and a future full of dark promises. I should have known better than to be swayed by Father's reminiscences or Finn's regret over leaving his own father to age and die alone." She sighed again. "We should have headed west to California. Or north. Anywhere away from Wilmington. Anywhere save here."

"Ye know full well ye never truly wished ta risk our lad's future by crossing the plains with wild Indians and even wilder frontiersmen."

Bridget's imaginings of the dire consequences such an adventure would surely offer always sent an exaggerated chill across Bethany's shoulders.

"Yer husband's misadventures in the north put paid ta that direction as well. The report ye found amongst his papers saying his father still headed

Glenmeade was scarce a year old. How could ye have known one was ta follow the other ta the grave so close despite the miles between them?"

The glow from the peat fire in the hearth grate wavered in Bridget's hair. Soft copper curls touched with gray released from her usual chignon tumbled down her back as she shook her head. She looked much younger lit by the fire's embers. As though just being here had brought back to life something she had been missing for too long. That feeling, at least, warmed Bethany.

"I am sure you are right. But Finn's cousin acts as though we came all this way to steal the very bread from his mouth."

Her marriage, her son, her very existence all came as bitter news to her husband's only remaining family. Bethany traced a finger against the cool windowpane, remembering the hot blaze of condemnation from Connal Delaney's gaze, scorching her with each new revelation she and Bridget delivered this afternoon.

"He's had a bit of a shock, is all." Bridget must have been mulling over his reactions as well. "Doubtless it's related ta the bad blood between him and that one ye wed. Jenna O'Toole hinted at some dark secret whilst we were clearing the dust covers from this nursery. I'll get the full story from her on the morrow."

Mrs. O'Toole did not stand a chance against Bridget's determination. Look at how Bethany herself had fared in deciding whether to come to Ireland or not. "I am quite certain you will. But, bad blood or not, he made it clear he had no care for the news that we intend to stay here. As if we have much choice at this point until the questions surrounding Ross's inheritance are settled."

"He'll come around, ye'll see." Bridget patted Bethany's hand. "Even as a lad, Connal Delaney always set about doing the right thing. I'm sure he's grown into a man of honor, totally different from his cousin."

A man of honor? Bethany could only hope. Her time with Finn left her skeptical regarding any Delaney being honorable.

"That Mr. Carey seemed concerned we were to stay here as well." She tried to divert her thoughts from the range of her reactions to Connal Delaney.

Face-to-face with the ghost whose supposed death haunted Finn's drunken ramblings, waves of recognition and fear had crashed in her chest, robbing her of breath and cogent thought. Knowing that it was imperative not to show fear or weakness when facing a Delaney had forced her feet forward to their awkward introduction.

Connal was so like Finn, and yet there were differences, too. Connal was leaner and more muscular. Straighter and taller. She'd gotten close enough to know he smelled different, like windblown grass and sandalwood, familiar and exotic at one and the same time.

Her introduction speech, rehearsed a hundred times on the voyage to Ireland, had disappeared completely. All she'd been able to babble was something about his eyes, a soulful brown that showed a depth of pain borne with steely determination. Eyes so very different from the cold, shallow gray of her late husband's she would never again mistake Connal up close for his cousin Finn.

"The Careys of Oak Bend always were a bit high in the instep." Bridget sniffed and rose from her rocker to poke at the peat embers. "Sticklers fer proprieties, especially if a young woman, even a widow, takes up residence with a bachelor—no matter the fact ye've as much right ta be here as any bearing the name Delaney notwithstanding. And as if I am not fit ta be yer chaperone after all these years."

Bethany shook off her reverie and rose from the window seat to slip her arms around her aunt, giving her a quick hug. "Oh, Aunt Bridget, I am probably just overwrought from the long journey. I just wish I could dislodge the feeling I have traded one set of disasters for another."

The faces of Finn and his cousin, so similar, merged, giving her goose bumps again. Some rift had torn this family apart. Who had been responsible? Finn, whose charm had quickly evaporated once they married? Or Connal, unpleasant from the start?

"There, now." The older woman squeezed Bethany back and glanced over at the small bundle curled on the bed. "Not everything has been a disaster. There's our lad, after all."

"Yes," Bethany agreed. At the moment, snuggled under the quilt with his dark hair tousled, her son looked like a babe still in his linens. "Ross is the one good thing Finn gave me."

"The only good that ever came from that one," Bridget snorted. "May the good Lord fergive me fer speaking ill of the dead. But that man—"

Ross stirred just then, his dark eyelashes fluttering open as he blinked and tried to straighten up.

Bridget held back whatever else she'd wanted to say, but Bethany felt certain she had not heard the end of the indictment regarding her erstwhile husband's many faults. It was a conversation they had held too many times for her to count, especially in the past months.

"Are we there yet, Mama?" Exhaustion still edged Ross's voice as he blinked in soft sleepiness at her. Dark circles smudged the underside of his blue eyes, so very like her father's. All this travel—the long sea voyage from Wilmington to Dublin and then two days jolting by carriage to reach here— had exacted a toll on him.

"Yes, dearest." She moved over to smooth his tangled curls and feel the warmth of his cheek. "We arrived at Glenmeade Stables just before tea. The coachman carried you in and you've slept half the night away, you were that tired."

Already the curiosity in Ross's eyes dulled and he settled back to lean against the pillows and peer at the darkened room. She poured a bit of honeyed milk into a mug for him and he drank it listlessly despite having missed both tea and supper. He finished the drink and sighed. "Papa said where he'd grown up there were lots of horses. You will let me have a horse of my own, won't you, Mama? You promised."

Another popular topic of conversation Bethany had engaged in far too many times lately. "We'll see about a *pony* once we have settled in, Ross. Would you like some more milk or one of the currant biscuits the housekeeper sent up for you?"

Ross shook his head, his eyes already closing as he drifted off to dream of his horse and pass the

remainder of the night. "We're home now, Mama?
We don't have to be afraid, do we? We don't have
to run away anymore?" he whispered as he nestled
into the downy depths.

"No, darling, no more running." His innocent
questions burned tears at the backs of her eyes. He
was too young to have such worries. "We are home."

She pulled the covers over his shoulders and
kissed his soft cheek, praying she'd made the right
choice in bringing her son to Ireland. Praying she
was telling him the truth about this new home.
Connal Delaney's visage still harrowed her nerves,
filling her with uncertainty.

Truth be told it wasn't just Connal Delaney's
frowns that frightened Bethany, nor even his resemblance to her dead husband, so much as her own
traitorous response to the similarity. When Connal
strode into the study it was as if the years had
melted and she was a girl again, catching her first
sight of her father's guest from the old country.

Finn Delaney's good looks and brogue seemed to
turn whatever he said into lilting poetry. Even
having grown up with her father and aunt speaking
much the same did not tarnish the appeal. She'd
been charmed by the attention he'd paid her
during his initial visit. He was the first adult who actually listened to her conversation, who sought out
her company and appeared interested in her
opinions.

At the time she'd found his Old World courtesy
and flattering attentiveness bewitching. She soon
discovered Finn's ploys for what they were: a
snare for her naivety so he could marry into the

prosperous business her father had founded in the New World.

She stroked her sleeping son's cheek. In appearance he looked so like his father. And his new-found cousin. She would have to prepare Ross for the shock of the resemblance between Connal and the father he'd adored, although Finn was more like an occasional playmate than a parent. She lowered the lamp flame and eased herself away from the bed, lingering to look at Ross a moment longer and reassure herself that she was willing to endure anything to secure his future.

Seeing Connal's chiseled cheeks, broad shoulders and firm jaw this afternoon had been like seeing Finn before the years of dissipation and indulgence took their toll. Her heart leapt in instant recognition and for a moment it was all she could do to keep her equilibrium. She'd practically clung to James Carey as if they were intimate friends and not acquaintances of only a few minutes.

Surely that sense of shock would fade as she grew used to Connal Delaney's appearance. If not, she would work to avoid his company—not seeing him any more than absolutely necessary.

Bridget dozed in the rocker, her head dipping to her chest, unwilling to seek her bed until Bethany went as well. Bethany poked at the peat in the hearth, adding a few more pieces, as Mr. Carey had showed her earlier. She was not yet ready to be utterly alone in the dark of an unfamiliar bed. Perhaps she would crawl in with Ross and cuddle with him. She felt the need for the comfort of holding her child this night. She might no longer be a gullible girl seduced by a smile, but she wasn't nearly as self-sufficient as she pretended for her aunt and son's sake either. This afternoon affirmed that.

Her thoughts kept turning over and over to her meeting with Connal Delaney. Emotions buried deep inside her flared to life in his presence. Caution, without a doubt. Dread, certainly. And yet, there was a heightened awareness, an odd sensation of excitement she had not felt in years.

"Foolishness." She put the poker back against the stone hearth.

"What was that, *isean?*" Bridget sounded so very sleepy, Bethany's conscience panged. It was not fair to make her aunt wait just because she was certain she'd find no rest in Glenmeade, at least not this night.

"Are you ready for bed, Aunt? You do not look at all comfortable sleeping in that rocker."

"I'm not the least tired. There's many a night I spent in this very room." A long yawn belied Bridget's statement as she pushed herself from the rocker. "But ye should get some rest. Our lad will be beside himself when he awakens in the morning and sees all the horses in the paddocks."

"Aye," Bethany whispered. She looked over at the narrow cot set up for her near Ross, doubting she would get much rest in it this night. "I am quite sure he will be up at first light demanding to be shown to the stables."

"Thank the Lord, Jenna O'Toole's daughter, Mary, will be taking up residence in the nursery maid's alcove after this night." Bridget chuckled as they slipped out the door into the darkened hall. "She's young enough ta still fancy early-morning forays to the barn."

Bethany clutched her shawl tight around her shoulders as she went out the door. The upper hall of Glenmeade Manor seemed so exposed after the intimacy of the nursery. "I want to take Ross's empty cup and the pitcher to the kitchen. Can I bring you anything back?"

"Nay, lass. All I want is a soft place ta rest my head." Bridget's pat on Bethany's shoulder reassured her even as she winced at the echo of her aunt's voice in the dark hallway. "The keeping room is off the kitchen. Can ye find yer way or would ye like me to light ye a candle?"

"Down the front stairs and straight back. There should be a light in the kitchen. Mrs. O'Toole said she would keep a lamp burning low on the mantel."

"We'll say our good nights, then." Bridget yawned and opened the door to the bedchamber opposite the one Bethany would occupy during the remainder of their stay at Glenmeade. "Stick yer head in and tell me when ye get back upstairs, but ye needn't whisper so. I'm sure I heard Master Connal climbing the stairs and heading ta the other wing hours ago. Meanwhile I'll keep an ear out fer our lad should he wake again."

Bethany checked on Ross, then scooped up the crockery and made her way cautiously to the main staircase. *Master Connal.* Her aunt slipped so easily into referring to Connal Delaney with a deference she had never shown Finn. But then, Finn had done little to endear himself to his new family once he had seduced his way into marriage. After two years working for her father in the warehouses, he'd used his charm to seduce her at a time and place where, she realized only in retrospect, they'd be sure to be discovered.

The fact that she came to her husband untried on their hastily arranged wedding night was a matter of happenstance only. She'd been foolish, flattered and naively eager to allow him the liberties that led to her downfall. Succumbing to the thrill of the moment and the tantalizing risk of the forbidden had cost her dearly. Bridget had blistered her ears for the entire two weeks between her being compromised and her marriage. And she had berated her own folly for most of the intervening years. Ross remained her saving grace through all the nightmares.

She gripped the banister, her fingers curling around the cool wood as she cradled the small pitcher and mug in her other hand. Her steps were muffled as she walked down the plushly carpeted steps. Turning at the bottom, she edged her way toward the pitch-dark kitchen passage, her fingers spread in front of her to warn of any furniture hidden by the night. If only she could do the same with the pitfalls lurking in their future here.

Twenty or so cautious steps and she felt a door in front of her. If Bridget's directions were correct, this led to the kitchen. Her stomach rumbled with sudden hunger as if realizing relief was close at hand. Pushing the door open, she stepped forward and blinked at the light flooding the room in front of her. Instead of being illuminated by a small flame from a lowered lantern as she had expected, the kitchen was ablaze with light from two matching lamps on the mantel and a larger one on the long planked table in the center of the room. Scattered across the table were a number of papers, a dirty plate and mug. A loaf of bread, an open crock of jam and a small wheel of cheese with a knife stuck in the top stood on a cutting block by the sink.

"Hello?" No answer. Had the kitchen been left this way until morning? No cook or scullery maid her father employed would have left such a feast out for late-night vermin. Nor left the lamps blazing, for that matter.

"Hello? Is anyone here?" she tried again, louder this time. Still no answer.

The room was warm from a fire in the overlarge stone hearth, no doubt used for cooking in the days before the installation of the modern stove that gleamed by the sink. Herbs hanging from the rafters gave a pungent, homey scent to the air, the first hint of anything familiar she'd found in this cold, forbidding land.

Although the amount of clutter left out here was nothing compared to Finn's, perhaps his cousin possessed the same bad habits. Finn's late-night forays into the larder had led to many mutterings between her aunt and her father's housekeeper until she'd begun slipping down to the kitchen to clean up after him before anyone else arose. Whatever the customary practices in this house, it did not feel right to just deposit the crockery she carried and leave the room this way.

"I am certainly no stranger to clearing up messes, thanks to you, Finn Delaney." She'd found setting the kitchen at home to rights oddly soothing. Perhaps performing such a task would work in this strange place as well.

A rag rug covering the slate in front of the sink felt warm on her feet as she deposited her contribution to the stack of other items waiting to be washed.

The cheese, flecked with dill, had an inviting aroma. Her stomach rumbled again. She'd tidy up the Glenmeade kitchens all right, but she was going to have a nibble before she got started. She whittled a piece of cheese from the wheel, eager to pop it in her mouth before attacking the bread.

"Please make yourself right at home." The sarcasm-laden comment spun her around with the knife still in her hand. Surprise pounded guilty fear through her veins.

Connal Delaney stepped out of the shadows from the back stairs with raised eyebrows and a raft of papers tied with string thrust under one arm. His resemblance to her husband struck her anew, sending further panic to twist her stomach and set her heart racing.

He was still dressed in his buff riding breeches and tall boots, but he'd shed his jacket and cravat. The stretch of linen across his shoulders betrayed powerful arms under his shirt, arms well-used to physical labor. Years of dissipation had robbed Finn of such a physique.

Very conscious of the fact that her host was dressed, whereas she was attired only in a cotton nightgown and wool shawl, embarrassment heated her cheeks. She curled her toes into the rug and fought the urge to flee the kitchen as if she was a thief caught in the act.

"Jenna . . . Mrs. O'Toole said . . . She offered—" She stopped, hating the hesitation that made her sound guilty of something far worse than assuaging her hunger.

"Ahh, there is your problem. There is really nothing here that is Jenna O'Toole's to offer." He stepped closer. The lamplight glinted in his dark gaze. "This is *my* home, Mrs. Delaney. Your claims to it, or any of its contents, have yet to be proven."

His tone twisted her name with edges as sharp as the dagger in her hand. Anger replaced fear as she looked up at him. "You actually believe I am perpetrating some kind of hoax?"

He shrugged and took another step toward her. "It is a possibility."

She spread her hands. "Why would I venture all this way on a lie? Why would I drag my child across the ocean?"

He set his papers on the table and tilted his head, quirking one brow at her. He moved closer. She fought the urge to take a step backward.

"Surely not solely to rob my larder at knifepoint?" His gaze fell to the knife she still clutched, forgotten.

She lowered the knife immediately. To her horror her stomach chose that moment to issue a loud rumble. Heat streaked across her cheeks again. "I beg your pardon."

For the first time a genuine smile curled Connal Delaney's lips as some of his frosty demeanor melted away. "I should probably beg your pardon for being a less-than-gracious host. Your presence surprised me. I am too used to having the run of the house on my own at this hour."

"Perhaps I should apologize first for foisting your role as host on you." She managed a tentative smile of her own.

His dark gaze intensified, as if he sought to peer directly into her thoughts. "Why did you leave America so soon after your husband's death?"

How much did she want to reveal to this man

who was barely able to restrain his hostility? And would he really be interested in the litany of her reasons for fleeing so headlong into the unknown? "I hardly think this is the time or place to exchange our life stories."

His eyebrows flashed up and he tilted his head slightly to the side.

"What better time or place than the dark of night to share intimacies?" His voice held a quiet calm she found anything but soothing.

He took a step closer. The clean scent of windblown grass and sandalwood that clung to him provided an odd comfort, given the circumstances. If she could have stepped back she would have, but the edge of the sink already dug into her back.

"I am sure you understand," he continued, "that your arrival, your claims, are at the very least unexpected. Until I learned of his death a few weeks ago, we have had no word from Finn in over ten years."

"And suddenly a stranger comes forward to claim his share of an inheritance you believed to be yours alone." She tried to look at the situation from his viewpoint. "How inopportune."

"Aye." His lips thinned. He grabbed the forgotten dagger from her grasp. "For one of us at least."

She flinched, both at the bitter honesty of his observation and his nearness. He was entirely too much like her husband at a distance, let alone this close. She pulled her shawl tight against her chest.

"So, shall we share Finn's portion of our sad tales? Establish our common ground?" His dark gaze bore into her, through her.

"If you insist." She tried to keep her tone light

and prayed he did not hear the little waver at the back of her throat. "Why did Finn leave Ireland? Leave Glenmeade and never look back?"

She blurted the questions that had bothered her over the years. Her husband had not suffered her curiosity over his past with any pretense at grace. How would she fare with his only remaining family?

Connal's intense gaze shuttered. He stepped around her and put the knife to work slicing the cheese. "What did he tell you?"

"That he loved this place above all others, but his father cast him out to make his fortune on his own. That he could never come back." Only in his drunken ramblings laced with bitter remorse and anger over some rash argument did Finn spill any information.

And even then, as it turned out, it had not been the truth.

She watched as Connal next sliced bread and put it on a plate beside the cheese. A pulse beat at the base of his neck as he held his peace, obviously waiting for her to continue. She took a deep breath. "He told me you were dead. Why would he say that when you are obviously not? Did you have a falling out? Did his father side with you and that is why he was sent away?"

Connal's jaw worked as he continued to fill the plate in silence. She had begun to think he would not answer any of her questions when he spoke at last.

"If you stay here you will learn all you need to know from the tattle mongers soon enough."

"I have little use for gossips." Twisted and inflated stories caused only harm and misery. "I would prefer to hear whatever truth there is from you."

"Truth? I think ladies should go before gentlemen."
Connal put the knife down and twisted to look at
her directly again. She swallowed and nodded slowly.

"Did you love Finn?" His hands gripped the side
of the cutting board as if he braced himself for her
answer.

The question shocked her. It had been the last
thing she expected. What kind of test was this? Her
heart pounded and she inhaled another breath as
she struggled to form an answer around the painful
lump in her throat.

"Finn . . . was my husband for almost eight years."

"But did you love him?" A strange urgency laced
his question. "Was Finn happy in his marriage? In
the life he made for himself in . . . Wilmington?
Was he good to you?"

She met his piercing gaze and tried to read the
purpose in this line of questioning. Did this man
really want the truth? How would he react if she
told him of his lost cousin's escalating drunkenness
through the years? Of his womanizing? Of the dev-
astation he visited on the once-thriving business her
father had left to them?

"He . . . was . . . away much of the time these last
few years." She swallowed against the bleakness of
her answer, torn between truths she'd admit to no
one and lies she could no longer bear telling. "We
led separate lives for the most part, after he gave
me Ross."

"Separate." Something hardened in Connal's
gaze. "Is that why he sought solace in the arms of
another woman so far from your home? Is that why
you allowed him to be buried in a potter's grave?"

Her stomach burned at his tone. How could he

question what she could not defend? Her husband had betrayed her numerous times. Consigned her to poverty, ashamed to bear his name, ashamed of the tarnished reputation he'd left as sole legacy to their son.

"I had no funds to bring his body to North Carolina," she answered with as much truth as she was ready to share. "I sent money to the curate at the church in Massachusetts for a funeral Mass. He promised to care for Finn's grave until I could send more for a headstone."

"No funds? Yet you had the means to travel overseas. To come here with your aunt and your son?" He faced her fully.

Connal's tone held shards of ice. The truths he sought burned against her tongue. Truths she had borne for most of her marriage and would carry with her for the rest of her life. Yet, she couldn't speak them. Behind his attack, in the deep brown depths of his eyes, she recognized grief and the need for this man to deal with the loss of a member of his family.

"I told you. I came here seeking my son's grandfather. To give Ross a sense of his family, his heritage. Finn was finished with me years ago." She couldn't bring herself to tell him the whole truth, that she had fled the shreds of the life she had shared with his cousin.

Connal studied her, the moments stretching toward eternity. Lamplight put shadows on his cheeks, deepening the harshness of his scrutiny. He was so much like Finn. The urge to turn and flee the kitchen swelled. She resisted, sensing such action would gain her little. Instead, she met his appraising stare with her own. *Did you love Finn? Was he happy?* Why had those been the questions he'd asked first?

He reached out and brushed a stray curl from her cheek. Her breath caught in her chest. His touch was unexpected and surprisingly gentle. "Why would Finn, why would any man, ever be finished with a woman like you?"

He asked the question gently, but the curl of his lip branded her as a liar. In this and everything else. His censure stung, echoing too many nights of dread and condemnation for her inadequacies she'd thought she'd escaped. She tugged her shawl tighter about her to hide her shivers of rage, past and present.

"My husband told me he preferred the comfort offered him by women who understood a man's needs. From *real* women." She nearly spat the least-colorful criticisms her husband had heaped on her as her throat tightened.

"You look real to me." Connal stepped closer. His hands grasped her shoulders.

"And you certainly feel real enough." His fingers bit into her arms as his breath fanned heat across her cheeks. His narrowed gaze dipped to her lips. Blood pounded in her ears and her stomach twisted.

No. The word sounded in her mind, but she couldn't get it past her lips as he pulled her closer.

Fear froze her. Habits she thought had died along with her husband surged to the fore. Suddenly it was Finn holding her, forcing his rights whenever he felt the need. This would go easier—quicker—if she cooperated. That much the years, their marriage, had taught her.

Relax. Just breathe and it will be over soon.

A hint of sandalwood filled the air she gulped. Finn was dead. Connal Delaney looked down at her. She would not let the shadows of the past hold sway over the present. She pushed against Connal's shoulders, winning an unexpectedly easy release. His dark gaze held hers for a moment as their ragged breathing echoed. Then he stepped back and let out a shuddering sigh.

"Finn was a fool," he said so quietly she almost didn't hear him. He reached for the plate filled with bread and cheese and offered it to her. "Take this and go before I am tempted to discover just how foolish he was."

Her hunger had long since fled. She spun on her heel and departed the kitchen with as much dignity as she could muster.

Chapter Four

He was a fool.

Connal pulled off his high-lows and stepped over to the basin in the mud room. The cold water he splashed on his face and arms might wash away the remaining signs of his early chores in the yard, but he couldn't rid himself so easily of the guilt and annoyance over his treatment of his guest last night.

The rigid line of Bethany Doyle's back as she fled the kitchen still haunted him. After Finn's supposed-wife disappeared into the darkened hall he had been left with the foul certainty that no matter how unwelcome her claims—of marriage and of having borne Finn an heir—his behavior toward her was unjustified.

She had caught him off guard when he came upon her in the kitchen clad only in a thin nightgown and shawl that did little to disguise her charms in the lamplight. But neither her appeal nor the length of time that had passed since he'd enjoyed a woman's company excused his behaving in a manner befitting his reputation. Even if

Bethany Doyle's halting professions of inadequacy had practically begged him to put her to the test.

That he had nearly succumbed to temptation irritated him; that she had been able to provoke even the possibility of such an encounter, and its ensuing guilt, infuriated him. Had these conflicted reactions been part of her calculations to keep him off-kilter?

He splashed more water on his face. "Calculations" might be a slightly harsh assessment, but Bethany Doyle had the same look of tempting beauty mingled with innocent appeal Rosleen carried when she came to him the day before she died. He could not afford to be deceived by beauty and an air of vulnerability again. Never again.

He reached for a drying cloth and scrubbed his neck. God, he missed Jack. The Wicked One needed to transform into The Wiley One if he was to have any success at refuting her claims, or at the very least negotiating a favorable settlement should her marriage lines prove true. He could not afford to turn her into an outright adversary until he had a strategy firmly in place. Seduction, especially as impulsive as the kiss he had so narrowly pulled back from last night, had no place in his plans for dealing with his cousin's widow.

Almost more disconcerting than the anger and mistrust he felt toward Bethany Doyle, though, was the realization that the scent of her skin, the way the lamplight glimmered red–gold in her hair, the way she'd melted in his embrace for just a moment, churned strange, unwanted feelings of longing in the dark recesses that once held his soul.

"Jest what were ye thinkin' last night?" Jenna

O'Toole's scolding tugged him back from the precipice of his unwelcome interest in his cousin's widow. "Throwing a perfectly good plate into the slops bucket as if ye've got crockery ta burn. I've a good mind ta serve ye yer breakfast on a plank."

He winced. He was in no mood to quarrel with his housekeeper. He'd stood in the darkened kitchen holding the meager plate of bread and cheese for too many minutes last night, tempted to either throw the plate at Bethany's back or to chase after her himself. Instead, he'd dropped the whole mess and stalked off to try and catch what little sleep he could before he faced her again in the light of day.

"Just coffee for me." He squeezed by Jenna standing in the doorway and reached for a mug on a peg by the stove.

She tugged the mug away from him, filling it before setting it on her worktable with a thunk. "Ye'll sit right here and eat a breakfast fit fer a man who spent the morning mucking stalls. Although why a man who has stable lads and horsemen aplenty would choose ta do such work himself is beyond me."

"With Jack still away and preparations for the new stock yet to be completed, we're a bit short-handed." He straddled one of the stools and took a sip of the rich black brew while Jenna cracked some eggs in a pan and pulled a meat pie and some biscuits from the oven.

He was not about to admit that he'd sought the solace of hard labor to help burn the edges from the anger and uncertainty the arrival of Finn's family had unleashed. Until he'd determined the best course of action where they were concerned, he did not wish to risk any further conduct sure to end in disaster. A second swallow of coffee failed to wash the bitter certainty that he could have spent the next week in the stables and still have failed to resolve the knot of emotions that froze his thinking. What was he going to do with his guests?

A tray set with a teapot and covered basket on the sideboard snagged his attention. "Is Mrs. Delaney playing the Lady of the Manor already? Surely she can descend the steps and eat in the dining room rather than require you to wait upon her hand and foot before her claims here are even proved?"

He could not disguise the irritation in his tone. Jenna turned sharply from the stove and followed his gaze, while he quashed a stab of guilt about last night's encounter and any role he might have played in Bethany Doyle's plans to remain above stairs this morning.

"Oh, that." Jenna shrugged and went back to her cooking. "Ye needn't fuss. That Bridget Doyle came down early to set the tray up fer her niece. Seems the lass did not sleep very well last night. And it's no wonder with all she's been through."

More guilt, compounded by the dawning reality that with additional mouths to feed and the concurrent household demands of extra chambers open, laundry and whatever else went into having guests, he was not the only one shorthanded. "You are free, as always, to order the house as you see fit, Jenna. I imagine you will need some additional help. Can you find someone in the village?"

"I can inquire." Jenna set a plate with eggs, a rasher and meat pie on the table. A furrow wrinkled her brow as she fetched his cutlery. "My sister's eldest is expecting in a month. Her younger daughter's yet ta wean the one she had last year. I think mayhap Andrew Cochrane's widow, Betsey, might be looking fer a few extra shillings til that boy of theirs gets a bit older."

Connal nodded his head as he dug into his breakfast. Jenna would know best who to approach. Not very many in these parts were open to having their womenfolk work for The Wicked One. The men, now, they appreciated fair wages in exchange for a fair day's or season's work.

"I need to take the mare and cart into town later this morning, if that suits ye, sir." Jenna had moved back to the stove before she made her request. "And one of the lads."

She turned back in time to catch his wince. Hadn't he just said he was shorthanded?

"If ye keep scowling like that yer face will set—" she started.

As usual, Jenna was not the least put off by his reaction, expressed or otherwise. She had run Glenmeade Manor for too many years to start accommodating the opinions of its occupants. Especially if they ran contrary to her own. Let Mrs. Finn Delaney learn so to her sorrow. That thought would give him a measure of satisfaction as he and the stable master adjusted the day's tasks to the further decrease in their workforce. For more than one reason he'd be glad when Jack returned.

"—and ye're likely ta scare the little one afore ye've been properly introduced." Jenna finished her remonstrance with a knowing shake of her head. As if summoned, there was a clatter of feet on the back stairs heralding an arrival.

"Slow down, young sir," Mary O'Toole's voice sounded from the top of the stairs. "Yer mam says ye must put on yer cap and jacket and we still must ask Mr. Delaney . . ."

A lad of no more than seven or eight skidded to a halt in the doorway, joined a moment later by a breathless Mary still trying to sort through a jumble of cap, jacket, shawl and bonnet she had clutched in her hands.

In dark serge knee pants and waistcoat, the boy gazing at him set Connal's pulse thundering and put him on his feet. It was as if the years had melted and his cousin Finn, the Finn who had been his constant companion and boyhood's best friend, stood before him. With his rumpled dark curls and the solemn set of his features as he studied the occupants of the kitchen, the boy was unmistakably a Delaney.

"How do you do, sir." He was also unmistakably his mother's son. After only a moment's pause, the lad stuck out his hand and advanced toward Connal by the table in a move entirely reminiscent of Bethany Doyle's greeting in the study only a day before. "I'm Ross Delaney just arrived from North Carolina."

Connal stepped around the table and dropped to one knee as he accepted the boy's hand. He had the bluest eyes, the same shade as his mother's, and the same soft lilt to his voice, otherwise Connal would have sworn he was grasping the hand of a diminutive ghost.

"How do you do, Master Ross Delaney. I am Connal Delaney, of Glenmeade Stables—"

"—home to the finest horses in all County Kildare," the boy said, finishing the old family credo. "My da always says that since Ireland produces the finest horses in the world, and since the finest horses in Ireland come from Kildare, that means Glenmeade horses are the best anywhere."

"So I have heard." Connal nodded, his heart hammering in his chest. How many times had he and Finn skipped that very boast over Kildare's hills and valleys? How many times had they waited eagerly for the words to echo back to them as if the land itself was affirming the truth behind the bragging?

He stood swiftly, no longer able to look at this apparition from the past. The boy was not Finn. Finn was dead, months ago. And dead to him, years before that. Even in the best of all worlds, he could not be expected to play the indulgent uncle on a moment's notice. And this was hardly the best of all worlds. The sooner they parted company this morning, the better. He focused his attention on the girl in the doorway. "What was it you thought you should ask me, Mary?"

"Master Ross is horse-mad, it would seem, sir." The girl finished tying her bonnet under her chin, then wagged a finger at Ross. "Come here, young sir, if ye please, and put these on even if it does not please ye."

Her no-nonsense tone and expression were all too reminiscent of her mother's at much the same age when Jenna had been put in charge of the Delaney boys. Ross's reaction evoked those long-ago days, too—instant obedience in the hopes of still being granted the longed-for treat. Under other circumstances, Connal might have found the comparisons amusing. As it was, his patience was stretched a little too thin and he sucked in an exasperated breath.

"Mary, Mr. Delaney asked ye a question. Answer him at once, girl." Her mother's scold saved the lass from anything he might have said.

Mary's fair cheeks flamed and she dropped a small curtsy that set her curls bouncing. "Beg pardon, sir. Mrs. Delaney wanted me to ask ye exactly where I might and might not be allowed ta walk with the lad on the grounds. She said she did not want him ta trespass where he was not welcome."

The boy stopped shrugging into his jacket and stared up at the man who now held his fate in his hands, and in more ways than the boy could possibly be aware. Unexpected sympathy twinged, Connal remembered how impatient he and Finn had always been to escape indoor boundaries for the freedom of the pastures and lanes that made up Glenmeade. But this boy was a stranger, no matter how undeniable his parentage, keeping him on a tight rein was surely best for all concerned.

"Try the orchard just beyond the kitchen garden, Mary." Bridget suggested as she stepped into the kitchen from the front hallway. For just a minute, the flash of her red hair in the doorway forced Connal's breath to catch in anticipation. But for the company, he would have cursed at such a foolhardy reaction.

"If that meets with Mr. Delaney's approval." Bridget winked conspiratorially at Connal as Ross skipped over to give her a big hug. She knew full well Connal would be hard-pressed to deny the boy the very same haven she and her young charges had sought on many occasions so long ago.

Ross looked up at her with pleading eyes. "But Aunt Bridget, the horses—"

"The orchard is a fine suggestion." Connal just wanted the boy gone. If both doorways had not been blocked he would have exited himself. "Stay on this side of the lane, away from the paddocks and stables. This is a working farm, not a play yard."

As if he was not horrified enough by this whole invasion of his home, never in his life had Connal thought to hear fall from his lips the very strictures Uncle Brennan and his own father had laid out a lifetime ago.

"But the horses are the other way, Aunt Bridget." Young Ross looked with rounded eyes first at Connal and then back to his aunt, hoping for some mitigation of his restrictions.

"I'm sure ye'll find a tree or two that needs climbing there, my lad." Bridget gave the boy's shoulder a little pat. "That will give ye a chance to have a look around without wandering too far off. The horses are here every day. Ye'll see them soon enough."

Hardly mollified, the boy studied the toes of his boots for a moment, mumbling something ending with what sounded like *bómánta*, Gaelic for stupid.

Connal's eyebrows rose. There was more Finn in this boy than just his looks. His father had never taken well to being thwarted.

All sympathy fled Bridget's features as she gripped his shoulder now quite firmly. "I am certain Mrs. O'Toole keeps a stock of good strong soap right here in this kitchen if ye've a mind ta speak thusly. Content yerself that we are no longer aboard ship or lose the privilege of leaving the nursery for the time being."

Master Ross is horse-mad it would seem, Mary had said. Looking at the horses from an apple tree was hardly as satisfying as being right there in the yard. Connal quashed his own sympathy. Self-discipline was the first thing a horseman needed to learn.

"Yes, ma'am." The boy twisted the cap in his hands for a few moments more, then lifted his chin to face her, clearly frustrated but anxious to please lest he forfeit his freedom. "I'm sorry I lost my temper."

"Then go on with yerself and don't give Mary a lick of trouble." Bridget released him with an indulgent twinkle. "Mind yer manners from here on. We're all a bit frayed from the long journey, but we do not want to be found lacking in civility."

She sought Connal's gaze. Did the slight arch of her brow convey a warning over repeating what had almost transpired in this very kitchen last night? He suppressed the urge to duck his own head and beg her mercy.

"Glenmeade horses are not playthings, lad." He focused his attention on the boy as he trudged past, his eyes downcast once more. "You must show that you can listen and obey before you will be able to go near them."

Ross paused and looked up as he jammed his cap on his head. "I don't think you look so much like my da, but you sure sound like him."

He sounded so forlorn, Connal could not help but ask, "How do you mean?"

"*No* or *later* was all he ever said to me, but later never came."

Ross made his way out of the kitchen with Mary O'Toole. Connal spun on his heel and stalked by Bridget without a word before he could call the boy back, put him on his shoulder and take him down to the stables himself.

Windblown grass and sandalwood filled her senses as his mouth moved with slow pressure against hers. Not harsh or demanding, but gentle, almost tender and giving. Heat curled in her stomach, then scorched a fiery path through her limbs in a way she'd never experienced before.

His fingers slowly traced the line of her jaw. His breath fanned her cheeks. She'd never felt so cherished, so treasured.

As their kiss deepened, waves of unfamiliar passion flowed through her. A wanton's moan, dredged from deep inside her innermost core, escaped. White-hot mortification shot through her and she edged her eyelids open to see familiar dark curls.

Finn? Cold fear sluiced away everything else. She froze. Finn never made her feel like that. Her eyes widened as he released her, pulling away. His dark, sultry gaze held questions, but no condemnation.

Finn had never looked at her like this.

It was Connal.
Not Finn. Never again.

Reality shot through Bethany as she sat up alone in a bed, far away from everything familiar save the dread pounding through her.

She swallowed hard against the lump in her throat. "Finn Delaney can never hurt me again."

She gulped a breath almost as shallow as her bravado. Drawing her knees up to her chest, she rested her cheek on one. But what about his cousin? With all his skepticism, his thinly disguised hostility, why on earth would she dream that kissing Connal Delaney would be so different from her husband's cold attentions? For that matter, why would she dream about kissing Connal at all?

"Ah, good, ye're awake *isean.* What were ye saying jest now? I didn't quite catch it." Aunt Bridget breezed in the door bearing a tray covered with a linen tea towel.

"Nothing important." Bethany extended her arms upward as if stretching and hoped her aunt wouldn't notice them trembling. She was still so tired she felt nauseous. She'd tossed on the cot in the nursery last night, so angry she'd barely been able to contain herself. How dare Connal Delaney pinion her with his doubting gaze while he pulled devastating admissions from her yet answered none of her questions? Then to top it all off, she'd reacted to him as if he was Finn and nearly acquiesced when she thought he meant to kiss her, something she'd vowed never to let happen again. That he'd let her go had been beside the point, in the wee hours. No wonder he'd invaded her dreams.

She pulled in a deep breath and exhaled slowly. "I can't believe I actually went to sleep after you sent me in here."

With one hand Bridget tugged open the heavy damask curtains covering the windows opposite the bed and let light stream into the room. Dust motes danced in the sunbeams. How long had it been since this room had benefited from a thorough cleaning? Certainly not the kind of question she could comfortably broach with their host, especially after last night. Was there any subject they would be able to discuss rationally?

"Ye've had it terrible hard these past few years with more than yer share of troubles." Bridget turned back to the bed. "Ye certainly deserve a more peaceful life than ye've had so far. It'll take us a bit ta settle in here, so I'm glad ye had a chance ta get a few hours' rest before ye face the rest of the day."

Rest? With the haunting echoes of her dream still vibrating deep inside her, Bethany felt anything but rested. Whether in sandalwood- and windblown-grass dreams or fixing her with his piercing dark gaze filled with accusations, Connal Delaney seemed determined to disturb any morsel of peace she might have hoped to gain from this journey. It might be cowardly, but between their very real encounter last night and her imagined one just now, she could do very well without seeing him any time soon.

She held back a self-indulgent sigh laced with self-pity, and pushed her hair out of her eyes. "So far Glenmeade does not appear to offer much relief from our troubles."

Life was hard and cold and lonely, anticipating problems was the only way to survive—those were the realities her marriage had taught her. Whatever led her to believe that coming to Ireland would change anything was beyond her now that they had arrived. She had to toughen up. She must gather her thoughts and prepare herself to meet Connal's hostility in such a way that her son would not suffer any further from his parents' mistakes.

Bridget set the tray on the nightstand, then sat on the edge of the bed and took Bethany's hand. "Things will get better, ye'll see. The sun is shining on the hills, there's hot tea, a bit of meat pastry and some stewed apples fer ye ta break yer fast, and things ta put in order. Ye've always been happiest when ye were organizing something, now ye've got a whole new life ta see to."

"Organize a whole new life? Not too tall an order." Bethany tried to smile with a modicum of optimism to match her aunt's. Not too tall if it meant securing her child's future. She could face Connal's scrutiny for Ross's sake.

"That's better. Start yer stitches as ye mean ta go on, like yer *mamó* always said." Bridget squeezed her hand. "See if ye can manage ta get everything done by the time I get back, will ye, my little bird?"

"Back?" Momentary panic seized Bethany. She was not ready to face Connal Delaney again, even in the light of day, at least not alone. "Where are you going?"

"I'm jest nipping into the village with Jenna O'Toole fer a few essentials. Master Connal has an appointment down ta the stables with someone interested in one of his colts. Ye can enjoy the morning and the house ta yerself fer a bit . . . unless mayhap ye'd like ta come along in the cart with us?"

After weeks aboard ship, followed by the dreary coach ride from Dublin, the thought of jolting along a country lane in a cart held little appeal for Bethany. Especially if Connal Delaney was otherwise occupied. "Perhaps next time. Where is Ross? I haven't heard a peep from him all morning."

Bridget smiled broadly. "Our lad and Mary O'Toole are playing hoops outside. He's as happy as a twink and will likely take a good nap after she brings him in for nuncheon."

Bethany pushed back the coverlet and swung her feet over to the side of the bed near her aunt. She couldn't stay in bed all day, her son needed her. "Did Ross eat a good breakfast? Has he been occupied? He certainly made a mess this morning when he set about exploring the nursery cupboards."

It was all well and good to borrow the housekeeper's daughter for an hour here or there, but she was used to being responsible for her son. Over the years as their finances had worsened, Finn had let go of more and more of the household staff, starting with the nursery maid and Ross's tutors. Each departure had added more chores for Bridget and her to shift between them. Spending her days with Ross, setting him on his lessons, had been the one joy in all the drudgery.

"Mary and he had it cleaned up in no time. That is, after they spent a lively hour or more setting up the miniature fencing and horse figurines they discovered in one of them. Master Connal's father carved them himself long ago, they are quite clever."

Bridget rose from the bed and removed the

covering on the tray as she talked. She poured Bethany a cup of tea and handed it to her. "The last I looked, he was busy chasing some chickens around the trees in the orchard behind the kitchen."

Bethany took a sip of the pungent brew and tried to let the warmth soothe her jangling nerves. "Did you get permission for him to play there? I don't want there to be any tension when he and Connal are finally introduced."

"Ye needn't fret about introductions. Both he and Master Connal handled their first meeting quite well, I must say."

"They've already met? How . . . How did that happen?" Bethany set the cup down onto the saucer with an abrupt crack, sloshing the tea. She'd asked Mary to make sure Ross did not disturb Mr. Delaney, figuring that warning would serve to keep them apart. "Was he frightened? Connal didn't speak harshly to him, did he?"

She knew she shouldn't have gone back to bed. She should have kept Ross with her. She should have just forbidden him from leaving the nursery. What must he have thought when confronted by a man who so closely resembled his father? She scrambled to her feet.

Bridget took the saucer from her hand before she could spill any more and fixed her with a stern look. "Bethany Doyle Delaney, ye must get a handle on yerself. Everything went fine. Master Connal happened ta be in the kitchen finishing his breakfast when Mary brought Ross down. They met as natural as can be under the circumstances."

"I should have been there. He—"

Bridget clucked and shook her head. "Children

take things far better than we ever expect. Fer Ross, the family resemblance between Connal and his father is nothing ominous, unless ye make it so."

"Unless Connal makes it so, more like." She'd be damned if anyone, especially Connal Delaney, thought to intimidate her son with glowering looks or harsh words.

Bridget fixed her with a quizzical frown. "I thought yer misgivings were rooted in yer exhaustion last night. Try ta set aside yer prejudice over his resemblance ta that one ye married and see Connal fer himself before ye judge him too harshly."

Was she being unfair? Judging him too harshly, given their sudden appearance on his doorstep? Bethany's thoughts had definitely tumbled over too many times to count since she had first caught sight of Connal Delaney. A soft tapping at the door saved Bethany from forming an answer. She reached for her shawl and wrapped it around her shoulders while Bridget went to the door. Bethany hoped it was Ross come in from playing already.

"Yes?" Bridget opened the door a crack.

"The boy's brought the cart around." Jenna O'Toole spoke from the other side of the oak-paneled door. "If ye still have a mind to come with me, we'd best be off."

Bridget opened the door wider. "Jest give me a minute ta fetch my bonnet and gloves and I'll be ready. Unless ye need me ta stay, Bethany?"

She turned back to face her niece with a concerned look. Mrs. O'Toole peered into the room from the hall with a curious look.

"I'll be fine, Aunt. You go ahead. Would you care to come in and wait for her with me, Mrs. O'Toole?"

"Thank you, Mrs. Delaney. That's most kind."
She and Bridget squeezed by each other in the
doorway. "Is there anything ye might like us ta try
to fetch fer ye?"

"Thank you, not today." Bethany shook her head
and smiled at the older woman standing just inside
the doorway, looking for all the world as if she was the
guest. Bethany searched for some small talk to set her
more at ease. "How . . . How often do you go to town
to do the marketing, if you don't mind my asking?"

"Generally speaking once every week or two." Answering a simple question about her routine
seemed to put Mrs. O'Toole more at ease. "We have
regular deliveries and we raise a good portion of
our needs in season."

Glenmeade's housekeeper took a good look
around the chamber. She ran her finger along the
sewing table by the door and frowned at the coating of dust she came away with. "I'm right sorry
about the state of affairs here. We rub along on a
fairly slim staff, being as we don't have much in the
way of visitors and there's just Master Connal's
needs ta see to."

"I hope we are not putting you out overmuch.
Bridget and I are certainly willing to lend a hand.
We did not mean to cause any trouble with our
visit." Although, at least from Connal Delaney's
viewpoint, trouble was certainly what they had
brought nonetheless.

"Oh, no, thank ye fer offering, but the ladies of
Glenmeade Manor have never needed to do so."
Mrs. O'Toole shot her a guilty look. "Master Connal
is sending me to the village to hire additional help.
And some of the stablemen's wives will be giving us

a hand with the laundry and heavy cleaning. Ye won't need to trouble yerself."

"Well, you will have to let us do some things. Neither of us is used to being idle." Connal Delaney was hiring on new staff. Would that cause more resentment or did this step hold the promise that they might achieve a modicum of peace between them?

"I'm sure ye will find plenty to occupy yerself with once ye settle in," Jenna replied. "But if not there is always something that needs tending in a house this large."

"That didn't take long." Bridget stood in the doorway with her bonnet already tied and a twinkle of excitement in her eyes, forestalling any further discussion.

"I'll take my leave, then, Mrs. Delaney. Pray visit me in the kitchen whenever ye have the time." The housekeeper gave her an awkward bob.

Aunt Bridget chuckled and gave Bethany a broad wink as she took Mrs. O'Toole's arm. "Oh, you don't want Bethany's help in the kitchen, Jenna. At least, not for meal preparations."

"That is hardly fair, Aunt Bridget," Bethany responded with mock indignation. "Father Lonigan always said my raisin biscuits were among the best in the parish. And Ross loves them."

"Raisin biscuits, is it?" Jenna asked. "Ye'll have ta teach me the recipe, ma'am."

"I would love to. Have a nice ride, Aunt, Mrs. O'Toole," Bethany called as her aunt reached for the door handle.

"I can hardly wait to see the village again," Aunt Bridget said as the door swung shut on the two ladies. "Has it changed much since I went away?"

It had been a long time since Bethany had been alone in as much space as this chamber offered. She would savor the peace and use it to gather her thoughts before facing Connal Delaney again. Ross's possible inheritance aside, she needed to determine how long this visit to Glenmeade might last. Ross needed stability in his life, if not here, then somewhere else. She had not crossed with her son an ocean to trade one miserable Delaney household for another.

She took her tea over to the window and sipped it as she looked at the mountains in the distance. It was no wonder Finn had loved this place. With the lush green of the pastures, the orderly paddocks and training yards outlined with white fencing, the cluster of barns flanked by neatly thatched cottages, Glenmeade was beautiful. It would be nice if Ross could come to think of this as home. But before that happened, before they settled here, she needed to know about this family, this place, and why her husband had left.

Now that the initial shock of their arrival was over, she and Connal needed to come to an agreement on how they would proceed. She could not let Connal's frustration or his hostility intimidate her, any more than she could allow his resemblance to Finn to throw her off balance. Surely she could ask her questions, and answer his calmly, without the riot of emotions the previous day's encounters had provoked.

She finished the last of her tea just as she saw him striding up the lane from the stables.

Chapter Five

Connal took the coin pouch from his pocket and tossed it on the desk, savoring the satisfying chink of money well earned. Joseph Champion had struck a fair bargain for the colt his man was leading home, and had promised to return at the end of the summer to look over the next crop of foals.

If not for the occupation of the Manor by Finn's family, Connal might have counted this a good day. He pulled open the bottom drawer and extracted the cash box and his ledger. There was little chance the tedious aspects of his business would help to clear his thinking, but that didn't negate the need to keep his records accurate and up-to-date.

At least that's what he told himself, but in actual fact he was willing to do almost anything to avoid seeking out Bethany Doyle. He wanted to postpone for a few more hours dealing with the reality that Glenmeade and its business would never be the same. And those facts did not even take into account the credit arrangements he and James had yet to go over.

He shifted his gaze to the clouds gathering on Kildare's hills. A storm hovered along the ridges, ripe with the promise of foul weather, an appropriate metaphor for this day.

With Jenna and Bridget off to the village and the boy still playing outdoors, the house had the quiet hush of emptiness he'd grown accustomed to over the years. Was it only yesterday he'd been lamenting that very emptiness due to lack of family?

Be careful what ye wish for, boy-o. One of Jack's favorite warnings came to mind as he turned his attention back to the ledger sheets before him without really seeing them. *Ye just may get what ye might not want.*

He'd wanted a family to fill Glenmeade, all right. "Just not Finn's."

"Not Finn's what?"

He jerked his gaze away from his desktop to find Bethany Doyle standing just inside the door, her gaze fixed on him with the same calculating detachment Joseph Champion had worn as he considered his yearling acquisition prancing across the training yard.

"Do Americans not believe in knocking before they enter a room?" The words came brusque with his need to force her as far away from him as possible.

"The door was open and, as you can see, I have yet to enter your sanctum. I had hoped we could attempt to be civil to one another this morning."

The fact that she did not quail in the face of his rudeness oddly pleased him, despite his deep desire to have seen the last of her. No good would come from the two of them standing at daggers drawn every time they met. At least, not until matters were settled.

"I beg your pardon. Let me begin again. Good morning, Mrs. Delaney. Would you care to come in?" He nodded his head to the side in a modified bow of greeting. The gentilities felt stiff and foreign.

"I hope your accommodations were suitable enough for you to rest a little after your late night." Was that civil enough to suit her?

"I managed as well as can be expected under the circumstances." She stepped into the study and offered him a brief smile that did not quite reach her lovely blue eyes. "Thank you for asking."

No sarcasm, nor even a note of censure lingering from last night's encounter, marked her tone. Good. While he had stepped over the line, he had no intention of giving any ground by apologizing.

Dressed in a drab brown outfit that did little to offset her fair skin or the light auburn curls she'd sculpted tightly away from her face, she looked like a governess. That appealing waif, who had haunted him through the intervening hours after he'd chased her from the kitchen last night, was gone. Could this type of outfit have prompted Finn's disparagement of her charms? If so, he still found himself hard-pressed to understand his cousin's blindness. No matter what she wore, an innate grace and elegance imbued this woman with an allure he found hard to ignore. Indeed she made his groin tighten every time he saw her.

The thought irritated him. He gave himself a mental shake. She had not sought him out so that he could stand here gaping at her. She clutched a packet of papers tied in a black ribbon.

"Is there something I can do for you?"

"We need to talk." She offered with prim gravity. "As soon as is convenient for you."

His gut clenched. An ordinary phrase, yet the last time a woman had said such words to him had been the day Rosleen died. Scattered thoughts and fragmented emotions crystallized into an icy rock in his stomach. Bethany Doyle Delaney had done nothing but cause him difficulty since she arrived. Was it only yesterday? There was little to be gained by postponing the inevitable. He was not sole owner of Glenmeade Stables. The boy was undeniably a Delaney and while nothing could be decided today, they needed to formulate a plan for handling an equitable division.

"If now is suitable for you, pray have a seat." He managed not to grit his teeth over the words as he gestured to a chair on the opposite side of the desk from his.

"Now that we are over the shock of our initial meeting"—her voice remained cool and steady as she continued—"I hope we can conduct ourselves with civility."

"Or, at least, without hostility? If only for the boy's sake?" He supplied the rest of the rules without adding the most important one: no physical proximity. If the discussion did not prove dampening enough, the expanse of wood and paperwork between them should discourage a repeat of what had nearly occurred in the kitchen last night. He was not about to let Finn's widow use feminine wiles to manipulate him.

Despite his caution, he couldn't help but admire the determined set of her shoulders, the way she kept her chin raised and her gaze steady as she crossed the room. Only a slight trembling and the amount of pressure she used to hold her packet of papers betrayed her unease.

She sat on the edge of the fading red velvet tufted chair. "We are, after all, family."

Did she truly have no idea how that word twisted through him? He sat in his chair but leaned forward, resting his arm on the desk, trying to achieve a reasonable air even if reasonable was about the last thing he wanted to be. "What would you like to discuss, Mrs. Delaney?"

She pressed her lips together and drew in a long breath. "As I told you yesterday, Ross is the only reason I came here. The only reason we are still here. We did not come seeking our fortune. Or, more accurately, yours. I brought my son to Ireland to find what was left of his family so the past could be put to rest."

The intensity in her voice was matched in her blue-eyed gaze as she searched his face, seeking his reaction.

"Which means exactly what?" He was not about to bare his soul willingly. No matter her protest he very much doubted she intended to turn down her son's rightful inheritance. Especially if Finn treated her as poorly as she'd hinted.

"I have so many questions. Questions only you can answer, since Finn's father is gone. Just as you must have more . . . more than the ones you asked me last night."

"So you came all this way for a history lesson?" He regretted the harsh sound of his words before he had finished uttering them. He might get more out of her if he remained as neutral as possible.

He tried again. "What is the point in revisiting old wounds, especially when the problems of the present and the future are far more pressing?"

"My father always said that ignorance of the past doomed us to repeat the same mistakes. Especially when the lessons to be learned were there for the asking. So I am asking." Her chin raised another fraction and she leaned forward. "And I intend to keep asking until I am satisfied. I would simply prefer to get my answers from you rather than the neighborhood gossips as you suggested."

"Your father sounds like a wise man. And you sound like a very determined woman."

Connal took a deep breath. Despite his reluctance, her point was well taken, it might be better for her to learn the basic facts from him before anyone else embroidered the tales. "Very well, proceed with your interrogation. I may not answer all of your questions—at least, not to your satisfaction. We may be related by marriage but that does not give you the right to invade my privacy at will."

He pushed back from the desk and paced over to the window, looking out at the grounds and the patchy clouds now obscuring the sun over the pastures. She wanted the truth to tell her son, to tell Finn's son. How much truth could he give her? How much could a boy bear? The basics should be enough to put her on notice that this was not the place for a woman and a lad to settle. He turned back to face her.

She rested her fingertips on the edge of the desk and nodded. "Fair enough. And I will try to answer yours to the best of my ability. Perhaps then we can discuss the future you are so concerned about."

He nodded. She chewed her lip for a moment, then took a deep breath. "Ross spent a good portion of the morning exploring the nursery you and Finn once shared. He is bound to wonder what it was like for his father, for you, when you were children here. I have no idea what to tell him."

So, she really was interested in delving into the distant past. He let the line of her thinking sink in for a minute and then shrugged. "Just like anywhere, growing up in Glenmeade had its share of joy and sorrows. We lost our mothers young. I am sure Bridget told you that much. She was with us the summer my mother died. Finn and I were born only two months apart. Our fathers were twins who raised us as brothers. We shared the nursery, our tutors, our ambitions for a time. The only way most people told us apart was the same way you did yesterday."

"By your eyes." Her gaze locked with his.

He nodded, looking past Bethany to another time. "Finn's were the same shade as our fathers'. After my mother was gone, my father said he could always find her shining in my eyes. He died the winter before I turned twelve. Uncle Brennan was the only parent left to us then. He did the best that he could, but he was better with the horses than handling two growing boys."

"Did you get into much mischief?"

How much had Finn told his wife? Never good at losing, had he shaded his tales so that he was the victim or the victor? Connal closed his eyes for a moment. Silence, broken only by the ticking of the mantel clock, stretched through the room. He'd fought so long to push the memories away, to choke them back, he didn't dare let them loose. When he opened his eyes at last, he found her waiting patiently for him to continue.

"We had our share of adventures, especially when we were out from under Uncle Brennan's thumb at school in Dublin. Finn was the risk taker, not that most people distinguished between us." He shrugged again. "Eye color is hard to see at a distance. Most people just called us by our last name."

The Wild Delaneys—that's what they'd been called back then, racing along Kildare's lanes or playing cards in a smoke-filled tavern. Finn had seen everything as a competition, a challenge to see who was best, who would claim Uncle Brennan's praise. He'd been galled every time he lost, but was even harder to live with if he thought Connal held back and let him win. Rosleen had been the ultimate prize back then although, in the end, none of them could be counted winners.

"That should be enough to satisfy the boy's curiosity about his father's childhood." His gaze locked with Bethany's for a moment. "What else was on your list? Or is it my turn?"

"I . . . I wanted to know about your uncle. About Ross's grandfather."

Any hope she had heard enough for one day was dashed.

"How did he die? Why did he never once try to contact his son after Finn left here?"

Connal could hardly bear her scrutiny any longer. The gray light did little to dim the luminous quality of her complexion, or the patent sympathy shining in her gaze. But it was wasted on him. She might not want to deal with the gossips but he had no doubt that even now her aunt was being filled in on all the sordid details. Her compassion would dry up in a matter of hours.

"Uncle Brennan died almost a year ago, just a few months before Finn." He looked out at the darkening skies. The rain would come any minute. "But from the day Finn left he seemed to wither. I have no idea if he tried to get in touch with Finn before his stroke. I was not around much those first years."

Those were the years when he truly earned his reputation. He'd drunk and wenched his way through Dublin's darkest gaming hells, living up to the brand of shame Finn and Rosleen left him to shoulder alone. He'd cursed them both for escaping, cursed Uncle Brennan for saddling him with the scandal. The Wicked One, in deed as well as ill repute, but that lifestyle had not satisfied the emptiness in his soul or assuaged his guilt. He'd let Rose down and he could never make it up to her.

Uncle Brennan's stroke sent Jack to find Connal, to rescue him from himself and bring him home to Glenmeade. He'd thrown himself into salvaging the business his father and uncle had built. He might not be welcome in the homes of Kildare's finest, their daughters and wives might need to be shielded from his corrupting influence, but men who knew horseflesh still found their way to his stables. Business was business, after all.

Bethany Doyle would learn all of this soon enough, but not from him. The truths and the lies he'd lived with all these years were too raw, too tangled one within the other. He glanced back toward her chair, only to find that she had moved around the desk and was standing just a few feet away, listening intently. Her packet lay discarded on the desk.

"Afterwards, when I came home, Uncle Brennan could not walk, let alone write anything. He barely spoke. He lingered for years, staring out the windows at the fields he once ruled. I had no idea where he had sent Finn or if he wanted him to come home. I made inquiries over the years, but they all proved fruitless until—"

"Until he was killed," she supplied, her tone matter-of-fact, almost indifferent.

His gaze locked with hers. Whatever she was thinking or feeling was not reflected in her eyes. What was it she had said last night? *Finn was finished with me years before . . . We led separate lives . . .* Was that really so, or merely what she said to insulate herself? To excuse herself. She had wanted the truth, hadn't she? Why should he be stripped bare while she stayed shielded?

"Shot dead by an enraged husband, who then suffered a fatal heart attack. That makes hard-to-miss headlines in more than one city."

She swallowed hard, but whatever she felt about her husband's death remained shrouded in the blue depths of her eyes. "Perhaps you can understand my reasons for coming here, then. I could not bear for Ross to grow up in the shadow of his father's sins."

"Pity you chose such a poor haven."

He turned his back and rested one hand on the window frame. The storm set to rage outside was nothing compared with the one he was struggling to contain within himself. It would be so easy to let the truth about her husband's sins pour out in a torrent, to let her know just how deep an error she had made by coming to Glenmeade, especially if she sought to protect her son from scandal.

The faint swish of her skirt told him she was on the move again. This time closing the distance to come and stand beside him. The maddening scent of cinnamon and vanilla assailed him. What about the unspoken rule? Hadn't last night warned her off? He was torn between wanting to shove her away and taking her by the shoulders to shake her for forcing him into this painful reverie.

"I wrote to Finn's father as soon as the news reached us in North Carolina." She wore a puzzled expression as she looked up at him. "That is when I mentioned my intention to come here unless he had an objection. You could have answered in his place. You could have prevented us from coming here."

This was one error he was not going to bear responsibility for. "If that is so, your letter never arrived."

Her eyes widened. "I had no idea the post would prove unreliable. No wonder you were so shocked by our arrival."

"Exactly."

She glanced over his shoulder, focusing on the portrait above the mantel. It was of Finn and him at about ten with their fathers. The artist had traded the painting for a prime gelding, getting the better of the deal by half, but he'd achieved a fair likeness. Not really all that difficult, given the family resemblances between men and boys. It had been a part of the décor for so long he almost never noticed it except

occasionally late at night when he'd imbibed too
much brandy.

"I suppose I owe you a thank-you." Bethany
looked back up at him, her lips pressed in a serious
line as she searched his face.

"For what, pray tell?" He could imagine the list of
apologies she could give him at this point, but gratitude? He still wanted to shake her, and to get
through this discussion and move on. But an errant
part of him wondered if he was just looking for an
excuse to take her in his arms again.

"It must have been a shock for you to meet Ross
this morning. I understand you handled it quite
smoothly, especially in light of not even knowing of
his existence only a few hours before. Thank you,
for his sake."

She seemed so sincere. Did she really think him
such a monster that he might take his frustration
out on a child? He hadn't kicked any puppies or
drowned any kittens today either. "Do you have
enough tales to spin for the boy for now, can we
move on?"

She took in a deep breath and nodded, her gaze
still studying his face. "I guess that would be fair.
Thank you."

"To what should I attribute your gratitude this
time?"

"For helping to fill in some of the gaps. I could
see it was not easy for you. Ross need not put Finn
on a plaster pedestal, but I also cannot bear the
thought of him knowing his father's perfidy while
he is still so young."

She drew another deep breath and clasped her

hands in front of her. "Now, what questions do you have for me?"

He studied her for a minute. She looked so demure. Clearly she was uncomfortable, as if she was a prisoner in the docket or a school miss standing for an oral exam. Indeed, Finn must have married her straight from her schoolroom; she hardly looked of an age to be the mother of a seven-year-old. He'd seen a flicker of temper last night when he'd confronted her in the kitchen, watched her deliberately tamp it back. This morning she'd all but raked him over the coals, claiming familial interest with a calm detachment, then thanked him, pretty as you please, with a sincerity that rang true.

Bethany Doyle Delaney was certainly an enigma. Under other circumstances, he might be tempted to try and draw her secrets from her. Or to explore the veracity of her claims that her husband said she could not offer the comfort of a real woman.

We led separate lives, she'd claimed last night. As impossible to believe in the light of day as it had seemed in the warm intimacy of the kitchen so late at night. She'd stiffened when he pulled her close, then acquiesced for the barest fraction of time, a dissatisfying cooperation that hinted at a disturbing depth of fear and dread. The realization had caused him to break away just as a small spark of something else flared between them. A flicker of possibility neither of them could endure.

Then or now.

He focused on the papers she'd left on his desk.

"What do you have there?" He flicked his gaze from the desk to her and back.

She followed his sight line. "These are papers for

your attorney. Copies of my marriage lines, Ross's birth record, Finn's death certificate. I assume you will want to have them verified."

His brows quirked up. She was definitely an enigma. "You certainly came well prepared for your *visit*."

"I told you, I plan to make a new life for my son. I brought all of my documents with me." She had the grace to blush as he stepped around her.

He picked up the packet and untied the ribbon.

"There is also notice of the bankruptcy I filed, and letters of satisfaction from our creditors."

"Bankruptcy?" He looked at her sharply.

"I had little choice. Finn ran my father's business into the ground, mortgaged our house to the hilt and borrowed against the trust my father left to Ross. If it were not for Aunt Bridget's own trust, we would have been virtually penniless."

"So this sojourn to County Kildare is indeed turning out to be most fortuitous for you and your son. You wash up on our shores and find the proverbial pot of gold waiting for you."

"That was not my reason for coming here." The temper he had seen last night flared again. "But I will not be bullied into failing to secure my son's future if I can."

Bullied? He nearly choked on his own anger. His hand fisted at his side, the nails biting into his palm. "You mean, not again."

She flinched at his jibe. Guilt washed through him. He was a bully. It was Finn who had robbed his son of a secure future. His wife had been just another of his victims.

"That was unnecessary. I apologize. I will send

these to the solicitor in Dublin who handles our affairs. He will know how to proceed."

She nodded and glanced out the window. "How will this work?"

Surely she had no interest in the day-to-day running of a horse farm. Would Bridget's funds stretch to allow them to set up a separate household? he wondered. If so, he felt quite certain they would be on their way as soon as she finished telling Finn's wife all the details she'd learned in the village. If not, they would have to rub along as best they could for a time. He certainly did not have the cash right now to advance them.

"A guardian for Ross's share will have to be appointed, I believe. Uncle Brennan was mine. He managed my financial affairs until I reached my majority."

"You and Ross will be co-owners?" At least she had the grace not to look satisfied at the change in her fortune.

His gut clenched as he tried to wrestle his thoughts around all the financial implications of dividing Glenmeade once again. Especially with the new stock and all the construction, not to mention the loan.

"I don't know how things work in America," he continued. "But in Ireland, all land must be divided equally among a man's sons. Our fathers owned Glenmeade jointly. Since my father's death I have been part-owner. Uncle Brennan's share would have gone to Finn, and will now pass to Ross. How long that will take is anyone's guess."

Once everything was settled she could take Finn's son and raise him anywhere she saw fit. Far away from any of the scandals Finn had wrought. The crunch of wheels on the drive outside signaled Jenna and Bridget returning with the cart just as rain splatters hit the panes like little whip cracks, only a few for the first handful of seconds, then the skies opened up in a massive downpour.

"I believe your aunt has returned."

"If you will excuse me, I must go and see if Ross and Mary made it back to the house safely." She was already heading to the door. "Can we continue this at another time?"

"Certainly."

He sat down at his desk and pulled out some stationery to write a letter to the solicitor. Surely they had covered all the basics. What more could there be? He was weary beyond measure, both from lack of sleep and from the toll of having to be sociable— if that is what you could call what he had been the last day—after so many years. The sooner he began the verification, the sooner he could get her out of Glenmeade and out of his thoughts.

"I did have one more question." She paused in the doorway, her hand on the doorknob as she turned back to him.

"What is it?"

He looked up at her as he sharpened his nib.

"Why did Finn say you were dead all these years?"

"He thought I was dead." Sometimes the simplest answer was the best.

She frowned. "Why would he think that?"

"Because the day he left Glenmeade, he shot me in the back."

Chapter Six

"They call him what?" The cool surface of the polished wood bedpost felt odd beneath Bethany's heated palm as she gripped it fast. Her chest tightened and air wasn't coming in fast enough. She sank onto the bed's quilted coverlet, still holding the post with her left hand while rubbing her forehead with her right.

"'That Wicked Delaney.'" Bridget shook her head, her lips pursed in disapproval. "Or, The Wicked One."

"How awful." Bethany's breath came a little easier, but the tightness in her chest dropped into her stomach. She wasn't sure which was worse: the actual circumstances behind the cloud of disgrace hanging over Connal Delaney's head, or the sinking realization she had just fled one life ruined by the stink of scandal, only to land her son in an even worse situation. Her assumptions that life would be easier to piece back together were shredding away before her eyes.

She was a terrible mother. Perhaps Finn had been right about that all along.

One look at Bridget's face in the kitchen had told her something was very wrong. But between assuring herself that Ross was safe and dry, and settled in the nursery with some bread and milk to be followed by a rest, and helping the two drenched older women bring the necessities from the cart into the storage room, it had been more than an hour before they could be alone and able to speak freely. She just hadn't imagined the reason for the shocked look haunting Bridget's features could be so dire. Or so immediate. She had brought her son into the home of a man who very probably was like her dead husband in more than his looks.

"I have ta say I agree with Jenna O'Toole." Bridget finished fastening the skirt she had exchanged for her sodden one and picked up her comb from the dressing table. "It's just not possible Connal Delaney could be responsible fer any such doings. There has ta be more ta the tale. Right up until the last letter she sent me, yer grandmam sang his praises. 'An upright young gentleman is that Connal Delaney,' that's what she always said."

Bridget joined Bethany on the bed, plopping herself on the mattress edge with a loud sigh. The ropes holding the mattress screeched a token protest.

"Not a bit like that one ye married," she continued. "Not that yer grandmam ever said a word against him. If only she had, yer father and I might have tumbled to his shortcomings sooner and put a stop ta things before they began."

"You must stop blaming yourself, Aunt. My misalliance with Finn was entirely my doing."

"Such things are seldom the result of just one

person's errors, *isean.*" Bridget put the comb down on the quilt between them and brushed her fingertips along the back of Bethany's hand.

If only she hadn't been so eager to be grown-up, so blinded by Finn's flattery, so stupid, the Delaneys and all their problems would have nothing to do with her life wherever she was. Of course, as Bethany always reminded herself when her thoughts turned down this dark path, then she wouldn't have Ross either. So she couldn't unwish her choices, she just had to find some way to fix them.

Again.

"We both know tales get retold and embroidered as they go along. Sometimes things are not as grim as is commonly believed." Bridget's comfort did little to warm Bethany.

"True," she answered. "Sometimes they are worse."

The entire Atlantic seaboard greedily devoured the salacious details of her husband's death. Discovered in bed with a business associate's much younger wife, the enraged husband had shot Finn dead, then suffered a fatal seizure of the heart. Wilmington's business community had not hesitated to pick the bones of the financial ruin Finn had made of her father's once-thriving naval-supply business, her personal fortune. But no one, not even Bridget, knew the whole, sordid truth behind her disaster of a marriage. Finn had been careful and she had been too ashamed.

"I don't see how they can get much worse where Master Connal is concerned." Bridget pulled the pins out of her braided bun and laid them on the quilt. "Jenna says he's not welcomed at any of the homes in the county. The menfolk come here for their horses, but they cross their women ta the other side of the street if they see him coming. Not that he actually goes ta the village often."

"He must be guilty." Bethany's heart sank. She'd so hoped his foul temper had more to do with his shock at their arrival, at finding out Finn had an heir, than with any defect in his character. She wanted to believe her aunt when she said Connal was not cut from the same cloth as Finn. She wanted to believe her instinct that he was not like Finn. But then her instincts had hardly proved reliable in the past—after all, she'd once believed she loved Finn.

"Everyone is guilty of something, *isean*. Things done, or not done. Those times haunt us all." Bridget sounded so reasonable, so calm.

"But he's lived with this for over ten years. Without speaking up in his own defense?"

"So Jenna says. And so did the greengrocer's wife and the clerk at the dry goods store. Everyone in the village has an opinion or two ta express where The Wicked One's concerned, it would seem. And none of them were any too high."

"Why? Why would any man suffer such treatment if it were not justified?"

The only logical reason Bethany could find was the black certainty he had no defense, Connal Delaney was guilty of seducing his fiancé and abandoning her when he found she was with child. Was that what might have happened to her with Finn if Da had not discovered them together and insisted on a wedding then and there? She felt nauseous.

"Jenna wanted to give me the true story—well, as

true as she knows it, Master Connal has never spoken about the events—before the others got a chance to wag their tongues, that's why she asked me ta go with her today." Bridget shook her damp curls out of her braid. "She says not ta take stock in the horrors ta be told. Even knowing the scorn he would face, Connal came back here after his uncle's stroke and saved the Stables from the brink of ruin . . ."

Bethany picked up the comb and started stroking the water out of Bridget's hair as she tried to rein in her racing thoughts and listen while her aunt continued recounting the information Jenna had shared with her. If he was being judged unfairly, how could he not have spoken up?

"And when the worst of the famine ravaged this county, he was responsible for providing the bulk of the foodstuffs the local parish gave out ta them who would have gone without. And he would not let the priests say who was the benefactor."

Bethany's head ached. She knew all too well that any protest Connal might have made through the years, any statements of the facts from his point of view, would fall on a certain number of deaf ears, no matter their veracity. Couldn't his actions since be viewed as just means to expiate his guilt? Wouldn't someone who was blameless at least try to clear his name?

"How could a man get the woman he already intends to marry pregnant, then repudiate her? How does that make sense?" The questions tumbling through her just poured out. And she'd thought she had too many questions about Connal Delaney when she awoke this morning.

"How many good deeds could wash away that guilt?" She continued combing her aunt's hair, talking more to herself than to Bridget. "Would he even *feel* guilt? Even if she died? Especially if she died. And the babe with her? How could he live with himself?"

"It's hard to say." Aunt Bridget hesitated, probably as puzzled by all this as Bethany felt.

"And what about that poor girl? To kill herself and her child, what could she have been thinking?"

"She wasn't thinking." Aunt Bridget stood abruptly and paced over to the windows. She hugged her arms around herself and shivered as she looked out at the storm. "She was feeling lost, alone, bereft of her dreams, of happiness."

With her hair curling around her face, then falling down over her shoulders as it dried, Bridget looked so much younger, almost fragile. Her face in profile wore such a sad expression it snapped Bethany's thoughts away from Connal's former fiancé. She crossed the carpet and stood behind her aunt.

"Aunt . . . How could you possibly know anything about how that girl felt?" She put her hands on Bridget's shoulders. "How could anyone know . . ."

Bridget tensed, then drew in a long breath and let it out. "I know. I was in love once. Before I left Ireland."

She fell silent for the space of several heartbeats. Bethany hesitated, unsure if her aunt was finished or searching for the right words to continue. So she just waited, trying to give Bridget the same patient support her aunt had always provided her.

"He was a fine figure of a man. Everyone said he

wasn't the marrying kind, but he was exciting, dashing, and not content ta jest be a crofter. He wanted more and he wanted me . . ."

Bridget's shoulders straightened and her voice lost its hesitance. "I caught his eye at the May Fair down in Kildare. He said he'd never seen anyone dance with such joy, that I fired his blood. My da did not approve. But I was headstrong and I wanted him ta be mine."

Bethany resolved to just listen as it all came pouring out of this woman she thought she knew. In fact, she had never quite looked at Aunt Bridget as a woman at all. As her rock, her comfort, almost a mother, always a friend. But not as a *woman*. A woman in love, a woman with dreams.

Bridget tossed her head to get some of her curls out of her eyes. "We managed ta meet in secret," she continued, her voice husky with emotion, "more than once. Then he went away on one of his trips ta the Continent. He was gone longer than he said he would be, so long that it became obvious I was carrying his child." She stopped again and drew in a shaky breath.

Shock poured through Bethany, mixing with sympathy and pain as she continued to hold her peace. She squeezed her aunt's shoulder, encouraging through the pressure of her hand and fingers, rather than through any words she could find.

Bridget glanced over her shoulder. There were tears glistening in the corners of her eyes. "That's when yer grand-da sent me ta make my home with yer parents. Yer mam was expecting ye. And yer grand-da thought Ross and Maeve could raise ye together, my babe and Maeve's. I had the babe on the ship going over. He was too small, too soon. He died after only a few hours."

"You had a son? I never knew." Bethany's heart ached for her aunt.

"Aye." Bridget managed a wavery smile. Her eyes had a faraway look.

"A wee lad with a thatch of black hair as dark as a raven's back." Her voice caught. "I barely had a chance ta hold him, ta christen him proper. Then he was gone."

Bridget held herself so stiff, so still, it was like she was frozen. Finally, Bethany mustered the courage to ask, "When you christened the babe, what did you name him?"

Aunt Bridget was silent for so long, Bethany was afraid she'd asked too much, that it was too painful.

"John," Bridget whispered at last. "I named him John, fer his father."

The rain drummed steadily against the window as Bethany held her aunt while tears, held back for far too long, welled. Finally, Bridget patted Bethany's hand and turned around. Tears streaked her cheeks but she managed the pouting smile that usually forced Bethany to reciprocate.

"Ah, there, *isean*. This must be a day fer secrets. Every family has their share of scandal. Everyone makes mistakes. And here I am spilling mine, when I never meant ta tell ye. Must be coming back here that did it."

All this time Bethany had been too wrapped up in her own mounting burdens to even imagine any painful memories Bridget might be carrying. Indignation and sorrow over the rough treatment life had handed her aunt burned in Bethany's breast.

Look at the price her aunt had paid for a few stolen encounters. She gave her a quick hug. "Did you ever see the man again? Did he try to find you?"

"Nay." Bridget shook her head.

She dabbed the tears on her face with her sleeve and sniffed. Squaring her shoulders, she raised her chin. It was like watching her dress herself in her usual demeanor.

"I left a letter fer him before I went, ta tell him I was expecting. Then . . . Then I wrote him after I reached Wilmington, telling him about the babe, but I never heard from him. Fer the longest time I hoped he would still want me, that he would come fer me, but I guess our fire had burned out."

"Is that why you never married, despite the men who seemed interested back home?"

"Aye." Bridget nodded, her smile a bit lopsided. "No other boy-o ever caught my fancy. Not the way he did. And I had the care of yer da and ye ta fill my days once yer mam passed."

Aunt Bridget seemed so brave. Bethany marveled at how easily she slipped back into her usual self-deprecating mode. It was as if there had been an-other woman in the room. A woman she'd never met before who had peeked out from behind the one she loved. One she wanted to know better. "Do you still wish sometimes you married John? That you could see him again and ask him what hap-pened? To get to the truth?"

"The truth?" Bridget shook her head. "Nay. The truth lies buried in the past. I know yer da was a strong advocate for studying the past, but I believe all we can look to is what we have now, and where we are headed down the road."

She gathered her hair and began to rebraid it.
"But I expect I may have a chance ta set a few things
straight by-and-by." Her gaze drifted to Bethany
with a hint of starch and determination. "He still
lives in these parts from what I hear."

Bethany couldn't help but smile. Now that was a
meeting she would give much to overhear, never
mind the lecture she felt more than ready to give
the unknown father of Bridget's child. But she held
her peace for the moment and went to pick up the
hairpins still scattered on the quilt.

Bridget squinted her eyes and frowned as she
wound the braid back into a bun. "It was quite odd,
actually—most of the people I met today, those who
remember me—seemed to think I had indeed
gotten married. Time and distance tend to muddle
things sometimes. And often the information
people think they know isn't right at all. See how
wrong people can be?"

They both shook their heads at the folly of
common knowledge. Bethany handed hairpins to
her aunt as her thoughts circled back to the questions that brought them here in the first place. "So
where does that leave us as far as finding a new
home? I cannot expose Ross to this, true or not.
Not if there is a chance Connal is cut from the same
cloth as Finn."

"Give things some time, *isean*. Time has a way of
sorting things out. Ross is still too young ta take
much of this ta heart. Did ye not say earlier that ye
and Master Connal had a chance to clear the air a
bit while we were gone?"

"I suppose so." It was no wonder Connal had

such a difficult time talking about the past. He lived in its cold shadow.

"Well, I say that if James Carey can find it in his heart ta still associate with Master Connal"—Bridget slipped her feet into her boiled-wool slippers and picked up the tea tray—"we could do worse than ta follow his example for a bit. After all, it was his sister who was most involved."

Bethany plopped herself down on the bed again. "The girl Connal was set to marry—the one who killed herself rather than live with the shame of having a child out of wedlock—was James Carey's sister?"

"Aye," Bridget answered.

Cool, damp air misted the windows this morning as Vivian finally honored James with her presence at breakfast. She had been with him for a handful of days, but this was the first time she had left her chambers.

Even after enjoying her charms to the fullest during her visit, he appreciated her ability to weave such a lovely spell about herself when she entered a room that the room itself seemed to grow smaller.

She looked every bit the calm, collected, though still-bereaved widow. Newly emerged from her year-long period of mourning, of course. They'd pushed back her husband's death so she could be free to dress in the colorful raiment that would show her to best advantage. Today she'd chosen a bright yellow-and-black-striped confection that seemed to fill the room with sunshine.

"Good morning to you, Cousin." He rose to greet

her as the maid filled her cup with chocolate. "You look lovely, as always. Did you manage to get some rest last night?"

"A bit." She met his smile with her own—wicked and knowing, with just a twist of pure innocence all at the same time. He loved that about her.

"Is that a new hairstyle?" he inquired. "It looks quite fetching."

"What about my dress?" Her pout of pique was belied by the twinkle in her dark eyes.

"You are a vision," he said as she took his arm and he escorted her to the table.

"We can manage to serve ourselves, Emily. You may go."

"Very good, sir. Madame."

The little maid bobbed and exited through the swinging door that led to the kitchen. Normally, he enjoyed watching the swirl of her skirts around her hips as she departed a room, but she paled in comparison to his guest's lush attributes.

Vivian took the seat next to him at the broad walnut table, set with shirred eggs, baked tomatoes, sausage on fine Irish lace. Cinnamon and jasmine teased him. His groin tightened. He leaned over and brushed his mouth against her jawline, flicking his tongue covertly against her skin.

She took a deep breath. "Who is being naughty now?"

"Guilty as charged. I throw myself totally on your mercy."

She giggled. The sound skipped around the room.

"You do look rested," he observed as he moved to take his place at the end of the table.

"Thank you." She smiled again. "After the rigors of . . . travel, I could not have asked for a better welcome. Your staff has been so very kind to me. And you have been the very soul of attentiveness. I cannot think of how I can ever repay you for your kindness in my hour of need.

"But I'd like to try." She leaned closer and whispered, "I do not have on any pantalettes."

His groin tightened further. "Naughty minx."

She sat back and sipped her chocolate. "Thank you for noticing my hair. Emily's sister, Maureen, I believe she said, has quite a way with a brush. Do you think I might borrow her to help me during my stay?"

He shrugged. "If it will make you happy."

Mrs. Mulrooney bustled into the room. The housekeeper smiled her satisfaction. "It's good ta see ye downstairs this morning, Mrs. Brown. And looking just as sunny as the day outside."

Mrs. Mulrooney addressed Vivian by the name he'd come up with on the night of her arrival, one that would prevent anyone from making any unnecessary connections.

"I hope ye find everything ta yer liking. I put out some of my special raspberry preserves ye seem so fond of."

"Thank you," Vivian murmured. "That was most thoughtful."

Ah, if only his very proper housekeeper had any clue of the inventive uses they had found for those preserves. Vivian's tongue flicked her lips. Her thoughts must have been following the same path as his.

"Will there be anything else ye'd be needing, sir?"

The housekeeper settled the fresh pot of coffee she was holding within his reach at the table.

"No, Mrs. Mulrooney, we are fine at the moment."

"As ye wish, sir, madam, enjoy yer breakfast." She bustled out in a swish of black wool skirts and closed the door to within an inch. Privacy with propriety.

Vivian buttered a fresh scone wedge and added some jam before biting into it.

"Much as I enjoy having you here, Vivian. I believe you also will be of enormous use to me as I adapt my plans."

She sipped the sweet brew in her cup, looking so intriguingly demure. "Indeed? You know I am always happy to help you . . . in any way possible."

He was surprised to feel her fingers graze the top of his thigh under the table. A thrill shot through him as she brushed them along his inner seam. Her gaze held his for a moment. No one looking at her would ever have guessed she was doing anything so bold.

"What is it you . . . require?"

"A simple task." He watched her take another sip before settling the cup back into its saucer. "There is a man I would very much like you to meet."

Her brows lifted, not at all put off by the unspoken suggestion behind his words. She was one of a kind, his dear Vivian. He knew he could depend on her.

"What man?"

Her attentions to his thigh had their desired effect as he felt himself hardening with eagerness for the satisfaction she was practically dangling before him.

"A dear friend of mine. I believe you will like him

very much. You should find him very easy to befriend. He's been, shall we say, alone for too long . . ."

"Really?" She smiled and took a tiny nibble of her scone. Oh so slowly she licked the jam off her lips with the tip of her tongue. The soft brush of her fingers against his trousers was driving him mad, and all the while she looked just as cool as could be.

"And what is it about this man that makes you feel—"

"He is the very image of your dear departed, former lover, Finn Delaney. In fact, he is his cousin."

She dropped her scone onto her plate. Her complexion grew paler still and her fingers hesitated in their featherlike attentions. "Finn?"

Interesting. He took a sip of his coffee to keep from asking her any questions. Had he underestimated the depths of their relationship? Vivian was so rarely discomfited. Perhaps it was the double loss. He waited.

After a moment she picked up the scone as though nothing had happened and her fingers on his thigh resumed their attentions. "Who did you say he was?"

"Finn's cousin, Connal Delaney. He owns a substantial amount of property nearby. Property I would very much like to acquire." His swollen member ached for release.

"Finn's cousin is a property owner while Finn was as poor as a church mouse without his wife to prop him up?"

"Aye, my dear."

"Would you say they resemble one another?"

"Practically a mirror image. Will that be problematic?"

Her eyes flashed at him, the message quite clear. How dare he question her abilities to handle just about anything he could throw at her?

"I withdraw the question." He soothed her ruffles before she could openly object.

Her gaze roved his features for a moment as she continued to nibble the scone. Raspberry jam smudged one corner of her lips. Her tongue darted to lick it away. The way she had him feeling right now he could definitely think of some better uses for that talented appendage.

"When shall I meet this image?"

He smiled. "I am quite sure I can arrange something very soon. I believe enough time has passed to let developments shake out a bit there. I am ready to give poor Connal some shattering news. I want you to pick up the pieces."

"Have I ever failed you?"

"Of course not. Shall we retire to my study to go over our plans in detail?" If he did not get some relief soon, he was afraid he might burst. One never knew around which corner a servant might lurk in this more public room. It would not do to have them overhear too much.

She allowed him to escort her out of the room and down the hall, the light pressure of her fingertips resting on his arm continued to tease him so that he stayed hard with wanting her.

She waited until he had shut the door with a click and flicked the latch. "Where would you like to begin?"

"Right here."

He pulled up her skirts, then lifted her onto the top of his polished rosewood desk. Just as she had

promised him, she was not wearing any pantalettes.
Good. Not that they would have proved much of an
impediment to what was about to happen.

He unfastened his trousers just enough so he
sprang free. Spreading her legs wide, he pulled her
to the desk edge and took her without preamble,
driving himself into her satin depths swiftly and
completely. She buried her face in his shoulder to
muffle her gasps.

Chapter Seven

"Let me see how you are doing, Ross." Bethany bent over the slate her son was using to practice his sums.

"Very good." Her praise had him beaming. "But you may want to check your third answer and the last one, too. Remember how I showed you?"

He frowned as he concentrated for a minute, then his brow lightened. "I see what I did."

He erased the final figures with the side of his hand, then scribbled quickly. "How is this?"

"Good job," she enthused. "Everything is correct now. Everyone makes mistakes, you know. Being willing to look at the things you have done, and fix them, that makes all the difference."

Her son looked more than a little lost.

The little lesson she'd just tried to pass on to him had really been meant for herself. *Everyone makes mistakes. Being willing to look at the things you have done, and fix them, that makes all the difference.*

But what about when the mistakes were as devastating as the ones that led to Rose Carey's death?

Was there anything that could make a difference? Finn had certainly been broken by the experience. He'd shot his own cousin in the back and been forced out of his home. The Finn Delaney she'd married certainly was not the type of man who risked everything to defend a woman. There had to be more to the story, the more that lay beneath the pain and reluctance in Connal Delaney's dark gaze.

"Mama, you're gathering wood again."

She looked down at her son and laughed. "I think you mean wool gathering. I also think you have done enough for right now. Put your things away and we can play a game until Mary gets back from helping her mother and Mrs. Cochrane in the kitchen."

"Can we go outside with Michael when he's back? We're going to dig worms so we can go fishing in the stream on Saturday. Michael says the best time to get worms is after a rain."

"Then you ought to find quite a few after these last days." Bethany laughed, pleased to see the sparkle in her son's eyes. It had been too long. Ross was too young to have anything more to worry about than picking up his toys and finding enough worms to go fishing with a friend.

The sun was out for the first time in the better part of a week. Ever since the day Aunt Bridget returned from the village with the news that Connal Delaney was a social pariah. Either by design or happenstance, their paths had not crossed since that awkward afternoon, although she'd been surprised at how often her thoughts turned to him. Bethany took most of her meals with Ross in the nursery and the master of Glenmeade Stables seemed to be absorbed in a flurry of construction down at the yards that continued despite the foul weather.

Ross had chafed at first over the confinement following his brief foray exploring Glenmeade's garden and orchard. He still had not had the opportunity to visit the horses, he reminded her daily. But he finally seemed to have settled into a routine of morning lessons and afternoon amusements.

"Michael says we have to make a bed for them to live in. Mary promised to help rake up a corner of the garden. Did you know that worms like to live in compost? Michael says . . ."

Ross jumped out of his seat and gathered up his lesson book and slate to put them on the shelf as he continued his chatter. Bethany only half-listened, paying more attention to the enthusiasm in his voice than to the subject.

Michael Cochrane, the new maid's son, provided a welcome distraction when he arrived with his mother two days before to take up residence at the Manor. Older than Ross by a couple of years, Michael trudged into the village with the stablemen's children each morning for lessons with the parish priest, but when he returned in the afternoons he and Ross played, quickly becoming friends.

The boys thoroughly explored the contents of the nursery cupboards and engaged in a number of imaginative games that entailed whooping and charging around the upper floors as pirates or Indians, or whatever struck their fancies. Ross had never had a playmate before and it warmed Bethany to see

him so happy, even if a few too many of his sentences
of late began with "*Michael says* . . ."

If only she could content herself so easily in these
new surroundings. It was as if she was holding her
breath, teetering on the edge of something, but she
had no idea what. Well, at least, none that might
make her more comfortable about staying here any
longer than necessary.

Neither she nor Bridget had ventured a return to
the painful subjects broached that first afternoon,
their conversations treading gingerly around any
but the most innocuous matters. Her aunt threw
herself into a project the next day, spending her
time in the butler's pantry polishing the silver service. Bethany hesitated to join her, not wishing to
appear to be taking stock of the family heirlooms.
Too wide a gulf stretched between the man who
had always called this home and the claims of a
small boy who would be just as happy at this point
to have his inheritance entail a rich supply of fat
worms to feed the fish.

Even with the addition of Mrs. Cochrane to the
staff, there were still any number of tasks needing attention in order to bring Glenmeade Manor back to
life. Bethany had contented herself polishing the furniture in the bedchambers in the wing she and her
family occupied. It was astonishing the number of
pieces that stood to benefit from a good coat of oil
and a thorough rubbing. Added to the satisfaction of
watching the rich hues of brown and gold glow back
to life was the bonus that by the time she reached her
bed at night she was too tired to have any further
dreams, involving Connal Delaney or not.

"Mama . . . Mama." Ross called her back to herself again. "Put your things away so we can play."

She turned to find him seated on the floor with the spillikins already spread on an uncarpeted patch of polished oak. His chagrined expression nearly made her laugh out loud, but she schooled her expression into contrition. "I beg your pardon for keeping you waiting, sir. I should have been paying attention to my chores."

She quickly gathered up her polishing cloths and the jar of beeswax and lemon oil Jenna O'Toole had provided her, along with the remonstrance not to try to do everything. So far she'd managed to get through only the nursery and Aunt Bridget's chamber. After putting her cleaning supplies in her basket, she joined her son on the nursery floor.

A gentle rap on the door startled Bethany just as she was extracting one of the spillikins from the bottom. The whole pile of sticks fell and Ross cheered and clapped his hands.

"I win, Mama. I win this time."

"You win indeed, young man." She tousled his hair.

"Beg pardon, Mrs. Delaney." Betsey Cochrane edged open the door. "I hate ta interrupt ye while the lad is at his lessons—"

Bethany scrambled to her feet. "Nonsense—"

"I won, Mrs. Cochrane." Ross gained his first and ran over to greet her. "I never won before, but Michael told me I would one day and today is the day. Is he home from school yet?"

"No, he's not yet." The older woman bent down to eye level with Ross, a big smile lighting her worn face. Life might not have been kind to her, but her spirit remained undimmed. "But I know he'll be busting with happiness ta hear yer news when he is. And I offer ye my congratulations right now in his stead."

"Thank you very much, ma'am." Ross beamed.

"Yes, thank you." Bethany gestured to the game they had just abandoned. "As you can see, lesson time is over. Was there something you needed when you knocked?"

"Oh, I'm so sorry." Alarm flashed in Betsey's eyes. "I nearly forgot in all the excitement. Mr. Delaney asked if ye'd mind stepping down to his study. He'd like a word with ye, Mrs. Delaney. A messenger just brought a letter."

"There is no need to apologize. We distracted you." Bethany waved away the other woman's consternation even as her own tightened like a coiled spring.

"Pray tell Mr. Delaney I will be down in a bit. I must change. She put her hand on her son's shoulder. "He looked up at her. "And we need to pick up our game, of course. Right, Ross?"

He nodded. "Do you suppose he'll let me down to the yard to watch the horses today, Mama? Will you ask?"

"I thought you were going to dig for worms this afternoon?"

She still felt uncomfortable allowing him too near such large animals, especially since for the most part, unless it was their turn for training or grooming, the horses here were not tethered or harnessed the way the horses he was used to from Wilmington's streets were. His eyes were her undoing as they gazed up at her like huge blue saucers. Huge blue, pleading saucers.

"Please, Mama. You know I have always loved horses. I just want to see them. I won't touch them or get in the way. Please."

"I will think about it."

"I'll wait fer Master Ross ta straighten up his toys, if ye'd like, ma'am," Betsey interrupted. "Mr. Delaney allowed as how he'd prefer ta see ye as soon as possible."

She took Ross's hand. "And after we're done, ye can come with me ta the kitchens. Mrs. O'Toole has some molasses cakes fresh from the oven. She was jest saying she was in need of someone ta sample them and tell her how they taste."

Ross nodded his agreement and skipped away. "Molasses cakes are my favorite."

Mrs. Cochrane laughed. "I do believe ye said the very same thing about the sugar snaps she made ye yesterday. And the cinnamon crisps the day before that, Master Ross."

"That's because yesterday my favorites were sugar snaps. Just like cinnamon crisps were the day before. But today, molasses cakes are definitely my favorites and I haven't even tasted them."

Ross's bubbly ease here warmed Bethany as she tried to think why Connal Delaney wished to see her as soon as possible. What could The Wicked One want with her that might necessitate haste? It was too soon to have heard from his solicitor, surely.

"Thank you, Mrs. Cochrane, I will go directly."

Betsey bobbed a quick curtsey. "It's me who owes ye the thanks, Mrs. Delaney. With my Andrew gone these past months, I don't know what my boy and I would have done without this new position."

"You need to thank Mr. Delaney. He is the one who hired you."

"I already tried, ma'am. He said I owed the position ta yer visit. He's been awful good ta us all along." She chewed her lip for a moment. "I don't mean ta keep ye, but could I speak frankly fer a minute?"

Bethany looked over at Ross, absorbed in his chore, and nodded, hoping the delay would give her a few more minutes to pull her scattered thoughts together.

"I've never been in service before, in case ye haven't noticed how clumsy I am, so I hope I'm not being too forward." Betsey stepped closer. "But I'm right glad ye're paying no heed ta the stories told about Mr. Delaney. That ye haven't let them scare ye off.

"When Andrew took sick," she continued in a low, confidential tone, "it was Mr. Delaney who sent the doctor around and paid fer him ta come back regular. Last fall, when the crops were due in, he sent almost the whole of the stable staff over ta bring in the harvest so we could meet our rent ta Mr. Carey. Connal Delaney's a good man, no matter what others may say."

Sincerity rang in her voice. Bethany touched her arm. "I will bear your words in mind, Mrs. Cochrane. Thank you for sharing your story with me."

As she headed toward the door she called to her son, "I will see you for tea, Ross. Enjoy your cakes and mind your manners in the kitchen."

"Yes, ma'am." His answer followed her into the hall.

Connal Delaney's a good man. Everyone is guilty of

something, isean. Being willing to look at the things you have done, and fix them, that makes all the difference. Kind words about Connal—Betsey Cochrane's, Aunt Bridget's and her own—words followed her, too.

Bethany's soft knock on the study door came much later than he would have preferred, but Connal schooled his tone to hide any hint of annoyance. There was little point in alienating her further than he already had, given his hopes to gain her assistance. "Come in, please."

He stood as she entered and gestured for her to take the same chair she had occupied during her first visit to his sanctum earlier in the week. "Thank you for coming so promptly."

He hadn't seen her since that afternoon. He'd been mildly surprised she had not packed her son up bag and baggage once Bridget had told her the commonly held version of the events that sent Finn running to America and into her arms nearly a decade earlier. His actions had done nothing to encourage her to do otherwise.

The state Finn had left her finances in no doubt played its part in her continued stay here. Connal had been shocked to see just how badly things must have been for her when Finn died. He'd jibed her about her failure to provide her husband with a headstone and it looked as if her husband had failed to provide her with anything beyond the barest of necessities. His cousin had not just bled their bank accounts, he'd hemorrhaged all their assets, especially in the past three years, if the papers she had provided proved to be even half true.

"Good afternoon." Bethany met his gaze with her own steady one as she took her seat. He could not detect any hint of horror or condemnation in their azure depths. There was nothing in her expression to betray anything but polite interest in his summons. "Mrs. Cochrane said you received a letter?"

The soft cadence of her accent slipped gently through him. "Aye."

He picked the folded vellum up from his desk and strode around to take the chair next to hers in front of his desk. He tapped the paper on his knees and sought the right words to begin.

He should have been surprised at how pleased he was to see her, but given the amount of time she had spent dominating his thoughts this week he was not. What had surprised him was that he'd thought of her so warmly rather than as an annoyance or a true impediment. He'd combated her frequent intrusions into his musings by throwing himself into helping his men complete the stable expansions. Pounding nails in the pouring rain had done nothing to alleviate his problems, however, save to leave him exhausted enough at night to sleep.

"Would you care for some tea?" He resolved to do the pretty before he got down to business with Bethany. Women liked that, didn't they? Not for the first time, he regretted how rusty his social skills had grown. "Jenna sent us a tray complete with freshly baked molasses cakes."

A soft smile creased her lips as she glanced at the tray set on the corner of the desk nearest them.

"No, thank you. Not right now. The cakes do smell delicious, though."

Her eyes sparkled when she looked back at him, as if she was enjoying a private joke. He was struck again by their beautiful blue shade. Small, wispy curls of burnished copper framed her face. Animation suited her features, she looked younger, less pinched. He realized in retrospect just how tense she had been during their other meetings. Not that she was at ease now, but something had shifted, relaxed in some small measure.

"You look well." He searched for a more specific compliment that would not seem too personal. "Your outfit becomes you."

He hoped the effort would please her enough to make her more amenable to his request. She looked down at her skirt and apron, then raised a skeptical brow. "These are the clothes I wear to do housework. You may cease with the pleasantries. I am sufficiently disarmed. Mrs. Cochrane said something about a letter being delivered. Is it some kind of bad news?"

"Not really a letter . . ."

I am sufficiently disarmed. He felt more than a little foolish for trying anything but the direct approach with this woman, especially in light of the intense questioning she given him the last time they met.

". . . I returned from the stables a short time ago to find a short note from James . . . Mr. Carey, informing me of his intention to visit Glenmeade this day."

Bethany kept her gaze fixed on him, trying to fathom his point. "Very well."

"He and I have some business to discuss which

will take up a good portion of his time here. It is business we postponed from the day of your arrival."

"And you want to make sure I do not interrupt you again? Or my son? Pray, have no fear. I will keep Ross busy and quiet in the nursery. You hardly needed to make your request for me to join you here seem urgent." She glanced over at the tea tray again and rose from the chair. "Hardly a matter that calls for soothing with tea and cakes, even."

He stood as well and caught her by the arm as she turned toward the door. The look of absolute panic in her eyes forced him to drop her arm immediately. "I have made a mess of this, please hear me out. I need your help."

Her chin raised. She remained tense, reminding him of her stance that night in the kitchen, but she nodded.

"Go on."

"I do not entertain often, at all, really . . ." He took a deep breath. "I know it is a great deal to ask, but would you join us? It may be very important for Glenmeade, for your son's future."

His request surprised her. "My father was in the naval-supply business. He arranged for sail cloth, rope, uniforms and the like to be shipped to Wilmington and stored in his warehouses until they were needed. He taught me to decipher ledger columns, which I suppose do not change much from one business to the other, but I doubt I would be able to add much to your discussions. I know almost nothing about horses."

"No, no." He scrubbed his hand through his hair. "I did not explain myself well. James has a visitor.

A widowed cousin, also from America. He is bringing her with him and hopes you will bear her company while we go over our business."

She was silent for what was surely an eternity, then frowned at him and shook her head.

"So, you asked me to come down here, offered me tea, and hemmed and hawed for the past five minutes because you want me to act as your hostess?"

Did she sound insulted or relieved? He wasn't sure. He looked over at the mantel clock. "I hardly think it was five minutes—"

"Closer to ten, at the least, I'm sure."

It took him a little while to realize she had just a hint of teasing in her voice. He looked sharply at her and quirked a brow. Her face held an almost serene, blank look.

"As you can tell, I am out of practice making polite conversation. James is a steadfast friend. I would like to honor his request. And would greatly appreciate your assistance. As I said, if all goes as it should, today's conversation is an important one for Glenmeade's future, and that includes your son."

"Very well."

The humorous note was gone from her voice. That he missed it so acutely surprised him.

"I believe I can manage to have tea and a bit of conversation with a dear soul," she continued. "She no doubt will want to regale me with stories of her youth or her lost love."

"At least you sound as if you have had practice. I would not know where to begin."

"For a time, after I was first . . . wed. Before my da took ill, Aunt Bridget worked as a companion for various older ladies in the parish. Many of them held on to their memories and their mourning black as a means of keeping their husbands alive. Talking made them happy and I never minded listening."

"As I said, I would not know where to begin. That is, provided she would even consent to address me." He refused to let his mind go down that worn path. If James was bringing her with him, surely his cousin was aware of the consensus regarding the owner— well, part-owner—of Glenmeade Stables and was choosing to ignore it in deference to James.

"Do you have any idea when they will arrive? Probably for tea." She didn't wait for an answer, which was just as well since he did not have one.

"I have to change my dress and fix my hair." Bethany was already heading to the door, talking more to herself than to him. "But first I must go to the kitchen and warn Mrs. O'Toole. It is a good thing Aunt Bridget spent so much time polishing the silver."

He failed to see why she had to change. He'd meant what he'd said about her appearance earlier. He thought she looked very presentable just as she was. More than presentable. Unless . . . Was she planning to change into widow's black to mark her status?

"Can I ask you a question before you go, Bethany?"

She turned back to face him. "Of course. You answered so many of mine the other day."

"You said the widows you knew hung on to their widow's weeds to keep their husbands alive. Did you take off your mourning clothes before the usual year because you want Finn's memory to die along with him?"

She took a few steps toward him. "Truth?"

He nodded.

"I never wore proper widow's black. I did not have the money to purchase new clothes. Not with a growing boy to clothe and feed." She smoothed her hands over her skirt. "I had too much to do taking care of our debts and trying to keep Ross insulated from all the talk without worrying about what color garments I wore."

Guilt tugged him. Even once he became aware of how dire things had been for her after Finn's death, the practical reasons she mentioned had not occurred to him.

"Besides—" The serious light was back in her gaze. He could have kicked himself for making the sparkle disappear. "—what you wear or do not wear has little to do with what you remember. I have only to look at my son and be reminded of his father."

"You are right. Thank you for your honesty. I am sure the wagging tongues did not make your decision any easier."

She chewed her lower lip for a second, then fixed him with an intent look. "Since we are trying to be honest with each other, can I ask you to clarify something you said the other day?"

Here it comes. He tensed and nodded. There was always a cost for letting someone know about the truth behind matters best left quietly in the past.

"You said Finn shot you. He certainly thought you were dead when he came to North Carolina in search of my father."

"Aye." He had yet to hear her question, but he knew what was coming, what he was going to have to live through again. He'd been surprised with the amount of grace he'd been granted since Bridget had surely related the gossip to her the other day. He already regretted not ever being able to see her look at him with humor again, with compassion or with anything but loathing.

"Are you sure it was Finn who shot you? Finn who challenged you to a duel?"

That was not the question he was expecting, not one he'd been asked before—at least not by any who had actually dared ask their questions out loud.

"Why do you ask?"

"Because the man I married would never . . . was not . . . the type to defend a woman's honor. Not at the risk of everything he held dear. Women were too interchangeable. Accessories."

He was not sure what it was costing her to admit the last, but from the tension in her stance and the haunted look in her eyes he guessed it was dear.

Her gaze searched his face. She took a deep breath. "I guess what I want to know is, what happened? What really happened to you, to Rosleen Carey?"

"Why?" He choked out the first word that came to mind. "What does it matter?"

"Because if the stories told here, the stories about what happened just before you were shot are not wrong, then Finn changed because of me. I made him the man he was."

It was an admission wrung from her soul, from so deep in her soul it surprised even her. It devastated him.

Besides himself, there were less than a handful of people who knew the whole truth about the events that had shattered Connal's life. Two were dead, one was a priest, and the others were Jack and James.

"You should sit down," he said.

He outlined the basic facts of that last summer, the summer he'd finally asked Rose to marry him and she said yes. They were waiting to set a date until James returned home from school in Edinburgh. One day Connal received a message from Rosleen asking him to call on her. Always charmed by her shy modesty, he'd been surprised when he got there and Rosleen threw herself into his arms begging him to make love to her, claiming she couldn't wait any longer to be his. A short while later she confessed she'd been having an affair with Finn and that there would be a baby. They argued. He'd been too hurt and angry to show her much in the way of compassion that day.

He rode away from Oak Bend to hunt for Finn. His search proved fruitless and he returned home to find another missive from Rose that sent him back to the Carey estate. Too late. One of the footmen had already fished her out of the river. She and the baby were dead. Connal grabbed James's pistols and tracked Finn down to challenge him to a duel, intending to kill his cousin.

"Finn turned too soon and shot me in the back. He claimed it was an accident, that his pistol misfired."

Bethany's face was an alarming white. He felt like he'd been riding at breakneck speed for days. She'd asked for the truth. Sorry as he was for shocking her with the sordid details, he knew she needed to hear them. Needed to know that Finn had already been broken when he arrived on her doorstep.

"Go on." She spoke so softly it tore at his heart.

He was not sure what else Finn had done besides betray and bankrupt Bethany, but she needed to know it was not her fault.

"My Uncle Jack carried me here. I swear if the horse had stopped he would have carried me on his own back. They all thought I would die. Uncle Brennan sent Finn away. He was very angry, but couldn't face losing us both. So he shifted the blame all onto me, figuring I could take it to my grave."

He scrubbed his hand over his face and blew out a short breath. "I survived. Living proof that the Devil gives luck to his own."

"So all this time, all the scorn you have borne, has been for Finn's misdeeds?"

"No." He shook his head. "Not for Finn. For Rose. Her parents were dead. James was away at school, and I was busy here with the foaling season. I left her alone. I left her vulnerable."

He stopped for a minute. Bethany came over to stand in front of him, waiting for him to collect himself and finish. Somehow, in her blue-eyed gaze, he found the courage to go on.

"In the end, when she came to me, she was afraid to tell me the truth. When she tried to seduce me out of desperation, when Finn rejected her, I was too noble. I wanted to wait for our wedding night. My rejection, my reaction to her confession, coupled with Finn's repudiation broke her. It was enough that she died in shame, a suicide no less. Buried in unhallowed ground just outside the churchyard. Most felt pity for her, sympathy even. How would they feel if they knew of her affair with Finn? Who would speak kindly of her then? I owed her that much. I failed her in everything else that mattered."

Bethany reached up her hand to cup his cheek. It was a small gesture of comfort that warmed him all out of measure. He looked down at her, afraid he might find pity or doubt, concerned she might be panicked again by his nearness. Her face was soft with sympathy, her brow furrowed with concern. Understanding, not fear, shone in her eyes.

She brushed his hair away from his brow. Once, twice, she stroked his temple, then she rested her fingertips on the edge of his hairline. No words she could have offered could have given him the comfort her silent companionship provided.

Before he realized what she intended, she stretched up on her toes, pulled his head down and kissed him, brushing her lips over his, ever so softly. Sunlight flowed into some of the dark, empty corners of his soul. The heady, comforting mix of cinnamon and vanilla filled him.

He pulled himself back a fraction and looked deep into the shining blue of Bethany's eyes. He could see no hesitancy, no fear. The desire he'd battled back just a few nights before roared back with a vengeance, fierce and swift.

He caught her to him and kissed her again, drinking from her lips like a parched man. And she kissed him back full measure.

Her hands clutched his shirt front and pulled him closer still while her lips demanded his complete attention. He cupped her cheeks with his palms, hardly believing that he could feel this way, that he could ever get enough of her, enough of this woman . . . Bethany . . . Bethany Doyle. Her name sang through his veins. Bethany Doyle Delaney . . . *Finn's wife.*

Like a cold bucket of water, the realization that he was kissing Finn's wife sluiced through him. He forced himself to break the kiss, to pull back slowly.

He set her from him, they were both panting, dazed.

"I . . . We . . ." she stammered.

". . . must not let this happen again," he finished the thought.

A knock on the door startled them both.

"Mr. Delaney? Mrs. Delaney? Your guests are arriving. Shall I escort them to the drawing room?"

Chapter Eight

"Finally, some decent weather." James Carey shook Connal's hand after climbing down from his horse. "Vivian has been quite chafing at the bit for a good ride."

Instead of the kindly, gray-haired woman draped in black bombazine Bethany had expected, James Carey's guest proved to be a devastatingly beautiful woman in a stylish merino riding habit. Fashioned in a rich shade of carmine red, it was trimmed with black velvet and showed her fair skin and ebony hair off to perfection.

She pouted from her perch, her mouth a lush confection, and then laughed with a soft twinkle that skipped across the Manor's front entrance. "Now, Cousin James, it is hardly kind of you to describe me thus. You make me sound like one of the horses."

"I beg your pardon, dearest of all my relations. I doubt even a blind man would dare confuse you with a horse. Certainly not our estimable host." His laughter joined hers for a second as he reached up and put his hands around her waist. "Allow me to help you down and introduce you. I should warn you, he has been quite horse-mad for as long as I can remember and might actually find the description adds to your attraction."

She arched a brow and tugged her formfitting jacket into place. Her skirt settled intimately around her hips, hugging them in a way that suggested she did not wish the encumbrance of numerous petticoats between herself and the saddle. She was tall for a woman, almost topping her relative as she stood beside him. Tall, but with a voluptuous figure most women would envy and all but the most wayward man was sure to find desirable.

She was exactly the sort of woman Finn would have found most attractive. He would have enjoyed pointing that fact out to his wife, followed by a long list of her own inadequacies in comparison, too.

Bethany was painfully aware that next to this glorious cardinal of a woman, she must look naught but a plain country wren with her brown skirt and white oxford blouse. She clasped her hands in front of her. At least she had been able to shed her apron, casting it onto a chair in the study as they had hastened to greet their guests.

"Vivian, I would like you to meet Connal Delaney, owner of Glenmeade Stables, home to some of the best horses in all the county." James placed her left hand on his arm. "Connal, may I present my dear cousin Vivian, Mrs. Sherman Brown."

Sherman . . . Brown? The name was surely unfamiliar, but raised the hairs at the nape of Bethany's neck nonetheless.

Vivian Brown extended her right hand to Connal

with a breathtaking display of even, white teeth. Her dark-fringed eyes seemed ready to devour his face as she studied him thoroughly. "I am so pleased to make your acquaintance, Mr. Delaney. I have recently grown quite passionate"—her cheeks turned the perfect shade of pink as she caught herself—"passionate about horses, that is."

Bethany suppressed a sudden wish to pull their visitor's gloved fingers out of Connal's hand. One kiss shared by two wounded souls, a kiss rooted in soothing some of the hurt and loneliness they had each suffered over the years, did not entitle her to jealousy. Not where Finn's cousin was concerned. *Especially where Finn's cousin was concerned.*

"It is good to meet you, Mrs. Brown." Connal's tone seemed a trifle overenthusiastic to Bethany's ears. "I am sorry for your loss, but I am sure you will receive a great deal of comfort during your stay with James at Oak Bend."

"Thank you." She looked down and ducked her head slightly. The feather on her bowler-style riding hat drooped at just the right degree to convey momentary sadness.

"I have found James to be a great comfort on a number of occasions, but none as profound as the loss of my dear Sherman." She looked up at both men through her lashes and they both appeared totally captivated.

Bethany had not seen such a fine display of acting ability since the traveling Shakespearean Company staged a performance of *MacBeth* last fall at Wilmington's Opera House.

Having sufficiently enthralled her male audience, Mrs. Brown raised her chin and widened her eyes as she appeared to notice Bethany still standing on the portico. "And who is this dear little creature standing there in the doorway, Mr. Delaney? Surely she is far too young to be your housekeeper?"

Both men swiveled to look at her. Vivian Brown was good, Bethany ceded her that. Not only was Bethany sure to pale in comparison to the vision they had just been admiring, but the beauty had managed to both condescend and insult her while veiling her small slights in seeming compliments.

Bethany stepped forward from the threshold with her hand out. "Welcome to Glenmeade—"

"I beg your pardon, Mrs. Delaney." It was James Carey who stepped forward to rescue her as he took her hand in his.

"This is my day for inadvertent discourtesy," Mr. Carey continued. "All the rain of late must have turned my brain to mush. It is my extreme pleasure to introduce my dear cousin, Mrs. Sherman Brown, to you. Is Boston anywhere near Wilmington? Vivian has a town home in that city and a rather large estate further out in the wilds of Massachusetts."

Sherman Brown . . . Boston? The hairs on Bethany's neck stiffened again. Something was definitely off kilter.

"Vivian." James turned to his cousin. "May I present Mrs. Delaney, our hostess. Mrs. Finn Delaney, late of North Carolina. Her family formerly hailed from this area although this is her first visit. She suffered the loss of her own husband not too long ago and is staying here for the time being with her young son."

"Oh, Mr. Delaney." Mrs. Brown touched Connal's arm. "You truly must be every bit the gentleman

James described to give a woman from so far away a consoling shoulder to lean on at the hour of her greatest need. Until I arrived in Ireland last week, I hardly know how I survived without such a shoulder myself."

Bethany nearly choked. Connal had the grace to look uncomfortable with the praise. He also had the forethought to hold his peace and merely nod his thanks for her compliment.

The full force of Vivian Brown's attention focused on Bethany next as she favored her with a broad smile that somehow did not quite reach the depths of her dark brown eyes. After the briefest instant, Bethany had the feeling she had been measured and dismissed as her guest's smile broadened ever so slightly.

"I am so pleased to make your acquaintance, Mrs. Delaney." A waft of exotic spices accompanied the small bow she made as she inclined her head in greeting. Jasmine and cinnamon in surprising strength. "James was quite taken with you the other day and when I heard that there was a fellow countryman, another new widow, no less, visiting so nearby, I insisted he bring me right over. I just know we have more in common than one or the other of us would guess."

She was so obviously making an effort to extend herself, Bethany hoped she had just misjudged Vivian. "It is good to meet you, Mrs. Brown. I, too, am sorry for your loss."

"Thank you, my dear. You know how difficult it is to lose someone you love so unexpectedly." She reached into her sleeve and produced a lacy handkerchief, which she then used to dab her lip. "I do

miss my husband, miss the life we shared, so dreadfully sometimes."

"Would you care to come inside?" Connal's invitation forestalled the need for Bethany to offer a
reply.

"I would actually love to have a tour of your
famed stables, Mr. Delaney. James tells me they are
quite modern and you designed your recent addi-
tions yourself."

"Well . . ." Connal turned to James.

"Perhaps after Connal and I have finished our
business, Vivian dear."

"You men and your business." The pout was back.
Mrs. Brown was definitely used to being the center
of attention and getting her own way.

"Well, go ahead, then," she said, "and get it over
with. Then perhaps Mr. Delaney will let me impose
further on his hospitality and allow me to see how
he treats his horses. My late husband always said
you could tell a great deal about a man by how he
treats his horse."

Both men raised their brows at that observation
but refrained from comment.

"I have arranged for my groomsman to bring
over the cabriolet in case the weather turns in-
clement by the time we are ready to leave. Vivian is
very susceptible to chills. He should arrive soon,
then leave with our mounts."

Connal signaled the stable lad walking the horses
in the yard to keep them there.

"I managed to survive the entire ride here on
horseback, did I not? I have just been fatigued from
my travels and unable to sleep uninterrupted at

night. You make me sound like some sort of exotic conservatory flower, James."

"I refuse to apologize for having a care for my only remaining relative in this world."

Connal's cheeks blanched at this not-too-subtle reference to Rosleen's death.

"Perhaps we should move indoors anyway. This way, if you please, Mrs. Brown." Bethany gestured to the door.

"I insist you call me Vivian. And I shall call you Beth. We compatriots must stick together. We have so much in common we shall surely become fast friends." She linked arms with Bethany. "Let us go in and have a cozy chat over a dish of tea while we wait for them, shall we?"

James and Connal followed them into the Manor while *Beth* tried to find the right words to correct her guest without insulting her over the choice of monikers she had just been given.

"There is no need to chaperone us, gentlemen." Vivian paused and glanced back at the men once they had all gained the foyer. "You go and seek your own refreshment while you conduct your business. You may join us in the drawing room when you have finished. Pray don't be long."

"Come along, Beth, or do you prefer Betty?" Vivian tugged Bethany's arm while she prattled on. "One of my dearest childhood friends was a Betty. Dreadfully plain, but the dearest little thing just the same. Mild as milk despite her red hair. I was quite fond of her."

"To be honest, I prefer Bethany."

"Well, of course you do. It is a lovely name, after

all. You must always be honest with me, Beth, how else will we remain friends?"

Bethany caught a look of sympathy in Connal's eyes as she turned away. He owed her for this favor all right, although for the life of her she did not see why he had felt the need to ask her to entertain this guest. Vivian Brown seemed perfectly capable of sustaining a conversation all on her own.

Ten minutes later they were ensconced on a blue tufted settee in the drawing room, drinking the tea Mrs. Cochrane brought them.

"I envy you your son, Beth. A living gift from your husband to comfort you. I hope I may meet him during our acquaintance. I was not so blessed." The beautiful widow set her cup on her saucer with a soft chink.

"Although not . . . I hope I do not make you blush"—Vivian gave Bethany a slow wink—"not from lack of trying, mind. Sherman was most . . . generous . . . in that regard."

Vivian selected one of the molasses cakes from the tray and took a dainty nibble.

"Ross is the greatest gift Finn ever gave me." Sherman Brown's very name niggled at Bethany. His name, the area he'd lived in, his age compared to his wife, all the coincidences shouldn't matter. Finn was long gone. He'd been in the wrong and paid with his life. It shouldn't matter, but it did.

That much was certainly honest. Bethany glanced at the drawing room entrance. How much longer would Connal and James take? She could barely stomach the idea of exchanging sad tales of her supposed loss with this shallow woman for very much longer. She did not want to be rude, however, especially in light of how important Connal said his business with James Carey was today. She drew in a breath, then attempted to keep the conversation directed toward Vivian Brown's favorite subject: herself. "I am sure your husband was generous in many ways."

"Generous? Oh, yes. There was nothing he would not give me if I asked. I owe everything I am to my dear Sherman." Vivian sighed and dabbed her lips with her handkerchief again. This time the move did not seem so calculated. Her features softened for the briefest moment.

"He taught me to dress properly," she continued after a suitable pause for reflection. "How to make polite conversation, how to arrange just the right menu for any occasion . . ."

Her eyes took on a faraway look as she spoke and Bethany felt her first twinge of sympathy for this woman's loss.

". . . Sherman took me from obscurity and turned me into the perfect hostess for his business functions. He adored me and I was quite devoted to him. He was a great deal older than me, but his death was still a shock. Quite unexpected."

"Would it be too upsetting to talk about what happened?" Bethany was willing to pry if necessary to keep the conversation away from being asked for her own summation of Finn's qualities. In her conversations with Aunt Bridget's various employers, this had been one question guaranteed to encourage a lengthy discourse.

Vivian drew in a deep breath. "A heart seizure. Sherman had a shock . . . His heart just gave out."

The hairs on Bethany's neck niggled at her again.

Sherman . . . Boston . . . heart seizure. So many co-incidences. Too many coincidences? The man who shot Finn had been named Sherman. He died almost immediately after when his heart gave out. But Vivian's husband had been dead for over a year, so surely . . .

"I came here immediately"—Vivian stopped for a second—"immediately after all of his affairs were settled. I knew James would be able to help me sort out what I should do next. I am at such a loss without Sherman. I wanted to get away from all the sad memories, see things in a new light. Surely, you can understand."

"Of course. That was one of my own reasons for coming to Kildare." Bethany gave her guest's hand a reassuring squeeze, suddenly anxious to disarm her and draw her into further conversation. If only she could think of the right tack.

"My husband used to travel in the Boston area quite frequently on business. He thought it was very scenic and lovely. Parts of it reminded him of this area where he grew up."

Vivian shrugged. "If you ignore the pine trees, I suppose the rocks and hills might be comparable in some parts."

"He was particularly fond of one town. Have you ever heard of Taunton?"

Vivian fixed a puzzled look on Bethany. "I believe Taunton is to the south of Boston. Quite the opposite direction of our country cottage, so I cannot tell you much above that."

"Would your husband have had any . . . connections there?"

Vivian's chin rose and her eyes narrowed briefly.

"Sherman? What an odd question. I . . . I knew many of Sherman's business associates, none that came from there, to my knowledge, however."

Something snapped in the dark-haired woman's gaze. She flicked an imaginary crumb from her crimson skirt. "Why ever would you want to know?"

"Finn mentioned someone with the same name as your husband in connection with his business there. I was thinking how ironic it would be if they were acquainted when they were alive yet we had to travel across the ocean to meet."

"Ironic, indeed. To think there might be another Sherman Brown so close by. Not that there could be another Sherman like my Sherman."

"Well," Bethany offered a limited confession. She knew full well Brown was not the last name of her husband's killer. "I am not sure of this man's last name, only that his first name was Sherman."

Vivian's brow cleared immediately. "Well, there you have it, mystery solved. Sherman is a fine old New England name and my Sherman was certainly a fine old New Englander, but he was also one of many. You might as well assume that every man with the name James is my dear cousin."

"What mystery is that, Cousin Vivian?" James preceded Connal into the drawing room by enough steps to overhear the tail end of the ladies' conversation. "I distinctly heard my name."

"Even if your name did come up, our conversation was private, Cousin. You should not have been eavesdropping. That should be mystery enough."

Vivian Brown's laughter filled the drawing room. Connal felt too sick to truly enjoy the light, airy sound. Or to appreciate the lovely tableau of the two ladies seated in his drawing room, both beautiful and appealing in their own right, yet so different.

To say that his conversation with James had not gone well would be to give the statement too much credit. Now there was a word choice he regretted— *credit.* All hope was not lost, but he was certainly teetering on the brink.

"I will ring for some more tea so you may join us." Bethany rose from the settee as he entered the room. Her expression carried more than a little hint of shock. Had her conversation with James's cousin included some version of the bad news delivered to him just now or was she simply worn out and overwhelmed by her guest's dominating personality?

The urge to put his arm around her to bolster her caught him by almost as much surprise as his own need to draw comfort from her. He had no right to expect her, of all women, to lend him her support when he was reeling from the enormity of the risky position in which he alone had put Glenmeade's future.

"Nonsense." Mrs. Brown stood and favored him a most charming smile. "Surely they have already refreshed themselves sufficiently while they were closeted away from us. In my experience, most men enjoy imbibing spirits while they talk their business. I was promised a tour of the stables."

She glided across the room to Connal and took his arm. The exotic aura of jasmine and cinnamon accompanied her. It was a heady mix, especially when combined with the frank sensual appeal she exuded. A mix she was clearly all too willing to use to get her way.

"You are the kind of man who keeps his promises, are you not, Mr. Delaney?"

"Well," he hesitated. James had hinted that Vivian might be convinced to invest in Glenmeade. Connal would have preferred to give his stable master some notice before bringing her through the training yards and barns. "Things are pretty chaotic there. Our new stock should be arriving anytime and we want to be as ready as possible."

He looked over at James, who pulled out his pocket watch. James raised his eyebrows and shrugged. "We need to start back to Oak Bend before too long, Vivian. We have a long ride ahead of us. I would hate for you to become fatigued on your first outing since your arrival."

"The longer the ride, the better, I always say."

She looked up at Connal through the fringe of her lashes. It was a devastatingly attractive sight.

"Honestly, James, you can be quite a tyrant at times."

"Far be it from me to think only of your comfort, Cousin." James favored her with a mock bow. "The afternoon is yours to dispose of as you wish. If you wish to expose yourself to the damp evening air, far be it from me to dissuade you."

"I simply wish to expose myself to some prime horseflesh, you goose."

Their lighthearted banter failed to lift the sense of impending doom surrounding Connal since he had heard the news from James. The investors James had lined up to back Connal's expansion of Glenmeade were likely to pull their support in light of the division of the estate, finding the investment too risky now that he was not sole owner. James said he still held out hope that they might be persuaded to provide their backing, given certain assurances and sufficiently increased financial gains. But the possibility that what had appeared a sure thing was about to collapse had Connal reeling.

"Let us be off." Vivian Brown tugged at Connal's arm. "Will you be joining us, Beth, dear?"

Only a hint of distress crossed Bethany's features at the continued shortening of her name.

"Please say you will," James spoke up before she had a chance to answer. "You can help me pass the time. I fear that once these two get started I will not be able to get a word in. Either of them could happily spend the rest of the afternoon discussing gaits and withers, or what have you, whilst I see horses merely as a means to an end, either to admire from afar or to use for my convenience."

"Have a care, Beth. I believe James holds the same opinion of the fairer sex," Vivian teased. "Although I am sure your status as a new widow may insulate you from his charms."

With her freedom dangling before her, the struggle about whether to accept or decline and flee was evident on Bethany's face for a moment. Duty won. "Let me fetch my bonnet and wrap and look in on my son. I will join you outside in a trice. Pray excuse me."

She exited swiftly, offering Connal a waft of her vanilla-and-cinnamon scent as she passed, refreshing compared with Vivian's heavier notes.

"She really is a dear thing, Mr. Delaney. You must positively dote on her," Vivian Brown observed as the door clicked shut. "So fragile and wounded by her loss. And so devoted to her son, she prattled on about him unceasingly practically the whole time we were together."

Wounded, certainly. Finn seemed to have seen to that. But fragile? One of the attributes Connal had only just come to realize he most admired in his cousin's widow was her determination to do the right thing, whether meeting her husband's financial commitments or raising her son. "Bethany is a great deal stronger than she appears."

"I believe I have observed that same attribute. Along with several others," James added. "Perhaps you are not so unfortunate as it would appear to have her arrive for a visit. Although, I, for one, wish it could have been better timed."

"Aye," Connal agreed as they exited the drawing room. Another day or two added to her arrival and he would not be facing the thorny financial situation he was looking at now.

A few minutes later Bethany joined them outside and they were off. The breeze had quickened since early afternoon, and it set the feather on Vivian Brown's hat fluttering and teased a few rebellious curls loose from beneath Bethany's chip-straw hat to dance across her cheeks.

Connal pointed out the roofline of the older buildings in the stable yard and what differentiated them from the newer ones under construction. Vivian Brown proved to be more than just attractive packaging, asking astute questions and really listening to his answers. On just about any other occasion Connal would have been more than flattered and intrigued by her interest, but he found his thoughts wandering to the couple strolling several feet behind them as he strained to hear the conversation between James and Bethany.

He paused to let them catch up when a loud cry

sounded from around the corner of the house. Bucket in hand a small bundle of dirt and energy came running to the edge of the lane. Finn's son, followed by Mary O'Toole, who halted a few paces away.

"Look, Mama! Look!" The boy held up his bucket. His boots and hands were caked with dirt. "It's full. Fat ones, too, just like you said."

"I see—"

The genuine warmth and smile Bethany gave her son was good to see. On almost every other occasion when Connal had been able to take note of her expression, she always seemed to hold something in reserve, a guarded wariness. Every time save just before she had kissed him in the study.

"But we have company. What do you say, Ross?"

The boy looked up at the adults standing a few feet away from his mother. Her skirts partially obscured him. "Beg pardon?"

"Yes. Now, please put down your bucket and take off your cap so I can introduce you."

"But, Mama. Me and Michael—"

"Michael and I," she corrected.

"Michael and I dug these just where Mary told us," he protested.

"Down by the chicken coop." Bethany wrinkled her nose as her son gave her an astonished look. "Now, do as I asked. Your worms will survive while you are being polite."

"Yes, ma'am." He kicked the dirt with the toe of his muddy boots, then put down the pail and took off his cap. He even suffered through his mother smoothing his hair.

She examined his grubby fingers. "You do not

need to offer your hand to anyone," she instructed as she turned around with her arm on his shoulder.

"Mrs. Brown, Mr. Carey. May I present my son, Ross Delaney."

The pressure from Vivian's fingers dug into Connal's arms with surprising strength. James tensed and sucked in a breath as he got his first look at Finn's son.

"How do you do," the boy spoke up, as he really focused his attention on the party of adults for the first time. His eyes lit up as he recognized Connal.

"He really does have the look of his father," James observed. His mouth was set in a firm line. Was he thinking about the child his sister might have borne thanks to his perfidious neighbor? Connal felt certain *he* would if he was in James's place.

Even being prepared by their earlier meeting, Connal found the boy's resemblance to his father astonishing.

"You may go on about your business, Ross. Take your worms and go back to the garden with Mary. We are on our way to tour"—Bethany winced as she seemed to catch herself—"to tour the worksite."

The boy tugged his mother's skirt. "Mama, did you ask my cousin if I could go with you? I have observed all the rules he said I must to prove I was old enough to go down there.

"See"—the boy looked down—"my feet aren't on the lane at all. I've only played where I'm allowed and we help Mrs. O'Toole with the chickens if they get loose. And I have stayed with Mary all the time except . . . except just now when I heard you coming."

He looked so crestfallen, Connal could not help

feeling sympathy for him. Not every Delaney needed to have a terrible day today. Someone should be happy.

"You must stay right beside me at all times," Connal said, "unless I say otherwise. Then you must obey me instantly. Do we understand each other?"

"Aye, sir." Ross's attention snapped toward Connal and his back straightened.

Thank you, Bethany mouthed. Her smile was thanks enough as her son skipped over to Connal's side, his worms all but forgotten.

"I'll take these, Master Ross." Mary advanced and picked up the bucket.

"Thank you," he called to her as they continued on their way. The constant flow of his questions on the rest of the walk nearly made Connal regret his invitation.

Nearly.

Chapter Nine

"Ride over for luncheon at Oak Bend three days hence. I could have more encouraging news by then." It had been a satisfying afternoon. James clapped Connal on the shoulder just before climbing into the cabriolet his groomsman had driven over. James managed to hide his smile but could not stem the anticipation inside.

He *could* have encouraging news, but in this instance he would not.

"Please come, too, Mrs. Delaney."

He smiled warmly at the woman who was suddenly playing such a prominent role in his plans for justice. Who would have expected Finn's widow to place herself so propitiously within his arrangements? Or that she would figure so significantly? The little nuances of circumstance never ceased to surprise him. "I am sure you will enjoy getting out and about for a bit. Connal can show you some of our childhood haunts on the way over."

As he expected, her gaze slid over to Connal momentarily before she answered. "I grew up in a city,

Mr. Carey. I am afraid I am not much of a rider. Especially across country. I would only hold him back. Thank you for the invitation, though." She shaded her eyes from the setting sun and gave him a lopsided smile that dislodged an unexpected curl of heat in his stomach.

Even with her plain clothes and simple bonnet, Finn's widow proved a disarmingly attractive bundle. Despite his preference for Vivian's vivacious and intoxicating charms, he could see how Bethany Delaney's aura of innocence managed to snag Connal's attention so often. How to put that to use was the next bend in the puzzle.

"Nonsense. Have Connal bring you over in his gig. It only takes another hour or so by the road. I am sure Vivian would enjoy furthering your acquaintance. Would you not, Cousin?"

"Oh, yes. Please do come, Beth." Vivian responded immediately to his cue. "It is so difficult for us city girls to while the time away here in the country. James tends to be a little dull."

She squeezed his knee under the blanket he had pulled over their laps. "Please say you will come and brighten my day."

Again the redhead's glance went to Connal's. How interesting.

"How can I refuse when you put it so prettily?" Bethany hid her dismay well, but not quite well enough to fool him. "I would love to visit with you, provided Mr. Delaney does not mind taking the longer route."

"We will both be there, then." Connal settled the matter with the efficiency he could bring to bear in almost any situation.

"That will be grand," James said. "I will send over a formal invitation with an exact time once I get home."

With a cheery wave he clicked to the carriage horse and they were off down the lane at a smart pace. Vivian's hand lingered enjoyably beneath the blanket. He adjusted his position to provide her better access to what she sought as he glanced back to see his hosts walking back into the Manor with a measurable bit of distance between them. Good. They might be forming a connection of some sorts, but he would wager a year's profit it was not a physical one.

At least, not yet.

Vivian's busy fingers continued their activity as they left the lane and Glenmeade Manor dwindled in the distance. He managed to make the first turn before he pulled the cabriolet into a small copse by the side of the road for privacy. There was little chance of anyone passing by on this part of the road at this time of day, but she did not know this. Fear of discovery was bound to add to the thrill for her.

Vivian's gaze met his and a smile parted her full lips. He was more than ready to discuss adjustments to his plans based on their successes and observations.

"First things, first." He took her in his arms and kissed her until she was breathless. Her eyes sparkled with expectation when he finally pulled back from her and lifted the coverlet. "Finish what you started, vixen, or I will not be able to form a coherent thought."

A few minutes later he readjusted his trousers while she dabbed her lips with the scrap of lace she kept tucked in her sleeve.

"You really are too good at that, you know." He tucked a stray lock of gleaming ebony back into place.

Vivian remained silent, pretending a pout she truly didn't feel. She might be the slightest bit miffed that he had only allowed her to tend to his needs, but she knew there would be recompense to come.

"Good things come to those who wait, the best things come to those who do not complain about waiting." He already knew what he intended to do to her once he had her alone and naked. Good things, indeed. He felt himself stirring to life again just picturing them.

She held out for just a moment more, then turned to him with a raised brow. "Promise?"

"Have I ever failed you, dearest?"

"It was hardly my fault, you know. There was that odious child demanding all his attention after I worked so hard to have the right questions ready so he would believe I was interested in his horses like you wanted. His horses, of all things, when he is almost a mirror image of poor Finn."

She shifted in the seat so she was facing him more fully. "And who would have thought he would prefer that little mouse to me? She is so plain. So totally unremarkable in every way. And that hair—"

"You certainly threw out enough lures." He interrupted her midtirade. Vivian was not often thwarted in pursuit of an objective. Especially if that objective was a man. Her recounting of Bethany Delaney's innumerable perceived flaws would doubtless cycle through many of their conversations.

"Lures, hell. I practically clubbed him over the

head with my interest and offered him sex on the nearest table. But *she* had fixed his attention totally on her, and not too long before we arrived."

"What do you mean?"

"When she crept out of the house, the little milk-sop had the bemused look of a woman who had just been thoroughly kissed by a new lover. How could you not notice?"

He stroked his mustache as he reviewed his impressions of the Delaneys's greeting on the portico. "Her lips were a trifle red and swollen. I had assumed she bit them to add color."

Vivian shook her head. "He smelled of her perfume. And there was a light in their eyes—part guilt, part thrill—that flashed whenever their gazes met."

"How unexpected. I would have thought Connal Delaney to be the last man she would want anything to do with after her marriage."

"Do not tell me you are taken in by her air of innocent simplicity?" Vivian shook her head and frowned at him. "Finn's wife is a sharp one. Do you know she tried to make a connection between my Sherman and the man who shot her husband?"

He touched her arm. "My dear, there *is* a connection between your husband and Finn's murder."

"No, James. Sherman Esterhazy shot Finn, not Sherman Brown. She tried to string the pieces together nonetheless. I fobbed her off with a story that New England is practically forested by men named Sherman. I have no idea how much of that she believed. But I don't have to tell you, I was more than a little rattled when she asked me about my husband's connections in Taunton."

"Well, well. So there is more to Finn's little widow

than meets the eye." She would bear watching. The notion intrigued him. As if what did meet the eye was not already pleasing enough.

"I know that look, James. And I cannot say that I like the idea of sharing yet another man with the likes of her. Not one bit."

Sharing? There was a thought. The woman Finn had married. The woman Connal desired. That Finn's wife had tried to assemble some of the pieces to the web of pain he'd woven through her life surprised him. She could not be that intelligent— she'd chosen Finn, after all. Given him a home and a son he did not deserve. She had earned whatever punishment fell her way as he went after her husband's family. Her own past choices governed her situation now and in her future.

He laughed at the worried expression on Vivian's beautiful face. Jealousy did not become her, but he refrained from pointing this out. Should the time come for a lesson, he would bring her to heel.

"As if she could hold a candle to you." He brushed his fingertips along her earlobe and across her jawline, which had the desired effect of mollifying her. "I was simply turning over the potential uses for the attraction you noticed between the two of them. How we can best use it to our benefit."

He traced his fingers ever so lightly down the column of Vivian's throat and along the line of her collar. She shivered and stretched in response to his attentions. Her responsiveness to even the simplest of his caresses was one of Vivian's finest qualities.

He brushed his fingers lower still. She sucked in an appreciative breath. "Take me home, James. Take me home, now."

He clicked to the horse and they were on their way. He had three days to test Vivian's charms, and to decide how to use Finn's widow, and her son, to extract an extra fillip of pain from Connal.

"So, that's the truth of it, then, is it? From his own lips?"

"Yes." Bethany nodded. "He bore it on his own shoulders all these years to spare her reputation. Speaking up after the first stories had gone through the county would have done more harm than good. Those who want to believe the worst will never let it go, and those who had some charity might give it up as throwing good after bad. Nothing would really change."

"It's like night and day." Bridget put down the bowl she'd been polishing and rested her hand on the counter. "God curse him."

"What?" Bethany's surprise filled the narrow butler's pantry, startling her aunt.

"Oh, *isean*, I'm speaking of the one ye married, not Master Connal. He's more than paid fer any mistakes he's made a hundred times over. And fer ones he never even thought of."

"I guess his preoccupation with making the Stables a success is understandable, too," Bethany continued. "This place, the horses, are all he had over the years."

"True." Bridget nodded. "Though Jenna O'Toole mentioned he's been more driven of late. She said he rummaged through the storeroom, digging out old ledgers and boxes of receipts last night. He has me ticking off this list of the silver service and cut-crystal pieces. And Betsey's cataloging the furniture in the unused chambers upstairs. Something's in the wind."

Bethany frowned. "Perhaps he needs to prepare a list of assets for the estate. He did not mention anything to me. He did not say anything at all yesterday after James Carey and his cousin departed."

Bethany hugged her knees as she sat on the small stool and watched her aunt. She half-expected to have seen him at some point last evening or this morning. So far he had been immersed in his work, leaving word he did not wish to be disturbed unless fire was involved.

Although they'd cleared some of the air between them, she supposed it was too much to hope that anything had really changed. She was still an intruder in his home. She might have a burning desire to explain the kiss she had forced on him, but he obviously had already dismissed it as unimportant.

Perhaps she was being unfair. He was not used to being open, especially on an intimate level. With anyone. They'd had quite a full day yesterday. His shattering confession, that devastating kiss, enduring Vivian Brown and, finally, the wonderful trip to the stables with Ross. Her thoughts had been so full last night, she'd barely slept. Connal, too, considering the hour when she heard him climb the main staircase and head off to the wing where his quarters were located. Perhaps he just needed a little time and distance to get used to all the changes.

"Our lad sure enjoyed himself yesterday. He's talked of nothing else ever since." Bridget took down a set of small crystal salts from the shelf in front of her.

"Yes. He has been beside himself with satisfaction."

Bethany picked up one of the soft cotton cloths to wipe the nearest, rubbing the fabric into the grooves and across its flat surfaces until it sparkled. "I would almost welcome one of his 'Michael says . . .' as a relief from 'Did you hear Connal say? . . .' Poor Mrs. Brown could not get a word in edgewise once we neared the stables. I tried to hush him more than once, but Connal kept encouraging him."

"I think Master Connal was not half so interested in Mr. Carey's fancy piece as she was in him."

"Mr. Carey introduced her as his cousin. Do you really think—" Bethany dropped her cloth and looked sharply at her aunt. "When did you even see Mrs. Brown? I did not catch so much as a glimpse of you during their visit."

"Aye, but there you all were fer the rest of us ta see as ye paraded down to the stables. There's not much that goes on, when ye live in a small place like this, that goes unnoticed. That one fairly fumed from the time Ross joined ye. And if she is Mr. Carey's cousin, I'll eat her hat."

Bridget's declaration made Bethany giggle. "It was quite a confection, was it not?"

Bethany's thoughts cycled back to the strange co-incidences Mrs. Brown had revealed yesterday. She'd really wanted to discuss her suspicions with Connal but was unsure of how. Anyway, maybe she was just trying to spin sail cloth out of moonbeams, as her da would say. She took a deep breath.

"What is it *isean*? There's more than yer usual share of worries that's been on your mind. Ye might as well spill all the details."

A loud ruckus outside forestalled the rest of the conversation. What sounded like an unending rumble of thunder shook the house, accompanied by loud whistles and whinnies. Bridget scrambled to grab the salts as they jumped across the marble countertop. Bethany also grabbed a couple that were dancing precariously close to the edge.

"What is happening, Aunt?" Bethany's voice sounded funny to her own ears as it shook.

"The horses have arrived. The ones Connal bought." Aunt Bridget gathered the rest of the salts into her apron. Her cheeks were flushed. "Now he's in fer it."

"Who?" Bethany said as some of the noise abated. "Who is in for it?"

And just what was whoever in for?

"Connal, Connal Delaney, ye'd best get out here. Quick as ye, can," a man called from the front yard. "Connal, where are ye, lad? I've brought ye as fine a harem of pretty lasses as ye ever did see."

"Him," Bridget said as she shifted the contents of her apron to Bethany's lap. With her mouth set in a grim line, she headed through the pantry door without another word.

Bethany settled the crystal salts well back from the counter's edge and went after her aunt. Skirting the massive table in the adjacent dining room, she crossed to the sliding doors and out to the foyer.

"Mama, did you see them?" her son called to her from the landing. "Weren't they the most beautiful ones you've ever seen?"

She looked up at him as he came to greet her, practically jumping from step to step in his excitement. "I have not seen anything save you as yet, Ross."

"Come on." He tugged her across the foyer and through the already-open front door. "Hurry."

They stepped outside into the sunlight and found Connal and another man standing together, admiring a magnificent bay-colored stallion in front of the portico.

There was no sign of Bridget, however.

Ross would have charged right over to the men, but she caught him to her by his shoulders. He nearly danced beneath her hands with excitement and impatience at the restraint, but she held him fast. The men were engrossed in looking the animal up and down. They might not notice if a small boy ventured too close to those massive hooves.

So this was what all the preparation was for, all the building down at the stable yard. The horse stood tall and proud as the two men admired him, commenting on his finer points to the groomsman who held his halter. His mane, tail and legs were a rich black and he possessed large, kindly eyes. If an animal could have kind eyes, that is.

"He sure is something isn't he, Mama?"

"He is indeed." Even a horse novice like Bethany knew he was something to behold.

Connal turned at the sound of her voice. He flashed her a broad grin that transformed his face. Gone was the careworn, wary man she had known since their arrival, replaced by someone with shining eyes and barely repressed excitement very much the same as the boy she was holding back with great effort.

"Bethany, there is someone I would like you to meet." He turned to the older man beside him. "My Uncle Jack."

"Black Jack Branigan," she supplied. He was not quite as tall as Connal, but possessed a lean frame with a strikingly handsome face. He was the type of man her aunt would call "a fine figure of a man." He was also the man who had saved Connal's life. "I am pleased to meet you, Mr. Branigan. Connal told me about you."

"I'm only guilty of half what he told ye." He stepped forward. His mustache and the hair at his temples were streaked with gray, but his dark eyes, so similar to Connal's, held a youthful twinkle that hinted at the reasoning behind his devilish name. "And that would be the half he told ye."

He gave Ross a broad wink. "Which is far more than he told me about ye."

"I am Bethany Delaney and this—"

"Connal, ye sly fox." His face lit up and he spun around and tapped Connal on the shoulder before she could finish. "Ye never so much as breathed a word."

"Uncle Jack, Bethany is Finn's wife . . . his widow," Connal corrected. "She came here from North Carolina—"

"I beg yer pardon, Mrs. Delaney." The joy in Jack's face had been exchanged for a wary look. "Doubly so, since I cannot offer ye my sympathies fer yer loss."

Bethany understood, she even appreciated his honesty. She just wished he had not expressed himself so openly in front of her son. In front of Finn's son. Jack must have realized the same thing as his gaze fell on Ross again.

"And this future horseman is Master Ross Brennan Delaney, Finn's son," Connal said, finally finishing the introductions without interruption.

Jack Branigan was certainly a brash, impetuous man.

"How do you do, sir." Ross stuck out his hand.

"How do ye yerself, young sir. Ye have the look of a Delaney, that's for sure." Jack put his foot on the step and rested his arms on his knees so he was face-to-face with Ross. "And if ye manage to be half the horseman of yer cousin here, ye'll grow to be quite a man, indeed."

He leaned closer. "But just between you and me, if ye ever have need of a real teacher, ye can come to me."

"Cousin Connal has already started teaching me everything he knows about horses, and since he said he learned everything from you, wouldn't that make you my teacher, too?"

"Why—" Jack took a moment to puzzle through Ross's logic. "Right ye are. I believe ye have me there, boy-o. Ye have the look of the Delaneys, but ye must have yer mother's brains."

He straightened up and turned back to the new stallion.

"My mother was a Doyle." Ross informed him.

He spun on his heel. His tanned cheeks paled a shade. "What's that ye said?"

"My mother was a Doyle before she married my father." Ross pulled away from Bethany's hands and took a step down. "I'm named for her father, Ross Doyle. Were the Doyles horsemen, too, when they lived here?"

Jack had grown quite still, almost as if frozen in place.

"That will be enough, Ross. Mr. Branigan is just back from a long trip. You must not be a pest."

"It's all right, ma'am. I've never minded a boy's questions. To answer ye, lad, I knew a family of Doyles once. They were drapers, not horsemen."

"That's what my mama and my Aunt Bridget said, but they are girls and I thought perhaps they just didn't know."

"Never doubt yer women, boy-o, yer mam and yer aunt . . . yer Aunt Bridget, did ye say?" Jack caught himself in midsentence. His face grew shadowed, his voice cautious. "Was she . . . well the last time ye saw her?"

"No, sir." Ross shook his head. "She was in a state."

"A what?" Bethany asked, trying, and failing, to decipher what was going on. Connal took a step closer to his uncle, clearly confused as well.

"You know, Mama, a state. Whenever Papa was muttering to himself and acting strange or walking into things, Aunt Bridget used to say he was in a state."

"Your aunt has been drinking?" Connal asked.

"Not so much as a drop. Not yet at least." Aunt Bridget stepped out of the house, her gaze fixed on the man in the driveway.

She'd removed the kerchief she'd tied around her hair while they worked, and had redressed it, winding her braid onto her crown instead of at the nape of her neck, where she usually wore it. She'd changed her dress, too. The one she wore to Sunday Mass, a soft blue trimmed with dark blue ribbons and white tatted lace certainly set her eyes off to a high sparkle.

"Bridget. Bridget Doyle!" Connal's uncle raced up the steps with a whoop. He picked up Bridget and twirled her around, then set her on her feet and kissed her, full on the mouth.

Ross's mouth dropped. Connal's, too. Bethany covered her surprise with her hand as the comments Aunt Bridget had made in the house clicked into place. Could Jack Branigan be Aunt Bridget's lost love?

She must have known—if not before, then soon after they got here—that she would see him again. Known and had not been afraid to stay and confront him. No wonder the shattering confidences she had shared the other day had been so close to the surface.

"Ye look grand." Jack set her from him, but kept his hands on her shoulders as if he feared she would disappear on him. "Haven't changed a bit. Just as pretty as ever."

She looked at him for a minute. Just looked at him as if she was memorizing every detail. "Well, ye have. Ye've grown old. Just look at those gray hairs."

Jack burst into a hearty laugh. "And just as feisty, too. I always loved yer fire, Bridget Doyle."

He made a move to pull her to him again, but she pushed him away. "Now, ye'll not get around me so easily with yer sweet talk. Not this time. Why did ye not come back fer me?"

She pressed her lips together and raised a brow, waiting for a suitable explanation.

"I got delayed. I came back as soon as I could, but ye'd already given up and gone away."

"I spent three months arguing with my father. Another two waiting for the seas ta be fit fer passage. And ye could not even send me word of what delayed ye?" Aunt Bridget was giving no quarter. Bethany could not blame her, whatever Bridget had to say had been waiting for over a quarter century to be said.

"I was in jail, sweeting."

"Don't think ye can 'sweeting' me after all this time. I left a letter fer ye here and posted another when I got to the States. I thought ye would come fer me."

"I never got the letters. In fact, yer father said ye had gone over there ta wed another man. Did ye wed another?"

Clearly, they had many things to discuss, a lot of air to clear. Connal must have been thinking the same thing as he caught her eye. They both looked down at Ross, who was drinking in the whole scene, his eyes as large as saucers.

"Would you like to meet my new horse, Ross?" Connal asked.

That snapped her son's attention away from the couple on the portico.

"Would I ever!"

Connal hesitated for a second, then scooped up Ross in his arms. He held him up so Ross could stroke the stallion's neck. Ross was entranced. Bethany tried not to think about the discussion going on behind them, choosing to enjoy this moment with her son.

"What kind of horse is he?" Ross asked.

"He's a Cleveland Bay," Connal answered. "Bay is his coloring and Cleveland is the district in England where he and the mares came from. Their blood-

lines will help create some very fine horseflesh,
I believe."

"Does he have a name?"

"Dunstan's Folly. Although now that he's ours we
can name him whatever we like."

"So he is going to live here? In the new barn with
the other horses?"

The conversation between man and boy flowed
naturally. Bethany was touched, not only by the patience Connal was showing his young cousin, but
also by the way he used 'we' and 'ours' in the de-
scriptions of his plans.

"Dunstan will have his own paddock, all to himself. Like Teagan, the white stallion I showed you
yesterday. The mares will join the rest of our breeders eventually. But for now we need to keep them
separate to make sure they do not have anything
that might infect the rest of the herd."

Ross patted the stallion's neck. "I think you are
going to like living here, Dunstan. I know I do. Especially when I get to pet you like this. Do you like
me petting you?"

"You can do this now," Connal warned him, "because he has a handler, but when you see him in
that paddock over there, even if he comes up to the
fence, what should you do?"

"Stay away?"

"That's right. You might spook him. He has work
to do in a few weeks and we need him to settle
down and feel at home. Stallions can be very fierce
and unpredictable when they are afraid."

"Why would Dunstan be afraid of me? He's aw-
fully big and I am not."

"That is the secret we use to keep them in our

control. They need to believe you are bigger than them, that you are in charge. That way they can trust you to take care of them."

"I see," Ross said. "Like I trust Mama because she always knows the right thing to do."

"Like that." Connal reached out and stroked the horse, too. The large hand and the smaller one matching their soothing rhythm.

"Dunstan and the mares are our chance to create a whole new, and better type of horse," Connal explained. "Ones we'll be able to sell to people who like to hunt and ride over the countryside. Do you see his feet? The muscles in his legs? I saw these horses years ago, on a trip to England, and I have wanted a fine specimen like Dunstan ever since."

Connal put Ross down. "You stay an apt pupil and in a couple of years one of Dunstan's foals could be yours."

"Mama says I am too young for a real horse, but she hasn't said no to a pony." Ross glanced over his shoulder. "Uh-oh."

"Uh-oh, what?" Connal looked back, too.

"Mama's got her unhappy face on, and Aunt Bridget's kissing that man again."

Chapter Ten

"It's about time ye came in fer a bite. Ye'll run yerself into the ground if ye don't take better care."

Connal was too tired to even explain himself at this point. He just nodded as Jenna set a plate of sausages, biscuits and gravy on the kitchen table in front of him, accompanied by the cup of steaming coffee he'd come searching for in the first place. He swallowed the aromatic brew greedily, welcoming the rush of warmth that flowed through him.

After spending most of the night with his stable master, checking over the new stock and getting them settled in, he was bone-weary and so tied up in knots he could barely think. To be so close to his dream. To reach out and touch those Cleveland Bays, to actually see them housed in his barns, eating his grain, but knowing he could very well lose them in a matter of weeks made him grind his teeth and twisted his insides into knots. He never should have taken the risk. He should have known better than to risk everything. He was so close. Able to see what he wanted, but not being able to actually have it.

"Eat up, Master Connal," Jenna chided. "Ye've got ta keep up yer strength, especially if yer going ta start insulting my cooking by failing ta do it justice."

He looked up. "What?"

"I was joshing with ye." Jenna's tone dropped from bantering to concern. "I don't claim ta fathom the whole of what's troubling ye. Just remember, no matter how bad things seem, ye still need ta eat and sustain yerself. Where there's life, there's hope. Ye've faced trials before. Ye'll get past yer troubles this time, too."

Her faith warmed him. He just could not see the way out of the tangle he had created. Not yet. He couldn't even talk things over with Jack. His uncle was preoccupied with his reunion with Bridget Doyle. Connal couldn't begrudge him the time he needed to sort things out with her. He owed Jack too much.

Besides, at least one of them deserved a chance at happiness.

A fleeting image of Bethany as she reached up to kiss him in the study—was it only a day ago?—taunted him. She'd felt so right, fit so well in his arms. Like a ray of sunlight breaking through the clouds, she'd warmed him with another tantalizing dream by offering him that kiss, a dream just as surely out of his reach as his breeding scheme. He was gambling enough on the horses, he wasn't about to risk anything else.

"Eat, Master Connal. Get a few hours' rest." Jenna tied a shawl around her shoulders, then picked up her gloves and hat from the chair by the door.

"Someone will fetch ye if there's a need. And I promise ta come wake ye myself when I come in."

"Where are you going?" He could ill spare any of the stable hands to go with her to the village, if that was where she was heading.

"I am going out ta the garden with Mary and the little lads. They are going ta help me with clearing the rows so I can get some of my planting under way. Not that the boys will be much help. They'll likely spend most of their time chasing the hens or adding to their worm colony."

"Do you want me to send up one of the stable boys to do the hard digging?" He offered her assistance though he could not afford to spare any.

She snorted. "As if that might really happen. What with the new horses just arrived, yer uncle's attention focused elsewhere—God bless 'em—and everyone getting ready fer the foaling and breeding seasons . . . If I wait on the stable hands we'll have nothing ta put on the table besides plain meat and potatoes come June."

"Sounds like a good meal to me," he ventured and gained a second snort for his effort, this time accompanied by an exaggerated roll of her eyes.

"By the way . . ." She tied the ribbons of her broad-brimmed hat under her chin. "Speaking of foaling, Lochie Tavis's wife tells me one of the maiden mares might be fixing ta drop early."

"Angelfire?"

Jenna shook her head. "I don't remember, ask Lochie, that's why he's yer stable master. He keeps the horses straight. I keep the spices in order."

With that she was gone and he was mercifully

alone with a full plate, a half-empty cup and more to think about than he could sort through.

It must be Angelfire, a gentle sorrel mare with a straight walk and trot, carrying one of Teagan's progeny. Lochie had mentioned early in the week that the first-time dam looked to be bagging up, but even with her udders swelling in preparation for feeding her foal, she shouldn't be due for at least another couple of weeks.

Great. Another worry to add to the scales.

"Could you spare a few minutes?" Bethany stood in the doorway. She looked wary, and weary, and a far-too-tempting target for his frustrations.

He toyed with the idea of telling her no, of picking up his plate and mug and quitting the room in search of another quiet spot, any other spot, where he could collect his thoughts in peace for a few minutes.

He nodded instead. "There should be water for tea on the stove or there may be coffee left."

"Thank you." She walked over to the stove without further comment, her skirt and apron made a soft swishing sound as she moved. After taking a mug from its peg, she reached for the coffeepot. She looked so at home in his kitchen, as if she belonged here, as if she had always belonged here. As Finn's wife he supposed she did. She was here because of Finn. Finn had married her, bedded her and made a son. Her connections with his cousin were like open wounds.

The realization that he wanted Bethany—untouched, untainted and un-everything that had to do with Finn—jolted him. He'd never cared this deeply that poor Rose had lain with his cousin.

Wished things could have played out differently, regretted his part in the despair which had driven her to drastic action, yes, but the fact that she had been intimate with Finn had not gotten under his skin the way picturing Bethany in Finn's arms did.

He'd far rather picture her in his own arms, kissing him, bedding him.

"Would you like more?"

Her question broke through his wayward thoughts.

He had so many irons in the fire, yet his thoughts kept circling back to this gamine beauty standing on the opposite side of the table. He frowned at her. "More?"

She held up the coffeepot. The soft scents of cinnamon and vanilla, as if from a savory confection, twined through him.

"Thank you." He shoved his uneaten plate of food away and held out his mug. The grease congealing from the sausage had nothing to do with his failure to eat.

He took a sip of coffee and waited for her to put the pot back on the warmer. "I do not have much time to spare. Have a seat. What was it you wished to discuss?"

She turned and drew in a breath, exhaling it slowly as she walked over to the table. She stopped without sitting down and pulled in another breath. Her eyes took on a haunted, defeated look as she hesitated. It was like watching someone draw the curtains closed.

"Never mind," she said. "I know you are exhausted. You must have any number of pressing matters requiring your attention. I am sorry I bothered you."

She took a step backward, turned and headed to the door.

"Wait." He was on his feet and around the table in an instant. He caught her by the wrist. "Go ahead. I have the time. What did you want?"

She looked down at his hand on her arm and pulled herself free.

"We . . . We never cleared the air after your visitors left the other day." She raised a pair of troubled blue eyes to meet his gaze. "About what happened just before they arrived."

Was she going to rail at him for taking advantage of her? Demand an apology?

She pressed her lips together for a moment. "I obviously upset you when I kissed you, and I want . . . I need . . . to apologize."

He'd been surprised when she kissed him, but he was even more surprised by her apology. "There is no need for you to apologize. You were just offering me some comfort in a difficult moment."

The warmth of sunlight filling empty corners in his soul, that's what she had given him for a moment.

"No." She shook her head. "That is not true. I kissed you because I wanted to. Because I wanted to know what it was like to kiss and be kissed on the spur of the moment, without any secret motives or hidden costs—"

A heady mix of cinnamon and vanilla flowing through him.

"—to share something on a whim because it might feel good. Because it felt right. Without any consequences or expectations beyond that moment."

"Did it?" He strained for her answer, needing to hear it in every fiber of his body.

"Feel right?" A rueful smile curved her lips. "Not to you. I am sorry I made you uncomfortable when you were already so raw."

He felt like he was looking at her for the first time. Looking at her in a completely new light.

"But did the kiss we shared feel right to you?" he asked her again.

She looked away from him, swallowed hard and whispered, "Yes."

That admission was all it took to shatter any claim he might have on restraint.

"Bethany."

Connal said her name so softly she wasn't sure she'd really heard him. She flicked her gaze back up to his. It felt like his dark eyes could see deep inside of her, as if he was looking at her for the very first time. She realized he meant to kiss her, how much she wanted him to kiss her.

Without motive or consequences, just on a whim.

He cupped her face with his hands and drew her mouth to his. He brushed her lips with slow, soft strokes that sent waves of gentle sensations through her. Her lips parted on a sigh of satisfaction that welled from the depths of her soul.

She flowed into him. One of his hands cradled the nape of her neck while the other laced into the hair at her temple. He deepened the kiss, circling the edges of her mouth with the tip of his tongue. She felt cherished, desired as she had never been before.

She was just venturing the tip of her tongue out to play across his lower lip when a horrified scream from outside reached through the aura surrounding them.

They pulled apart as another cry split the air.

"Merciful heavens!"

"Master Connal!"

"Mrs. Delaney!"

"The children!"

"Somebody help!"

The alarms jumbled together. They were both on the run by the time the most frightening of all reached them: the high-pitched shriek of a horse in full panic.

They tore out the mud-room door at the back of the house. Connal cut directly toward the front, already a good ten paces ahead of Bethany. One glance at the empty garden was all she could spare as she followed him as swiftly as she could, hampered by her layers of skirts and petticoats.

As she rounded the corner of the house, Mary O'Toole was attempting to climb the fence to the pasture on the other side of the lane while her mother held on to the back of her skirt, preventing her from topping the rails to the portion of the paddocks assigned the new stallion.

"Ye'll only make matters worse, girl. Just wait!" Jenna shouted as her daughter struggled to get away.

"Let me go. They'll both be trampled!" Mary's hysterical answer sent a chill through Bethany's heart.

They'll both be trampled!

A small figure lay crumpled faraway on the grass. Standing a few feet from him was another small figure, jumping up and down and waving his arms in the air, jacket in hand like some sort of banner.

Ross! She would have screamed. She should have

screamed. She screamed inside her head. But her throat was too clogged with terror to make a sound.

Far too close to both figures pranced the massive bay stallion.

Connal reached Jenna and Mary.

"Come down, Mary." He used a low, soothing voice. "Come down now. And be quiet. We'll take it from here."

The girl glanced down at him even as she continued to try and break free of her mother. "But Master Ross, little Michael—"

"Ross is doing everything that he should right now to keep the horse back—"

Bethany kept her eyes fixed on her son as he kept jumping and waving and roaring at the horse currently standing several dozen yards away, pawing the ground.

They need to believe you are bigger than them. Wasn't that what Connal told Ross just yesterday? Was that what he was doing? Making himself as big and scary as possible? Dear God.

"We'll spook the horse if we don't go about this just right." Connal reached up as he continued to talk in that soothing tone, so at odds with the dire circumstances they faced. He nodded to Jenna, who released her hold on her daughter. Putting his arm around Mary's waist, he pulled her down and put her into her mother's arms. She burst into tears, but stuffed a fist against her mouth to muffle the sound of her sobs.

"Oh, Bethany," Aunt Bridget put a comforting arm around Bethany's shoulder. "We came as soon as we saw the way of things."

Bethany couldn't look at her aunt. Couldn't sink

into her embrace. She couldn't do anything but keep her gaze fixed on Ross and remind herself to gulp an occasional breath.

Connal's uncle joined him at the fence to survey the scene. Both men carried grim looks as they made their assessment.

Please . . . Please . . . Please . . . Her heart pounded her voiceless prayer against her chest. *Please let them bring him safely back to me. I cannot bear to lose him. Please . . . Please . . . Please . . .*

"My boy! My boy!" Betsey Cochrane's hysteria echoing from the portico reminded Bethany that she was not the only one with so much to lose. "How did this happen! Why aren't ye going ta fetch him back!"

Mary stepped back from her mother, sniffing, releasing Jenna to go and meet the older maid as she rushed to join them by the fence, screaming at full volume.

Even then, Bethany kept her gaze fixed on Ross.

"Hush now, Betsey," Jenna said, attempting to calm her. "Mr. Delaney and Mr. Branigan know best what ta do. Ye must trust them. And ye must try not ta make so much noise, lest ye scare the beast more."

"Michael's all I have left of my Andrew. Ye must do something, Mr. Delaney," she implored.

Bethany winced. The maid's hysteria grew louder instead of softer. If she—

Too late. Aunt Bridget sucked a breath in through her teeth as the stallion charged straight for the boy prone on the grass.

Bethany's heart stopped beating altogether as

her son ran between his helpless friend and the menacing beast.

"Heah-heah!" he yelled as he waved his jacket in a huge arc. *"Heah-heah!"*

Bethany went blank. She couldn't move. Couldn't think.

"Miracle of miracles." Aunt Bridget breathed as the stallion swerved at the last moment, missing Ross by inches.

Bethany could have sunk right down on the lane with relief, but she held herself upright, her arms wrapped around her.

The horse stopped, turned and pawed the ground only a few strides away, keeping a wary eye fixed on the boys as he tossed his head and shook his mane, clearly still agitated.

"Not another word, Betsey Cochrane," Jenna told the maid sternly but quietly. "Ye'll make things worse."

"But—"

"Not a word," Jenna repeated.

Ross stopped all motion. He didn't look at the men by the fence. He didn't look at the women standing in the lane. He just kept his attention focused on the horse. Did he know help was coming? He must be nearing exhaustion. He had to be so very scared.

Connal was stripping off his jacket and unbuttoning his waistcoat. "Give Jack your apron, Betsey."

Having something to do, even something so illogical, gave the maid a purpose. She straightened her spine and practically tore the apron off her back. And she held her peace.

"The white should gain the animal's attention,"

Jack explained as he took the apron and handed it to Connal.

Connal looked at Bethany. "He is very brave and very smart. I will have him back to you in no time."

She couldn't speak. Couldn't thank him. All she could do was nod.

"There's Lochie with a rope." Jack flicked his head toward the far side of the field.

"Wait until I get about halfway there," Connal said to his uncle.

"Aye," Jack nodded.

Connal climbed through the rails and walked slowly on to the field. He covered half the distance, clutching the apron behind his back. His pace was excruciatingly slow, so as not to startle the horse too soon.

"I'm so sorry, Mrs. Delaney," Mary spoke up. "They—"

"Hush, girl. Not now," her mother silenced her.

Jack entered the pasture, heading for the boys from a different angle than Connal or the man they called Lochie. The men matched each other, pace for pace.

All the women standing on the lane held their collective breaths. Connal signaled Lochie to halt, then began waving the apron over his head to catch the animal's attention. By taking off his jacket he added to the mass of color he planned to use to challenge the stallion into leaving the boys alone.

Please . . . Please . . . Please . . . She'd never ask for another thing.

The horse's head came up. His attention shifted from the boys to the man in white. He whickered, clearly uncertain about what was happening.

Connal advanced, still silently waving the apron in languid arcs. The stallion whickered again and backed up. Connal kept coming, the horse kept backing up. It was like watching a strange dance. A strange, dangerous dance.

Ross stayed as still as a statue, guarding his friend, apparently aware that any motion might send the stallion charging back their way.

Please . . . Please . . . Please . . . Just keep him safe a little longer.

Michael's loud moan split the silence and he struggled to sit up. The horse whickered and reared, renewed panic tearing his attention from Connal's advance.

Bethany had nothing left. No prayers. No bargains. Her world depended on Connal Delaney. A small part of her hung on to that, kept the rest of her intact because of that. Because of him.

Connal ran straight for the horse, waving the apron and whooping at the top of his lungs. Jack darted forward and picked up the injured boy. He headed back to the fence, leaving Ross standing like a lone sentinel in the center of the field.

The horse turned away from Connal and ran back toward the barn and Lochie. Connal dropped the apron and ran full tilt for Ross. He scooped her son into his arms and also headed to the fence.

Joined by two members of the stable crew, the new stallion was quickly roped by Lochie and the other men and held firm.

"Praise heavens, *isean*." Her aunt gathered Bethany into a big hug.

Bethany still couldn't breathe, couldn't move. All she could do was wait.

Mary's tears turned into smiles as she hugged her mother. Jenna was all smiles, too.

"Oh, Michael, my Michael!" Betsey ran forward to reach through the railings and take Michael from Jack's arms.

"My boy, my boy," she kept repeating. "Mama's got ye. Ye're safe now."

She clutched her son to her and showered him with kisses. "Thank ye, Mr. Branigan. Thank ye both."

"Be careful with him, ma'am," Jack warned. "Set him right down on the grass so we can check him for broken bones."

"Ye can't imagine how scared I was when I looked out the window to see what all the ruckus was about as I was sweeping Mr. Delaney's room. There ye were, lying in a field with a rampaging horse." Betsey put Michael down.

Bethany knew exactly how the other mother felt.

Jenna joined them. She ran her hands over his arms and legs. "Where does it hurt, lad? Did that great beastie step on ye or kick ye?"

Michael shook his head, then put his hand to his temple. He squeezed his eyes shut. "Where's Ross?"

"He's right behind ye, boy-o. Ye're both lucky lads." Jack climbed through the fence. "Does yer head hurt? Are ye dizzy?"

"Everything is spinning." Michael opened his eyes. "I tripped. The horse was chasing us. Is Ross really all right?"

"We'll give him the once-over in a minute. Ye'll likely see him later."

"Do you think you can walk?" Jenna asked Michael. He nodded. "Best get him inside and to bed, Betsey.

Mary, you go, too. Help Betsey, then go to the kitchen and put the kettle on. We'll send for the doctor."

Betsey helped her son to stand as he protested. "But I don't want to go to bed. Me and Ross are going fishing later. Mary promised."

"I doubt ye'll be going anywhere fer at least awhile," Betsey answered. "Yer lucky I'm not fishing fer a switch. After the doctor pronounces ye fit, we are going to have a long talk about where ye may and may not go, ever."

As the Cochranes departed, Connal reached the fencing at last. His dark gaze locked with Bethany's as he handed Ross over the fence to Jack.

Then all she could see was Ross. Ross out of the paddock and safe. Everything frozen inside her broke free. Her fear, her joy, her tears. She stepped away from Bridget and opened her arms wide. Ross ran into them and she held him fast.

"You were so brave, so smart," she finally managed to choke out as she kissed his dark curls. Her tears were still flowing. "I'm so happy you are all right."

"Then why are you crying, Mama?"

"Because you scared her, Ross." Connal frowned deeply at Ross as he joined them. He had his jacket slung over his shoulder. Ross's jacket and his own waistcoat were clutched in his hand.

Bethany stood up, but kept her hand on Ross's shoulder, unable to let him go now that she had him back. "Thank—"

"Don't thank me for the boys. I was protecting my investment. Getting the children out of the way was the most expedient means."

He turned to Ross. "You disobeyed my instructions to stay away from the animal." Barely repressed anger shook Connal's voice. "You frightened your mother. And just look at all the people you pulled away from their work. What do you have to say for yourself?"

Ross's lips trembled the tiniest bit before his chin went up. "I had to help Michael. He's my friend and he was hurt," he answered, truth ringing in every word. "I tried to do what you told me. Be bigger than the horse."

"You have good instincts." The words were close to praise, but the hard line in Connal's tone was cutting. "But next time, think before you act. Run for help. Do not try to solve everything on your own. We all need each other." His gaze flicked to Bethany and then away. "That is a lesson I learned too late."

Chapter Eleven

The air grew heavy with anticipation for the tumult to come as the threat of rain hovered in the distance. Again.

The weather in Ireland seemed to shift more swiftly here than along the warmer shores of North Carolina. Almost as swiftly as the far-flung emotions swirling inside her. Fear, longing, desire, anger and relief cut wide swaths through the confusion in her thoughts.

Bethany paced away from the windows, twisting her hands together as the peat fire hissed softly in the grate and Bridget's knitting needles clicked together. Today's events tumbled through her over and over. The fear clutching her when the stallion charged Ross. Those hooves, so large and deadly, thrashing the air. Connal's quick reactions, saving her son's life.

She'd been frozen, rooted in place. Unable to move or speak or think of anything beyond the horror playing out around her. She had been unable to save her son, even when his life depended on it. Her very soul trembled with that certainty.

And with the realization that she had behaved the same way in her marriage. As Finn spiraled down, delving deeper and deeper into his dark excesses, she had frozen herself—willing herself not to think, not to care, not to hurt as her life deteriorated around her. Ross had been her only hope, her only salvation, the reason she got up each day, the reason she endured. The reason she was here. And she'd nearly lost him today.

She wanted, needed, to see Connal. To thank him, to make him understand just how much his actions meant.

After bringing Ross to her, he'd stalked away to the stables and stayed there the rest of the day. His uncle had gone down to fetch him as evening approached, but so far neither of them had returned.

"Why are they still out there, Aunt Bridget?" The need to see Connal consumed her. "Do you think there is a problem with the horses, with the stallion the boys spooked?"

"I think there is always something to worry about. What makes the difference is how you handle those worries." Bridget put down her knitting. "Jack said the stallion was fine when he came back the first time. The doctor said our lad had nary a scratch from the incident and little Michael will be out of bed in a day or two. No real harm was done, so put yer fears aside."

"Connal was so angry. He has so much invested in the new horses." She paced the length of the rug back to the window, treading lightly as she sidestepped the toy horses strewn near the edge of the nightstand where Ross had been playing with them earlier. "He would not even let me thank him. He just stalked away."

"Bethany Catherine Doyle Delaney."

The impatience in Bridget's voice surprised her. She called her niece by her full name only when she was truly exasperated.

"Ye cannot judge all men against that poor excuse of a husband ye married. Connal was not angry because his investment was endangered, he was frightened for Ross. He was frightened for you. It was fear that made him angry."

"Do you really think so?" She sat on the edge of the window seat. A sharp breeze puffed the curtains beside her. "But he seemed so certain of what to do."

"Then ye haven't yet tumbled ta the whole of it."

"What do you mean?"

Her aunt picked up her needles again. "There was a time when both ye and Connal were too trusting and ye've both been slapped pretty hard fer that trust all these years. The realization that he cared so much about both Ross and ye scared Connal. Knowing how much losing ye would hurt him is what will make him keep his distance."

Aunt Bridget's words struck true. Could her aunt be right? Was she not the only one who had frozen? She nibbled her lip as the idea that Connal had been frozen as well filtered through her thoughts. Frozen by the guilt he had piled on himself, and the shame others heaped on him. "Do you think . . . he is as afraid of me as I am of him?"

"Aye. Now, what are ye going ta do about it?" Bridget raised an eyebrow.

What was she going to do? "How did you forgive

Jack Branigan so easily, after all the years? How did you get past all the pain, all the fear?"

"There is nothing ta forgive. Not in a balance-scale way, where one has or needs more than the other. He was delayed. I left. We both need forgiveness. We never really tried ta find each other. We need to learn ta trust all over. We've suffered enough ta know ta leave the past in the past and start fresh."

Starting fresh. That sounded so appealing but practically impossible in Connal's situation, in hers. At least not in the same way as Jack and Bridget. Unless . . .

"Connal sees himself through the eyes of everyone around him who condemns him as The Wicked One." She gave voice to her thoughts as they formed. "Just as I see myself as inadequate through Finn's reproachful glares."

"And, so?" Bridget waited for her to come to the answer on her own.

"And so . . . We need fresh eyes. We need to look at ourselves, at each other, in new light."

Bridget smiled broadly. "Ye always were a clever girl. Ye need ta look at yer choices and decide what's best fer ye. What will make ye happy. So does Connal."

"Is that what you are doing with Jack Branigan? Making a choice?"

"Aye." Her aunt's gaze softened in the lamplight as her gaze shifted to a spot only her thoughts could see. "I loved a man, once, and lost him. I had a child, once, and lost him, too. Neither were by my choice. I've chosen ta be alone for almost a quarter century. Now we have a second chance and I choose not to let it slip away."

"Bridget?" Jack's soft call as he knocked on the door could not have been better timed. Bridget was on her feet in an instant. "Bridget, would ye like ta come down ta share a bite with me?"

"Of course." She opened the door.

"Did Master Connal come back with ye at last?" she asked after Jack swept her into a passionate kiss.

"Nay." Jack shook his head. "He's sitting out in an empty stable, all torn up and too stubborn to take a risk. I told him—"

Bridget's hand on his cheek halted him before Bethany could glean too many details. He spotted her sitting by the window then. "Oh, hullo, Bethany. Are ye hungry? Would ye like to join us?"

"Thank you, no. You go on."

Jack slipped his arm around Bridget's waist. Bethany had never seen her aunt look so . . . so happy. *We have a second chance and I choose not to let it slip away,* that's what she'd just said. Could Connal Delaney be Bethany's second chance? Could she be his?

"I'd be happy to keep an ear out fer our lad if ye have something else ye'd like ta do," Bridget offered as they left.

"I have everything set up for a late supper in the drawing room . . ." Jack said as the door clicked shut.

So Connal was out in the stables, all torn up, while she paced the floors here feeling much the same way. Things needed to change, but how could they if they were both frozen? A lamplit stable might provide enough light for fresh eyes, enough for them to see if they could thaw just a little.

She grabbed her slippers and a shawl, then headed to the stairs. There was only one way to find out.

It was cooler outside than she expected. She tucked the shawl over her head and shoulders and braved the first splatter of raindrops anyway, holding close to the basket dinner she'd packed for Connal.

She was damp and breathless by the time she'd traversed the lane and made it to the nearest stable door. The one with light shining through the cracks. She hesitated outside the door. Should she knock? What if he wasn't alone? What if he was in one of the other buildings?

She was considering just leaving the basket outside when the door opened and Connal stood before her. He was dark and brooding and dangerously handsome silhouetted by the light inside.

He didn't say anything, just stepped back from the doorway to let her pass.

With only the slightest hesitation she moved inside. He left the door open behind her. An unspoken offer of respectability despite the late hour and the probability that there was no one around to care that they were alone in the stable together.

Silence held between them for the span of several heartbeats as she fought to catch her breath. She realized she was clutching the shawl tighter than necessary around her as though the damp wool might protect her from what she was about to do. She forced herself to loosen her hold and let the shawl drop down her shoulders.

His gaze ran over her hair, her face. The ridge between his brows tightened.

Fear and longing twisted inside her. She hugged herself.

"What are you doing here?" His question was quiet and noncommittal.

"Jenna left your dinner for you." She held out the basket as if that would explain her delivering it to him on a dark, rain-swept night.

"Oh." His mouth tilted ever so slightly and then straightened out once more. His gaze held hers.

She shivered.

"Perhaps you would be better off back in the house."

"No, I . . . that is . . . I really wanted to talk to you." Her voice came out shaky and uncertain. She felt naked, as though all the hidden emotions she'd tried so hard over the years to keep inside were seeping out of her very pores. She was thawing all right.

She stopped and drew a slow breath. "I wanted to thank you for what you did. For all that you have done for me . . . for us . . . for—"

"There is no need." His flat tone gave nothing away.

He looked so shadowed. Bridget said it was fear, but it certainly looked like anger. Exactly like the anger she had seen too many times from a man who looked so much like this one.

Old panics gnawed at her middle. She squeezed her arms against her stomach again and winced. Finn was in her past. Finn was in Connal's past. The only way Finn could hurt them here, now, was if they let him.

"Are you all right?"

"Yes, I—"

"You should not be out here. Not after what happened with the boy."

"The doctor said Ross is fine and that Michael will be completely recovered in a day or so."

Her voice trembled again. She wanted to stamp her foot in frustration. She'd acknowledged her fears. She knew what she wanted to change. So when would she be able to control her nerves? When would she see herself with those fresh eyes she thought she wanted so much?

"That is good to know, but the news could have waited. Now that you have delivered it"—he eyed the basket she still held—"and the dinner, I should escort you back to the house."

He took her elbow and half-turned her toward the stable door. His grip was strong and firm, yet gentle. So much like the man himself.

He won't hurt me. He saved Ross. He is not his cousin. Connal wasn't angry, he was afraid, too. These snatches of thoughts raced through her as he urged her to follow his lead.

Ye need ta look at yer choices and decide what's best fer ye. What will make ye happy. Leaving was not what she wanted. She wanted Connal to see that she could look at him with fresh eyes and know him for the man he really was. The man. Not the reputation.

She placed her hand against the door frame to halt her forward progress and felt him brush against her. Heat rushed over her at the contact. She glanced up and caught his dark gaze with her own. He was so close.

She drew a deep breath. "I am not going back to

the house right now. I need to talk to you. And you need to listen. You need to trust me."

His gaze held hers in the semidarkness of the lantern light for what seemed an eternity.

"You should be careful not to speak aloud things better left unsaid," he warned.

She held her breath for a moment longer, gathering her courage. "There seems to be more than enough of not saying what needs to be said around here already."

"Indeed."

The cold light in his eyes shifted, warmed just a little after that torturous sentence. The edge of a smile curved his lip, giving her hope.

"What do you know, Bethany Delaney?"

She smiled. "I know what kind of a man you are."

He raised a brow. "What kind of man is that, pray tell?"

"You took us in when it was the last thing you wanted, you risked your life to save Ross, you shoulder all the burdens here and keep the worries to yourself. You are an honorable man."

"Is that how you see me, pretty Bethany?"

He leaned toward her and heat washed over her again. She so wanted him to kiss her. She wanted him to do more than kiss her. And she wanted to do so much more than just kiss him.

"There are those that would be happy to tell you dark and forbidding tales of Connal Delaney."

"No."

"You think you know better? Better than what is common knowledge?" His hands gripped her waist. He leaned closer.

"Yes. Because I see you with fresh eyes." Her

breath quickened in her chest and the coiling snake of heat writhed in her middle, blotting out the fear that lived on after Finn. Her hands gripped the edges of his shirt and she pushed up on her tiptoes. "Can you see me with fresh eyes?"

"What?" He dipped his head the slightest bit toward hers.

He was so close. So very close and yet he wasn't close enough. Her heart sped fast in her chest. He held himself still, waiting for her as though he knew the battle inside her. A truth he couldn't possibly know.

"Fresh eyes. Outside expectation, reputation, the past," she explained. "We need to look at ourselves, at each other, in a new light. With fresh eyes."

"And what if we do not like what we find in the new light?" he asked.

"Then we go on, try something else, a little wiser, a little warier. But no longer frozen by the same old fears and expectations."

"This approach sounds quite drastic and more than a little reckless."

"You need a sharp blow to crack ice," she explained.

If anyone saw them now, together, in this half-embrace, would they think her as reckless as he made her feel?

Her need to feel his mouth on hers made caution a pale, flaccid thing. His gaze held hers, dark and deep and unreadable. And she knew without the words needing to be spoken he would not make the next move. He would not send her away. He would not ask her to stay. Whatever happened next would be up to her.

She parted her lips and wet them with her tongue.

His gaze dipped to watch her. Fresh heat blazed in those fathomless brown depths. Fire raced over her skin at his reaction to her. She felt naked and vulnerable, yet more alive and powerful than she had in a long time, in a lifetime.

Connal was not Finn. Not the least bit like Finn. She was done being frozen, done with fear and uncertainty. Something in Connal's eyes, his stance, his very soul, bespoke a freedom she had never known but always yearned for. Freedom she could no longer wait to taste.

"Connal." She breathed his name and tugged him down toward her, pressing her mouth hotly to his.

His lips were warm and firm and velvety. He allowed her full reign of their kiss. This encounter was hers to control. The realization was heady.

She slid her arms around his neck and leaned up and into him; tilting her head and coaxing his mouth open with her tongue in that delicious, teasing way he had used as they kissed this morning.

No hidden costs . . . without consequences. Isn't that what she'd come to him looking for this morning? Honesty. Freedom. No expectations beyond the moment. Beyond this moment.

The muscles of his chest and thighs pressed close against her, his body cradling her intimately but with a gentle restraint she found sensual in a way she had never experienced before. The power of this man came not from his control of her but in his command of himself. She longed to be closer still. As close as possible in every way.

She stretched up on her tiptoes as her tongue tangled slowly with his. She still wasn't close enough. A whimper of frustration escaped her.

His hands slid up along her rib cage, a slow trail of fingers that set fire to her skin despite the layers between them. He reached up beneath her arms, lifting her, pulling her so very close. Her toes barely brushed the floor as he pulled her against him, shifted her in his arms and leaned back against the wall. She lay fully against him, his legs on either side of hers. Desire welled, hot and deep, and she moaned into his mouth.

Never had fashion, or her lack of it, seemed so raw and sensual. The thin stuff of her gown, her scant petticoats, did little to hide the raw-boned feel of the man. Her breasts were pressed against the muscular planes of his chest. Her belly against the flat trimness of his own. The hard swell of his desire pressed plainly against the softness of her thighs. A piece of her melted as she took pride in how quickly and completely just kissing her, holding her, had gained his full attention.

She wanted this kiss to go on and on and yet she wanted so much more. Never before had she felt like this. Never. She pushed away the darkness of before, of the past. All she wanted was now. Here. This man.

She arched closer to him still. His kissed her over and over. Suckling first her upper, then her lower lip. Tasting her, letting her taste him, feel him, fully. The need to open to him, to welcome any desire he held, to meet his needs willingly with her own, was overwhelming.

He lifted his head. Rain might beat against the outside of the stables, but pure heat pulsed between them inside. Despite the cool dampness so pervasive in the crisp Irish air, she had never felt so warm or so safe in her entire life.

"Bethany."

The way he said her name, raw with emotion and need, was joy. She wanted nothing hidden in this moment between them.

"Yes." She breathed her agreement, giving him a wide smile. It was not so much an answer to the question in his voice as consent to anything he might ask of her.

His eyes slitted and he brushed his lips over hers ever so slowly. White-hot spirals of longing swirled inside her.

He lifted his head once more.

Silence beat between them as his gaze locked with hers. "I want you."

Simple words and yet they scorched her from her toes to the roots of her hair. A moan of agreement escaped her.

His mouth tilted up at one corner. "You have no idea what you do to a man when you make that exquisite little sound."

"What I do to *you*." She couldn't stop the accusatory tone in her voice.

"Aye."

His fingers threaded up into her hair, loosening her pins until they showered into rushes at their feet. Her curls fell around her shoulders.

"I want you," he repeated himself. "And if you do not leave this stable right now, I mean to have to you."

The old fears suddenly seemed far, far away. She wanted him more than she could express in mere words.

"Make love to me, Connal Delaney."

"Aye." His mouth covered hers again for long, slow moments. He kissed her so thoroughly and so very

slowly she was caught between wanting it to go on
and on, never ending, and wanting to move forward.

His hands swept down her back, molding her to
him. He cupped her hips and rolled them toward
him. She was cradling his member, but there were
too many layers of clothes between them for her
to feel anything other than frustration. And all the
while his lips kept up their slow, tantalizing caresses
on hers.

His fingers trailed up to the buttons at the back of
her gown. He began to undo them. One, two, three.
Each button gave with no protest beneath the touch
of those mesmerizing fingers. Cool air kissed the
skin of her back. She felt no chill. No fear.

Only the longing for more.

He nibbled his way from her lips, her jaw, to the
skin just below her left ear. The heat of his mouth
against her pulse beat was heavenly and so teasingly
wonderful she was sure she would die from the
pleasure. Four, six, ten, in moments the buttons
were no longer an impediment to the desire raging
between them. He eased the gown from her shoulders. It drooped down her arms. She pulled back
from him enough to let it flow down her arms, over
her hips and onto the floor.

She stood before him now in naught but her petticoats and corset, with her hair flowing free. His
eyes devoured her, appreciated her. She felt free.
Freer than she ever had in her life. There was no
hurry, save the driving compulsion to become one.

Her breath came fast in her throat, the corset
had never felt so confining, separating her from
the caresses, the attentions she craved. She had
never stood before a man like this. The infrequent

marital relations pressed on her had never held this level of mutual desire, mutual needs and concern expressed by a man who worshipped her and asked her to want him in return.

She was amazed and awed and stunned. His gaze roved her body with slow heat. She felt beautiful in ways she had never realized possible.

She reached behind her back to undo the lacings of her corset, eager to be shed of this impediment, eager to return to his arms, to his lips.

"Bethany."

Her name on those lips was hoarse and low, betraying his own impatience, firing hers.

She could only get so far in the lacings with her trembling fingers. She paused for a just a moment, took a breath and turned her back to him. "Could you help me?"

He reached for her without hesitation. He ran his hands over her shoulders and down her arms, sending more white-hot spirals through her. She sucked in a breath.

His fingers made short work of the rest of the lacings. Her corset gave way with a sigh and he tossed it to the side. He stood behind her now, resting his hands on her shoulders. The cool air played over her exposed skin, raising gooseflesh, but the shivers racing down her spine were from his touch.

He slid his hands downward along her arms to the tips of her fingers. Locking his fingers between hers, he tugged her backward. She leaned against him. He was so warm behind her. The air on her front provided a sensual contrast that took her breath away.

She tilted her head to the side, resting against his

chest and his mouth found her ear, then her neck, the curve of her shoulder—giving each soft, languid kisses.

His mouth nudged aside the lacy strap of her camisole. His fingers teased the strap down on the other side. The camisole dipped low across her breasts and hung for the span of several heartbeats against the tightened points of her nipples. His fingers kept tugging until it dropped to her waist, baring her breasts to the lamplight.

"Sweet heaven." Connal groaned against her shoulder. "Sweet Bethany."

His arm snaked about her waist and pulled her tight against the rigid planes of his chest. "You are so very lovely."

She felt lovely. In his arms, she felt lovely in ways she had never thought to feel. And she wasn't afraid. The desire to be with him, to know him as fully as she could, was intoxicating.

He turned her to him and covered her mouth with his. The drought between kisses was over. She moaned into his mouth as his tongue delved into hers to dance against her own. Slow, soft and wonderful.

His hands slid to her petticoats. In moments she was naked in his arms. His hands slid over her thighs, her hips, her belly and upward. And all the while his mouth lingered on her own. She ached for him. Could hardly bear the anticipation by the time his fingers first brushed her breasts.

Then he cupped them, fully, massaging them so gently she wanted to melt.

He released her lips and bent his head. The warmth of his breath against her nearly drove her mad with longing. Then his mouth covered one nipple.

"Connal." She shivered in his arms. Pleasure shot through her, whole and complete as he kissed and suckled first one breast, then the other.

She clutched his shoulders as the shudders continued unabated. She had never felt anything so overwhelmingly wonderful. Not once.

Long moments later her breathing came under control and she could feel the ground beneath her feet once more.

"Oh, my." Her voice was shaky and low.

"You are exquisite. Perfect." Connal's awed voice held a smile.

"I have never . . . What did you? . . . Oh, my." She swallowed and fought for rational thought there amid the stables, naked in the lamplight. "I didn't know there could be so much . . . feeling there."

"That was just the beginning."

She liked his quiet confidence, liked the promise that it held.

"There is?" She felt virginal, inexperienced, despite her marriage and child.

"Aye, much more, lovely Bethany."

She pushed away from him ever so slightly, finding her footing despite the weakness lingering in her knees, and reached for the buttons of his shirt. One by one she undid them, ignoring her trembling fingers. Impatient.

"Then you must show me this *more,* Connal Delaney, for I do not think I will be leaving until you show me every bit of it."

"Demands, already?"

"Aye," she answered him definitively. "I want you to show me everything."

"I shall be happy to do so, sweet Bethany."

His shirt parted beneath her hands. He shrugged and she drew it down his shoulders before tracing her hands, palms, over the broad, flat planes of his chest and belly.

"And I want you to demand the same from me. Pleasure for pleasure."

She leaned against him and watched his eyes narrow as he sucked in a breath. His heat and hardness pressed against her softness. She could hardly wait.

"So very—"

"—perfect," she finished for him, agreeing completely.

She lifted her chin and pressed a kiss against his mouth. Her fingers drifted downward to the fastenings of his trousers. As she began to open them, he gripped her shoulders and pulled her tight against him, kissing her with that deep, unabated passion that was his alone.

"Make love to me," she said again when his mouth left hers.

"Aye, I intend to." He scooped her into his arms.

Chapter Twelve

He carried her to the smaller room off to the left of the stable entrance. The room that would be reserved for his hands if they needed to be in the stables overnight for a foaling.

Fresh hay covered the floor, scenting the air in this unoccupied portion of the new construction. In the far corner he tugged a folded quilt blanket from the wall and tossed it open amid the hay. The feel of Bethany against him, so soft, so real, overcame any shreds of rationality he could have called his own.

She tucked into him so perfectly. Her lush curves fitting against him as if this was exactly where she belonged, had always belonged.

He released her legs from his hold. She slid down the length of him.

For just a moment, sanity threatened the lust-filled haze surrounding him. He was about to make passionate love to his cousin's widow. A woman with a child and responsibilities of her own. And he had the financial care of this entire estate and its business, the welfare of the people who lived and worked with and for him to look out for. Giving in to impulse like this was surely a step on a reckless path to disaster.

He set her from him and tried to ignore the lovely glow of her skin, the tumbled sultriness of her hair, the enticing warm scent of cinnamon and vanilla. "Bethany, are you sure—"

Her fingers covered his lips before he could finish.

"Now is not the time for such a foolish question." She moved forward into his arms.

"Foolish?"

"Yes." Her laugh was shaky and sultry at one and the same time.

"I am naked in your arms. I may not be sure of everything. I may not be sure of much. But I am sure that I want you, here and now. I want you to see me with fresh eyes. I want you to make love to me."

All the while she was making her declaration the tips of her breasts were brushing his chest each time she drew breath. Silken locks of her hair fell against his arms. The warmth of her breath fanned his skin. And most of all, the knowledge that she was indeed naked and willing in his arms, all combined to drive him to madness with his desire to push her down on the quilt and do exactly as she asked.

She reached up and put her mouth against his, kissing him slowly. "I want you as I have never wanted anyone before."

He slid his arms around her at that and pulled

her closer, kissing her deeply, letting his tongue and hers slide together in slow passion.

This was heaven and hell in one neat little package called Bethany Doyle Delaney. Surely he would lose himself, his mind, his soul, everything, in the pursuit of loving her as completely as his body cried out for him to do.

But it was the little moan she gave as he edged her lips with his tongue, that unbidden sound that thrust him over the edge.

He released her only long enough to shrug himself out of his trousers and kick them away into a darkened corner. Then he drew her back into his arms to feel the whole length of her against him. Bare skin to bare skin. Luscious softness to hardened muscle.

"Dear God, I want you."

"I am right here," she whispered back to him, trembling ever so slightly.

He knelt on the quilt and pulled her down with him. He stroked her softness as he kissed her, her lush breasts, sleek legs, firm bottom. He wanted his fingers to learn every inch of her as he traced lazy paths that sent shivers racing through her and rewarded him with those moans he already loved.

When he could stand the temptation no longer, he delved his fingers into the hidden silkiness between her thighs. She opened to his questing fingers between her curls. He slid them down and touched her damp readiness. Slick and wet and open.

He rubbed her first, then slid a finger into her wet sheath. She moaned and arched her back. He loved how she reacted to his every touch.

He dipped his head to taste her breasts. The full, high curve, the tight pink nipple. He circled and suckled her above, stroked and slid within her below.

"Oh, Connal, oh." She shuddered in his arms as she experienced this next climax in her pleasure.

He was awed and amazed. He had never been with any woman so responsive to his touch. To have her experience the ultimate just from his touch slid into his heart and dug anchors into his soul. Giving her pleasure became an aphrodisiac of its own.

She licked her lips and focused on him, her eyes dazed with satisfaction.

He couldn't hold back any longer. The need to claim every inch of her in the most ancient, unexplainable way drummed in his very blood. His soul.

He drew her beneath him, settling himself between her thighs. She was open and ready as he slid deeply into her. Her silky sheath hugged him tight. She fit to him and he fit in her as though they had been made just for this purpose. Their twin groans of pure satisfaction split the air.

He held himself still, held himself back, enjoying the anticipation, enjoying having her so close, so totally his. She was so hot, so tight, so right, he needed to savor this moment to its fullest.

She took a deep breath, reached up a hand and drew his head, his mouth down to hers. She kissed him, melting his resolve to go slowly as she drew his tongue into her mouth and suckled his lips.

He longed to give in to the pleasure, the completeness, of moving inside her but he remained still. He returned her kiss, savoring the exquisite willingness of her mouth, the sensation of stroking his tongue against hers.

She trembled in his arms, her own locked around his neck. He drew her legs up around his hips. The longing to move inside her built to a fever pitch and yet he forced himself to stillness, prolonging this initial sensation, anticipation, as long as he could.

He released her mouth to nuzzle her breasts and was rewarded with another moan and the upward thrust of her hips. He sucked in his breath as she rocked against him, up and back and up, in time with the suckling motion of his mouth against her breast as he tasted her nipple.

"Oh, Connal, oh." Her breathless voice shivered through him. She arched her back and groaned his name again, then subsided into wordless little cries as she again knew the fullness of pleasure.

Her body convulsed him, writhing with the sensations he wrought in her. She gulped for breath, lying beneath him sated and satisfied and melded so completely around him.

He could hold back no longer. He had no thoughts beyond this woman, this moment, nothing but the satisfaction looming ahead.

"No secrets," he told her and took her lips once more. She sighed into his mouth.

"Nothing hidden." He began to thrust in and out of her sweet little body in a rhythm older than time itself.

"Just you and me and now."

He tasted her agreement against his lips and in the shuddering acceptance her body gave him as he thrust and withdrew, thrust and withdrew.

"Oh, oh. Oh!" she cried out and clutched him as he quickened his movements, thrusting hard and fast, letting her feel his need for her in each pounding motion.

"Connal. Connal." His name flew from her over and over as he loved her with the full force of his body, moving toward the unseen crest of his own desires.

She twined her legs around him and arched against him as the crest broke and the climax rose inside him. He shuddered in the throes of his own release as he poured himself into her.

Moments later there was naught but the mingled sound of their breathing and the distant sound of the rain.

Bethany stared up at the crossed beams of Glenmeade's stables and felt a kind of satisfaction she had never thought to feel. Making love with Connal Delaney had been something far different from what she had experienced in the unyielding arms of her husband.

This man had given her pleasure, cared for her satisfaction, while Finn . . . She stilled her thoughts. He didn't belong here in the warmth of Connal's embrace, with her body still linked to his. She banished all thoughts of anything before these past few moments.

Smiling against Connal's neck, she felt his body twitch deep inside her. She laughed, her body squeezing around his in reflex, and he groaned weakly.

"Thank you," she whispered, unable to stop herself.

"That would seem an odd thing to be saying at a time such as this." His words were muffled against her shoulder.

"Not at all. I never knew . . . what lovemaking . . . could truly be. Now I do. I appreciate you showing me the difference." She sounded prim even to her own ears. What an odd conversation to be having with a man who even now was deep inside her body.

"Is that what I did?" He propped himself up on one elbow to gaze down at her.

His hair was tousled, a lock of it drooping over his forehead. Sweat still glistened along the top of his lip. She had never seen him look more devastatingly handsome. Her heart gave an odd little flip in her breast.

"Among other things, yes."

He dipped his head to kiss her very softly.

"Your pleasure was my pleasure." The words rumbled against her breasts as he chuckled. "Especially the other things."

He dipped his head and began to leisurely nuzzle her breasts, nipping and licking and tasting her. She closed her eyes, enjoying each flick of his tongue, each nibble of his lips.

"I suppose I should release you," he said in between a lick and a suckle. "But I don't think I will at the moment."

"Oh? Why is that?" Her breath had begun to quicken inside her as he continued his teasing enjoyment of her breasts.

"Because you have such sensitive and delicious breasts, lovely Bethany, and I would like to enjoy them at my leisure."

"Oh." She couldn't think of anything to say as

he latched on to one nipple, suckling vigorously. His fingers pinched and teased the other nipple into tight attention.

"In fact"—he lifted his head, his tone slightly husky—"I think I shall spend the rest of the night feasting on your breasts. Would you like that?"

"Oh, yes, please do." She managed the words in a breathy tone as he rasped his teeth against the nipple he had been suckling.

"Ah," she moaned, and wriggled beneath him, her desire for him quickly rekindled beneath his teasing ministrations.

He thrust against her in answer to her motions, his member engorged and swollen within her again. She moved upward in answer to his thrust, enjoying the hard feel of him so deep inside her.

And then the teasing was gone. His hand slid beneath her, arching her up to accept him as his mouth fastened hungrily to her breast. He suckled and nipped and tasted her to the point of madness while he thrust into her again and again.

She cried out as the pleasure waves broke over her anew, passion shuddering through her over and over. He followed her once more, the hot flood of his semen streaming into her.

They didn't have the strength for conversation after that and drifted to sleep nestled together on the quilt covering a soft bed of hay.

She awoke some time later. Connal was no longer at her side. He stood by the window, trousers on, shirt off, looking lonely and handsome and unreachable. Her throat tightened around the certainty that their interlude together had won them nothing but lust satisfied. That nothing had truly changed.

What was it she had promised him if looking at each other in a new light did not work out? That they would go on, try something else, a little wiser, a little warier. Could she really do that?

"Connal?" Her voice sounded thready, uncertain. She swallowed.

He crossed the space between them and knelt in the hay next to her. She sat up, longing to reach out for him and draw him back into her embrace. She didn't move.

"You must be cold." He slid his shirt over her shoulders, ignoring her nakedness. There was a wall back between them. She could feel it, but had the surety that if she reached out she would encounter its cool, solid confines with her fingers.

"We need to get you back to the house. I have work to do."

Her breasts were sore from his attentions. The stickiness between her thighs gave testament to their time together, yet he addressed her as though she had accidentally invaded his study and he was shooing her away.

So much for fresh eyes.

He held out his hand.

She took it and stood. Some distant crumb of rebellion inside her moved her to shrug the shirt from her shoulders as she stood. She straightened her spine, standing before him in the same lack of dress that had so entranced him earlier.

His gaze drifted over her and his features tightened. Having lain beneath him now, she recognized the signs of his desire. So, the wall he'd erected between them did not offer him immunity.

Why this careful civility? Somehow she could not bring herself to ask the questions hovering on the fringes of her heart.

His gaze flicked down to hers just before he pulled her toward him. His mouth took hers without any of the gentleness he had shown earlier, yet she knew in her soul the raw need she tasted held no malice. She relaxed in his arms and opened her mouth beneath his.

He groaned and gathered her more fully against him, deepening the kiss to the shared passion she had been looking for when she awoke. Then he set her from him.

"I cannot tell you how much this, us, has meant. I enjoyed tonight as much as you did. Perhaps more." He raked a hand through his hair and bent to retrieve his shirt. He draped it over her again. "We need to get you back to the house. And this is definitely not the way to go about it."

"Then what is the way?" She shrugged off the shirt again. "Perhaps I should put my own clothes on again instead of traipsing through the stable yard in naught but your shirt?"

She walked into the other room and picked up her corset, then her pantalettes. Crossing before the doorway he now occupied to find her petticoats she bent over again, granting him a full view of her derriere. She felt very daring and defiant.

He came up behind her and grabbed her shoulders. Surprise made her drop the things she'd gathered. He pulled her back against him and let his hands drift down over her breasts, cupping and fondling. She melted back against him, more than willing to spend the rest of the night as they had started out, despite the slight soreness between her legs.

"You know you tempt me at every turn." He growled against her ear, annoyance touched his words, but his hands were gentle at her breasts.

She arched back against him, discovering his arousal with the mounds of her bottom and rubbing him to earn his groan as a reward.

He turned her in his arms and kissed her again, more thoroughly than the last time. When he released her their breathing was ragged and she was more than ready for the entire episode to move forward to its natural conclusion.

"Bethany, there is more between us than what happened here tonight. But I have responsibilities. Going on like this will only complicate things."

"Complicate?" Dismay cooled her ardor. She pushed away from him as her words from earlier, her unspoken promises stung her. "Yes, of course, your responsibilities. I understand."

She turned her back to him as her throat tightened and tears burned the backs of her eyes. One evening of passion changed so little and at the same time changed everything.

She was a fool. Promising no hidden motives, no consequences. She was eating those words now. Eating them and choking on them.

She'd asked only for the moment, only for the now. He'd tried to warn her. It hardly seemed fair to expect him to hold to a different standard now that she had gotten what she asked for.

She slid into her petticoats and chemise, not

bothering with her corset. She couldn't wait any longer to be covered up in front of him.

Nothing hidden. No secrets. She'd only been kidding herself.

Aunt Bridget's suggestion that he had been keeping his distance because losing her would hurt too much rang true in a whole different light. A fresh light. She shook her head. She would have to take a page from his book and do likewise from now on.

She flung the gown over her head, getting lost in a maelstrom of fabric as she struggled to get it into place.

His fingers guided her into the garment, gentle and firm. She struggled to hold back the words burning in her throat and the distant sob threatening deep inside her.

She would not cry in front of him. Not now. If there was one thing she had learned from her husband's hard-taught lessons it was that. But the touch of his hands was so tender, and hard to resist. She just wanted to melt back into his arms, take up where they had left off and forget he had interrupted anything with words she didn't want to hear.

"Good evening," she managed, sounding stiff and formal to her own ears.

"Bethany." He reached for her and drew her back toward him.

"Yes?" She turned her gaze up to his, willing herself not to respond.

"I am so—"

"No." She pressed her fingers over his mouth. She didn't want any apologies. She had certainly walked into this with her eyes wide open, determined to make love to the man. She had thrown herself at him in the most wanton of ways. He would have been a fool to turn away what she had so easily offered him.

She would not brook his apology. "Just say good night to me."

His gaze held hers for a moment. At last he dipped his head toward her. She couldn't stop herself from tilting her chin just the slightest bit. He pressed his mouth to her forehead. His breath stirred the hair at her temples.

"Good night, Bethany Doyle Delaney." Then he released her.

She ducked her head and hurried away from him, the corset cradled in her arms like something precious.

He watched her go and regret tore at him. He wanted nothing more than to call her back, pull her back into his arms and spend the rest of his life making the last five minutes up to her.

But he couldn't do that right now. Not with things the way they were. Glenmeade had been his life for so long, he couldn't imagine not giving his heart, his life, his very soul to the Stables. It was the only thing that had kept him going after the loss of Rose, after Finn's betrayal, after Uncle Brennan's part in the whole sorrowful mess. Glenmeade had been everything.

Still was everything.

How could he turn his back on it now? Accept that he could not save the Stables from his mistakes? Accept that he was not the man his father was and never would be? Accept that he was more like Finn than he had ever imagined?

Bethany disappeared into the darkness and he heard the distant slam of the kitchen door. Lovely Bethany. He had been only too eager to take her in his arms, to let her blot out the thoughts and plans he'd been pondering out here on his own.

He did not regret what had passed between them. He would carry the memories of these past few, sweet hours with Bethany for a long time. But he could not afford to let them be repeated. He had to hurt Bethany now, he needed to hold her at arm's length, in order to protect her.

Vivian Brown, James's cousin from America, was looking to invest in something, possibly the Stables. But there was more to it than that. James had hinted she might be interested in more than investing. Was he ready to sell himself into marriage?

Vivian Brown was beautiful, wealthy and, most importantly, attracted to him. He read that much in her eyes, her flirtatiousness. James himself had all but offered her to him after breaking the news that his original investors would most likely pull out of the arrangements they had made all his plans around. Pull out because of Bethany and her son. Pull out because he was no longer sole owner of Glenmeade.

"You could do far worse, Connal. She looks the part of a vain, capricious woman, but she is interested in investing her funds. With the right persuasion, she could be interested in Glenmeade. In you," James had said. "Vivian needs distraction. The old man who was her husband indulged her, but she has never known the touch of a young and virile husband. You could do far worse."

Connal raked a hand through his hair again and longed for a stiff drink. But the whiskey was in his study and he didn't think he could trust himself to enter the house right now. Not with Bethany right upstairs. Lovely Bethany, who had given herself completely to him tonight with no demands beyond the physical act itself. With no commitment between them.

The way Rose must have gone to Finn so long ago.

The comparison stung more than anything else. He was every bit the cad Finn had been. Worse, because she was under his protection here. A family member.

"Damnation." He growled and fisted his hands before pounding the nearest post in his frustration. Again and again and again until his knuckles were scraped raw and the pain was throbbing up his arms. Sweat dripped into his eyes. Horses whickered nervously in the deep recesses of the neighboring stables.

There was no answer, no salve for his conscience, no fix for the mistakes he'd made this evening, and the ones that prevented him from correcting them.

Morning shed no new help on any of the happenings from the previous night. He rose at first light, hoping to eat quickly and escape the house before anyone had arisen. Such was not the case, however.

"Good morning, Cousin Connal."

Ross Delaney—so like his father it was still unsettling to face first thing in the morning—sat at the kitchen table with a mug of milk in his hands and the remnants of an early breakfast askew on his plate.

"Good morning," Connal managed, despite an immediate desire to turn and walk the other way. "How are you feeling?"

"I am fine, sir. Mrs. O'Toole is in the garden. So is Mary. I'm supposed to sit right here and not move until they get back."

Connal was not surprised. "After yesterday's escapade, you are lucky you are not back in leading strings."

"Don't give them any ideas." Ross laughed, then drank the contents of his mug in one big gulp.

Finn all over again. The memory made Connal smile in spite of the concerns that went along with it. At what point had it become acceptable to smile over memories associated with Finn?

"Ross Delaney, I told you before to wake me before coming downstairs. You know we do not want to disturb your . . ." Bethany entered the kitchen, then halted in her tracks. She was pale and luminous in the morning light. One stray curl had escaped the hair she'd obviously pulled back in a hurry.

She looked so lovely. He wanted nothing more than to take her in his arms and cart her away to the nearest bed, to strip off her clothes and make passionate love to her again. He wondered if she could read the lust on his face.

"Oh." She glanced from him to the boy. "Ross—"

"I know, Mama." Ross scooted down from his seat

at the table and rounded the side to reach her. "But it was bright this morning and Mr. Black-Jack said he would take me out to the stables the first bright morning."

"The stables . . . Oh, I do not think—"

"Aye, boyo, we're stables-bound." Jack chose that moment to enter the kitchen. "Good morning to ye, Missus, Connal."

He nodded to each of them before turning his attention back to Ross. "Ye'd best ask yer mam before ye make any plans on those horses, lad. Ye gave her a fright yesterday that she's not likely to forget anytime soon."

"Mama." Ross turned his blue eyes on his mother. "Could I please go to the stables with Mr. Black-Jack? I promise to listen to everything he says. He said it's best to confront your fright with horses right away rather than let it get bigger in your mind by waiting. I don't want to be a coward. How ever will I get my pony to behave when I get him?"

"Pony?"

Her gaze strayed to Connal for just a moment. He waited to see if she would ask for any assistance.

"I did tell him that." Jack attempted an apologetic tone. "Though I'd hoped to talk to ye about it first."

"All right." Bethany blew out a soft sigh and sifted her fingers through Ross's hair. "To going to the stables. We'll talk about a pony another day. Stay with Mr. Branigan and do exactly as you are told. If I hear anything to the contrary . . ."

"Thanks, Mama." Ross rewarded her with a big hug.

"I'll take good care of him," Jack offered over his

shoulder as he accepted Ross's hand and let the boy lead him out of the door. "Or Bridget will have my ear to chew on."

Bethany watched out the window as the man and boy walked down the lane past the paddock and the horse where the whole drama had unfolded. She watched until they disappeared around the corner.

"He will be fine with Jack," Connal said.

"I would not have let him go if I had no confidence in your uncle." She didn't turn from the window. "Or in Ross."

What was she thinking about as her gaze continued in the direction of the stables? Was she worrying about her son? Was she reliving any of the previous night? Was there anything he could say to assuage the sting of the distance he had deliberately put between them? Without removing the distance?

He took a step closer. Cinnamon and vanilla teased him. The longing to draw her into his embrace grew stronger. He wanted to hold her. Just hold her here and watch out the window as the sun gradually rose higher to bathe Glenmeade in fresh-washed light.

"If you are tired—"

She turned to face him. "You need not worry about me."

She stopped as she realized how close they were. Then her chin lifted. She focused the wide blue of her gaze on him. "Last night . . . was something that should not have happened, but I am quite certain we can manage to avoid any further unnecessary entanglements."

Unnecessary entanglements?

"Indeed?"

"Yes." Bethany nodded, so cool and calm, not at all the heated wanton she had been in his arms a few scant hours ago. She turned to walk away.

"Where are you going?"

"You should come upstairs, too."

Really? Was his wanton hiding in her after all? Irrational hope flared. "What do you have in mind?"

She turned and gave him half a glance. "We are invited to Oak Bend today. Remember James Carey and his cousin asked us both to lunch. I need to get ready."

She disappeared around the edge of the kitchen door, leaving it to swing back into place.

Oak Bend with James Carey's cousin. And sitting in the gig with Bethany all the way there and back. Sitting with her, but not touching her. Not taking her in his arms. He gritted his teeth over the day awaiting him. At this point he'd rather spend the day mucking stalls.

Chapter Thirteen

The doubtful look Aunt Bridget bestowed on her hung in Bethany's mind as she trailed down the steps to meet Connal and depart for their afternoon at Oak Bend.

She had done the best she could to assemble a fitting outfit within her limited wardrobe, but she was certain she would look a pale, drab thing next to James Carey's flamboyant cousin.

An afternoon with Vivian Brown would never be her choice for a day's entertainment. Especially when the day included rides to and from Oak Bend alone with Connal Delaney. It would not only be exceptionally rude to cry off, however, it would be imprudent, given how important this appointment might be for Glenmeade's future.

Connal stood outside the Manor with a sweet-looking black mare and a gig ready to go. Her heart lurched uncomfortably at the sight of him, despite her resolve to be unmoved. He looked dashing in a black brushed-wool jacket and slacks. And with a bowler perched on his head, no less. Great. Even he looked to be better dressed than she. Her serviceable green Kerseymere skirt and jacket had seen better days.

"Mrs. Delaney, don't forget yer bonnet." Mary appeared behind her in the doorway and Bethany's quiet perusal of Connal Delaney was at an end.

"Thank you, Mary." She took the proffered bonnet and tied its ribbons under her chin, glad of something to do with her suddenly trembling and uncoordinated fingers. She pulled on her gloves and descended the steps to the drive.

"If you please?" Connal held out his hand to her.

Within moments they were both seated in the gig. He coaxed the horse forward and they set off at a trot past Glenmeade's rolling pastures. They were next to each other, but Bethany made sure they did not touch at any point. No point in unleashing any wayward longings. Any *more* wayward longings, that is.

She'd gotten only a few hours' sleep, gaining those through sheer exhaustion when her restless mind could no longer churn through the events of her time in Connal's arms. She had never experienced anything so wonderful as the melding of her mind and body with this man. Surely there was nothing in the world to compare with it. The entire experience left her more certain than ever that whatever she once felt for Finn, it had never been love.

Cresting a final hill after almost two hours spent blanketed in silence, they arrived at the Carey estate at last. From the hillside the grass rolled down to a winding river, with small copses of trees clustered here and there like little groups of gossips

standing in a town square on market day. Situated
on a knoll above one of the river's most prominent
curves was a majestic Georgian brick mansion, reminiscent of some of the homes on North Carolina's
tobacco plantations.

Connal brought the gig smartly to a halt before
the wide steps and double-oaken portals of Oak
Bend's manor house. He stepped down from the
carriage and turned to offer his assistance. His dark
gaze held hers and her breath came harder in her
chest. She forced her fingers into his. It seemed to
take an inordinate amount of time for him to draw
her forward, then place his hands at her waist.

Her world tilted beneath his touch and she bit
back a sigh. How could she even have considered
attempting a day of cordial visitation with thoughts
of his lovemaking so fresh in her mind that her
body still ached from his touch?

He set her on her feet and his hands lingered for
heartbeats longer than necessary. She gazed up at
him and knew to the depths of her soul he wanted
to kiss her just as badly as she wanted him to kiss
her. No consequences, that's what she'd promised
him. And that included demands for things he was
unwilling to give no matter his reasons.

"Welcome to Oak Bend, we had begun to fear
you had quite forgotten us." Vivian Brown's elegant
tones slid between them like a knife. Connal released her and turned to their hostess as she descended the steps to join them.

"Mrs. Brown." Connal bowed over Vivian's hand.
She was resplendent in a blue sateen gown, surely
more suitable for the ball room than for daytime
visits. "How good it is to see you again."

"Now that we are no longer first-time acquaintances, I insist we use first names, Mr. Delaney. Both James and Bethany call you Connal, and I shall feel quite left out all day if only you and I are on formal terms."

The sunlight played on her lustrous, ebony coiffure, so dark that some of her curls seemed almost midnight blue. Her eyes sparkled in the fresh air. She was more than lovely. Even Bethany would be hard-pressed to find fault with her appearance.

"Whatever will make you most comfortable will certainly please me, Vivian." Gone was the man who spent the drive over in complete silence. Suddenly, Bethany longed for him.

Vivian's delighted laugh was a pleasant caress.

"You remember my cousin's widow," Connal said, finally remembering to include her in the greetings. Vivian had the nerve to look startled as if she had forgotten she and Connal were not alone.

"Of course I remember dear little Beth." Vivian smiled, displaying her beautiful white teeth. "You look lovely today, my dear. Utterly charming. Is that style bonnet all the rage still in North Carolina? I believe I had one very like it three, maybe four, seasons ago. It never suited me, but it looks divine on you." Vivian prattled on, not really needing or expecting any answers.

Lord, this woman can talk. Bethany felt dowdy next to Vivian's striking coloring and fashionable gown. She certainly must pale compared with their vivacious hostess.

"Morrison," Vivian called over her shoulder to the rotund butler hovering in the doorway. "Please go and see what is keeping Mr. Carey. Make sure he is not so absorbed he does not realize our guests have arrived.

"He has been very busy with a thorny piece of business these past few days, trying to keep a deal from unraveling," Vivian informed her guests after the butler scurried away to do her bidding. "I cannot keep his affairs straight."

"That is because they are my affairs and I do not burden you with the details." James walked down the steps to join them. "I am sure Vivian has been keeping you well entertained, but I apologize for not coming out immediately to welcome you myself."

"You have news?" Connal tried to ask in a casual tone, but Bethany detected the urgency behind his question.

"We can discuss matters later," James reassured his friend.

"Oh, this is lovely," Vivian gushed. "We do not have enough company out here in the country. I was just saying to James we need to have an excursion, an outing more extensive than the church gatherings they have locally. Was I not, James?"

"And I believe we will pursue something along those lines very soon." His gaze doted on his cousin.

James winked then at Bethany as though they shared some unspoken secret. "Vivian does not know what a recluse our Connal has become over the years."

"There is no fun living like a hermit. We must rescue him from his own clutches if that is the case." Vivian laughed as though life itself were some grand adventure. "What do you think, Connal? Could we pry you from your rustication and entice you to join us in a search for joys elsewhere than your wonderful horse farm?"

"I have many demands on my time at Glenmeade," Connal offered in a noncommittal tone.

"Beth dear, do let James escort you inside while I run off with your marvelous cousin."

Connal raised one dark brow as her fingers gripped his arm in a proprietary manner.

James Carey's arm was beneath Bethany's palm before she could agree. He pressed her hand as Vivian tugged at Connal.

"Vivian, they have had a long drive, let them come inside and have some refreshments before you drag the man back to the barn to examine that hoof that has you so concerned."

James led Bethany into the salon behind Vivian and Connal. A tea tray awaited them on a lovely cherry side table.

"Do sit down, Beth dear, you look exhausted." Vivian frowned ever so slightly, managing to look both concerned and disapproving.

Bethany sat, trying to ignore the niggling irritation of Vivian's comments. Connal chose the settee on the opposite side of a plush Persian rug in gorgeous hues of blue.

"How do you take your tea, Beth?"

Vivian offered tea to all of them with practiced efficiency. She was quite a charming hostess in an odd way. No doubt she had spent a great deal of time entertaining when her husband had been alive. Each dip and sway of her body as she poured tea and handed it around seemed like a dance. Bethany felt all the more awkward in her presence and struggled to ignore the feeling she was a child invited to the grown-ups' party as she sipped the hot brew in her cup.

Connal certainly appeared to enjoy their hostess's tantalizing dance. He smiled into Vivian's dark eyes as he received his cup. "Thank you."

"Oh, no, darling." Vivian pressed his hand. "I want to thank you."

She poured her own cup of tea and took a seat next to him. "I understand from James you are his closest neighbor and dear friend. As James is my very dearest cousin, despite the ocean separating us, I must thank you for bearing him company since he is so very alone when he is in residence here." She leaned closer, her breasts nearly brushing his arm.

Bethany swallowed more tea than she intended and scalded the back of her throat. Her eyes watered, but she managed not to cough. James settled himself on the settee beside her. "Vivian loves company almost as much as Connal shuns it. They make quite a pair, do they not?"

Was James shopping for a new husband for his widowed cousin? If so, things would become more complicated and uncomfortable at Glenmeade very quickly.

"Yes," she managed to answer despite the pain in her throat. "They certainly do."

If matchmaking was the reasoning behind today's invitation, it would prove an even longer day than she had envisioned. She had certainly misunderstood Connal when he had stressed how important this day might be for Glenmeade's future.

"Tell them about that Curragh, James. Connal is sure to find the details fascinating."

"In a bit, dearest."

James favored Vivian with a look of amused indulgence. He turned his attention back to Bethany.

"Curragh boasts one of the finest courses in Ireland, or anywhere," he explained. "It is home to the Irish Turf Club, which, among many other things, hosts an annual horse fair and masque ball the first Monday in May. Attendance is always high because of the quality of the horseflesh traded there."

"And, it is also a prized social event." Vivian's eyes sparkled with excitement. "Horses by day, dancing by night, who could resist?"

"Not me," Connal said. "I admit the event is something I have wanted to have Glenmeade participate in for quite some time."

"Then you are in luck." James leaned forward toward Connal with an expectant air. "I wrangled an invitation for you, for all of us, to attend this year."

"Truth?" Connal's stunned pleasure showed in his broad grin and excited tone.

"Aye," James said, nodding.

"I am in your debt once more, James. How did you manage this?"

"Well I—"

"Oh, what difference do the dreary details make? Glenmeade Stables will exhibit at the Curragh Horse Fair this year." Vivian preened for Connal again as though she had provided this opportunity herself. "To thank us, you must promise to partner me at the ball. James is a horrendous dancer."

"That is a wonderful opportunity for Glenmeade," Bethany offered.

"Oh, yes, of course it is." James patted her hand

and then let his fingers linger over hers. "Come now, I have yet to show you my home. Connal practically ran tame here when . . . at one time. I am sure he has no interest in a tour. We can safely leave him with Vivian to discuss all the important details."

Like what color gown she should wear, or how she should dress her hair? Bethany realized she should be ashamed at her catty thoughts, but she just wasn't.

"Do indulge James and take the tour, Beth. He will be crushed if you refuse him." Under the guise of settling her skirts, Vivian moved closer to Connal.

"Do show her everything, James"—she smiled prettily—"while I find out all Connal knows about Curragh. I confess I find the entire enterprise fascinating. Not just the ball."

James's pressure on Bethany's fingers drew her to her feet. There was nothing she wanted less than to leave Connal alone with Vivian Brown. And Connal did not exactly look displeased by the voluptuous woman's attentions.

The direction of her thoughts brought Bethany up short. She had known Connal hardly any longer than Vivian had, yet that had not stopped her from having wild relations with him in the barn when the opportunity presented itself. Heat flooded her cheeks and she stopped resisting James's lead, turning dutifully to follow him out of the room.

Connal's gaze stayed fixed on the door as it closed behind James and Bethany. Why on earth had his friend needed to take her on a tour of his home?

"There now, this is certainly better? We can have a comfortable coze without interruption." Vivian's fingers squeezed his arm familiarly. Was he supposed to woo her while James occupied Bethany with a tour of Oak Bend? And if not, exactly what was James planning for Bethany?

The direction of his thoughts was anything but comforting.

"Connal?"

"Forgive me, I was momentarily distracted. You were saying?"

"I am so glad they are gone." She enunciated clearly. "James is a dear, but he is sometimes dreary company."

She leaned against Connal's arm again as she stretched to put her teacup down next to his. Her full breasts pressed against him for a moment and the lace along the edge of her gown's bodice fluttered, offering him glimpses of the full, soft roundness within. He was quite certain the beauteous widow would make a charming bed partner. But seducing her in the parlor beneath James's nose did not seem the correct thing to do.

"I hope you do not think I am being too forward, but might I ask you a question or two of a personal nature?"

Considering the level of his distraction as his mind was busy providing him with images of Bethany and James, the least he could do is allow his hostess to lead their conversation as she saw fit. He nodded.

"Following . . . Rosleen's . . . tragic passing, I can well understand why you did not marry right away. But after so much time surely you have considered settling down to a family of your own. I find it so hard to believe every eligible woman in the county has not cast their lures your way. You are such a handsome devil of a man. So strong. And virile, I have no doubt."

Her interest in the subject was clear, but her reference to Rose surprised him even though he knew that she had been Vivian's cousin also. Rose was one subject he and James never discussed, never mentioned.

James had returned from Scotland a month after the tragedy and ridden right over to Glenmeade, not seeking vengeance, instead offering his hand in quiet support as he had in all the intervening years. As he had today with that invitation to participate in the Curragh Horse Fair. The least he owed a friend like James was to indulge this relation he was clearly so fond of.

"I have considered marriage, Vivian. More often of late."

"Really?" She managed to rub her breasts against his arm again as she reached for her teacup. "I must confess the marital state was one I enjoyed quite fully. I have felt the lack quite keenly since the passing of my own dear husband." She took a sip, but kept her wide-eyed gaze fixed on him over the rim of her cup.

"I am sorry for your loss." He didn't bother to draw away from her, wondering just how far she would go if he did nothing to encourage her.

"Yes, it was a dreadful time for me."

She leaned into him. How much longer would this teacup dance last? Had she reached the dregs yet?

"There are times when I long to be held, just to be held and nothing more. And then there are times . . . when that is no longer . . . enough."

She turned her face up to his. She was so lovely and clearly willing. He had the keen sense that he could take her right here and she would be eager for him. This was going in a distinctly uncomfortable direction.

"Again . . . I am sorry for your loss."

He could not keep his mind from mentally following the tour James and Bethany were on. Although he had not been inside Oak Bend in years, he was familiar enough with the house to know how long a *tour* should take.

Not wanting to offend Vivian Brown was becoming more and more difficult by the moment. The woman seemed determined to offer herself to him in the most blatant manner. Indulging his friend's relation would stretch only so far. Still, if she was really interested in investing in Glenmeade she might prove the only option available to him at the moment.

He tamped back the desire to follow after James and Bethany. No matter the irritation he felt, he'd known James all his life, so if he could not trust the man alone with Bethany . . . The thought would not complete itself.

"Connal?"

He realized with a start that Vivian was still speaking and he had lost the direction of her conversation, if not the pressure of her breasts against his arm.

"Yes, Vivian." He focused his gaze on her once more.

She pouted up at him, a slight flush hovering on her lovely cheekbones. "I do not believe your attention is entirely here with me."

"You are right. I am a cad of the first water." He bowed to her, managing to extricate himself from her partial embrace at the same time. "When one is as absorbed in his enterprises as I have been of late, social niceties tend to fall by the wayside. I apologize."

He took her hand and struggled to find a topic of conversation that might ease her pout without encouraging her blatant seduction. He silently counted the minutes until James returned. With Bethany.

"When opportunity comes your way, you must be ready to seize it." James chuckled. "I believe your uncle used to say that often enough."

"Aye." Connal took a final sip of his whiskey. "Aye, I am quite sure he did. Thank you, James, for making this happen."

"Now, I must insist, Beth. I have too many gowns for this part of the world anyway and if they are not out of style already they will be by the time I return to anyplace where fashion matters." Vivian's endless stream of chatter grew closer.

Bethany had a distressed look on her face as the ladies joined them after retiring to refresh themselves following a bountiful lunch. Her expression practically screamed for rescue.

"I will find something in a shade that will be as flattering as possible, given your unfortunate coloring, and send it over in a day or two. That should give your seamstress at least a week to shorten the skirt and take in the bodice."

Vivian's gaze fixed on Bethany's bosom was enough to send Connal screaming for rescue. "Unfortunately, as inviting a day as this has proved to be, we must be on our way."

Vivian pouted. "So soon?"

James laughed at her. "This is probably the longest Connal has been gone from Glenmeade Stables for anything other than business in years. We are lucky to have pried him away for this long."

"But today had to do with business. What about our trip to Curragh?"

"We will meet again there, Vivian. Thank you for an entertaining afternoon."

After sending for the gig they were on their way back to Glenmeade. Bethany was exhausted. Scrubbing floors was more relaxing than dealing with Vivian Brown for any length of time.

Connal guided the gig over the rutted road in silence, no doubt mulling over the coming trip to Curragh and the effect it would have on the Stables. Or, perhaps, dreaming of the voluptuous widow who clearly longed to occupy his bed.

Having spent the afternoon with Vivian, his silence was a relief. The tension that had remained unchecked on the long, lonely ride to Oak Bend had not eased—too many things to say, too many feelings to suppress—but they had new worries to occupy their private thoughts.

Questions seethed in Bethany's middle. All of them centered on the trip, the ball, the entire outing. How were they to be ready for such an important enterprise in less than two weeks? Vivian's castoff aside, there would be a need for her to buy things she hadn't purchased in years if she was to represent the Stables properly.

Of course, Vivian would be there. She would be more than capable of comporting herself in a manner best suited to attracting attention. Especially if she truly was interested in investing money in the Stables. But if Connal—no, not just Connal anymore—if Ross needed the Stables shown in their best light, then his mother needed to be ready.

Clouds thickened overhead. Even given her limited experience with changeable Irish weather, she knew there would shortly be a storm. The only question was, just how bad of a storm would it be?

Sure enough, the wind began to pick up as the distance between them and Oak Bend became greater and greater. She glanced at Connal's profile. His jaw was set and his gaze stayed focused on the road ahead. He continued to ignore her as though she was not so close to him that the brush of his thigh occasioned hers.

Pictures from the lamplit stable flashed through her thoughts, tearing new holes in her heart. She would have marveled at his self-control, but she was too busy reminding herself not to be pathetic.

She sighed out loud before she could catch it back.

That snagged his attention. He glanced at her ever so briefly. "We are not going to make it."

"I . . . I beg your pardon?"

"The weather." He jerked his head toward the

clouds swirling thicker above them. "The rain is going to come faster than we can travel."

"Oh." She pursed her lips. So, now, after that lovely afternoon, she would come home wet and bedraggled the same way Aunt Bridget had after her first trip to town. What a perfect end to a less-than-perfect afternoon.

"There is shelter ahead."

"Shelter?"

"Aye, this is going to be a flasher. We will not be able to continue until it is over."

Shelter? Dear Lord, please let it be a farmhouse, an inn, a tavern—because if there was one thing she did not need it was more time alone with Connal Delaney. Trouble was, she did not remember enough detail from the trip over to know what they had passed or where.

He glanced at her again as the first fat raindrops fell, and offered her a grim smile.

In moments the rain came in earnest, pelting them as he turned off the main path and down a slight hill. At the bottom and to the left he pulled the carriage to a halt.

"Come with me," he shouted as he jumped to the ground and crossed quickly to her side.

He plucked her from the carriage without ceremony. The ground felt slippery under her feet. His hand gripped hers and she had no choice but to hurry along behind him. She was grateful now for the coat Bridget had forced on her and the bonnet that kept most of the water from drenching her hair completely. In a few steps they were out of the immediate downpour.

"Stay here, I must take care of Astrid."

"What?" The rain muffled what he said. She didn't understand the last. In front of her was an earthen wall. She looked behind her at the sheets of rain.

"The horse." Connal ducked back out into the downpour.

She turned to survey her gloomy surroundings. It appeared to be a cave. Thick rock walls and an uneven floor, but toward the back there appeared to be bit of a hearth and there were signs this had been used as some type of habitation. She shivered. Did anyone still live here?

"There." Connal stamped back into the cavern and took his greatcoat from his shoulders. Water pooled at his feet. "What a mess."

He turned toward her. "Take your wet things off. If we're lucky there will be something to start a fire with and we can dry our coats while we wait for the rain to stop."

"If we are lucky?" She removed her bonnet and coat and followed him back toward the little hearth.

"Aye, I have spent many a rainstorm in here. Though not for quite some time. It made a handy shelter for us on more than one occasion."

She watched him assemble bits of wood and strike a flint to light the kindling. The spark took and began to spread. He turned up toward her. "Bring your garments over here. Mine too, if you please."

She scooped up coats, hat and bonnet. He took them from her and arranged them on rocky outcrop near the fire. Their coats hung at odd angles but near enough for the fire to actually be of some help. "Who did you spend rainstorms here with?"

She wished the question back almost as soon as it left her lips.

For several moments he didn't answer and she had begun to think he would ignore the question altogether.

"Finn," he told her quietly. "And Rose."

Finn and Rose, the two people who had hurt him most and the man who had almost destroyed her. Specters out of the past that did not belong here in the present.

"I'm sorry."

"For what?" Connal pushed to his feet and stood opposite her. "What went on between Finn and Rose and me happened a very long time ago."

"Yes, but what they did has not left you in peace in all the time that has passed. Just as Finn's deeds have not left me."

His gaze held hers in the flickering firelight of the darkened cave. There was something intimate and otherworldly about the rocky surfaces surrounding them. As though they existed in a time out of time, as if anything that happened here could not affect life outside these walls.

Is this where Finn seduced Rose? Is this where Rose and Connal fell in love? She couldn't bring herself to ask.

"These are matters we should not be discussing." There was a warning in his tone.

He was too close for comfort and yet not close enough. For just an instant she was afraid, of him, of herself, of everything. Anger boiled through her, displacing the fears.

"Why not?"

"This is why." He pulled her to him and his mouth closed over hers, blotting out the storm, the past, there was no room for anything but the feel of his arms around her and his mouth on hers.

Chapter Fourteen

James stood in front of the parlor's mullioned windows and gazed at the drive long after his quarry had disappeared from sight. The late afternoon breeze stiffened through the trees, carrying the promise of yet more rain as it whistled in through the panel he opened.

With any luck his departing guests would get a good soaking on their way back to Glenmeade. The image of them bedraggled, plodding along through the mud, supplied scant satisfaction following their thoroughly unsatisfying visit.

He accepted the glass of whiskey Vivian handed him and tossed back the contents in one swallow. "Another."

"But—"

He quelled her protest with a raised brow. He'd been thwarted enough for one day. When she returned he took the glass from her but took only a sip of the contents this time before returning to his scrutiny.

She stood next to him, joining him in his perusal

of the drive, although she was probably not aware that was what they were doing. Her exotic jasmine and cinnamon scent so nearby provided a comfort nonetheless.

After a few minutes she shivered, making a delightful display that set the lace at the edge of her bodice dancing and offered a tantalizing glimpse of the milk-white flesh below.

Vivian sighed. "More rain. Do you suppose the Delaneys will reach Glenmeade before it breaks? A soaking will not be kind to that bonnet and Bethany's curls will frizz all out of control from the dampness."

"Bethany? Why so formal? You called your new bosom beau 'Beth' all afternoon."

Mischief lit Vivian's ice-blue eyes. "I call her Beth to annoy her. It throws her off balance every time."

Although he shouldn't have been surprised— Vivian's instincts made her the ideal partner in so many ways—he was nonetheless. "Clever girl."

Vivian beamed from his praise. "I wanted to be sure the dear little thing had more to think about than my stealing her man right out from under her nose."

He turned to face her more fully. "I hate to be the one to enlighten you, dearest, but you have not made many inroads in that respect."

Vivian pursed her lips into a delicious pout, but held her peace. This was the first time she had failed him and she was most likely not yet ready to give up the ghost on the task he had set for her.

"I fully expected to return from dragging your *dear little thing* about the place to find you thoroughly compromised."

"It was not from lack of effort, let me tell you." Pique wrinkled her nose. "Hard as I try to fathom it, he is simply not showing any interest in me."

The breeze caught the lace on her neckline again, eliciting another round of shivers, offering his imagination an enticing image of the delights beneath her blue satin bodice. He traced his index finger slowly along her jawline. "Perhaps you would benefit from a little refresher tutelage in the art of seduction."

She sucked in a breath through her teeth as his fingertip barely grazed her skin while he trailed it down the column of her neck. Her gaze held a sultry, wanton cast as she looked up at him through her lashes. "I always enjoy your . . . lessons."

"In a bit, then." He dropped his hand back to his side and took another sip from his glass. The look of disappointment on her face made him chuckle. "Apparently I must remind you, Vivian, dear. The cardinal rule of any seduction is to promise delights to come, then to delay them for as long as possible."

Her lips formed another little pout, quickly replaced by a smile of anticipation. As always, her willingness to fall in with his plans—whether they concerned what to have served for a meal or how to gain the edge in a business deal—pleased him.

"You should not take today's failure too much to heart. I believe I also owe you a reward for being so astute earlier."

"A reward, you say?" Vivian stepped closer and slipped her arm into the crook of his elbow.

"The observation you made the other day after

our visit to Glenmeade is correct, the Widow Delaney has designs on keeping herself in the family."

"Well, of course." She practically glowed with her small triumph. "That would certainly explain why a man as viral, but isolated, as Connal would not respond to me. His desires are being sated for the moment by that drab little thing. And right there in his own home, no less. With a woman who came to him seeking his protection."

"Apparently taking advantage of those closest to them runs in the family." The idea stung, angering him in the process. He gritted his teeth. "We will just have to make sure Connal Delaney regrets soiling his nest. Along with all his other sins." Rosleen's face drifted through him, dragging pain in its wake. Enough, he tamped the emotion back into the recesses of his mind. He patted Vivian's hand.

"Did you say something about a reward?"

"Ahh, yes. I was certain if I mentioned it you would not let me forget. Pray open the drawer on that side table by the mantel and fetch it for me, will you?"

He remained by the windows, awaited her delighted squeal as she opened the small leather box. The skies overhead were thick with dark, menacing clouds. The kind that produce hellfire and thunder. He wondered if Bethany clung to Connal even now as the storm raged around them.

"They are beautiful!" Vivian raced back to him, her eyes dancing. She gave him a very heartfelt kiss to thank him before holding them up to admire them some more. "I have always wanted sapphire ear bobs. Sherman had promised me a pair for my next birthday, but . . . but that was just before—"

"You can model them for me, later," he interrupted her, unwilling to go down the path of dear Sherman just at the moment. He bent and tasted her lips again, this time edging her lips open with his tongue.

"What about the lesson in seduction you promised me?" She flicked the corner of her mouth with her tongue.

"We have all night—"

A knock on the parlor doors stopped him from continuing. They separated and Vivian held her gift behind her back as the downstairs maid slid back the door. "Mr. Carey?"

"Yes, Emily. You may come in."

"Beg pardon, sir, madam." Kindling bucket in hand she bobbed a quick curtsy. "Mrs. Mulrooney asked me ta see if ye wanted me ta lay a fire in here and light the lamps."

"Not tonight. You may do so in my study. Mrs. Brown was just telling me how fatigued she is after tending to our guests. I'm afraid she is getting another of her headaches. Would you ask Mrs. Mulrooney to arrange for her to have a bath set up in her room, along with a tray of cold meat and cheese if she regains her appetite? Then make sure she is not disturbed for the remainder of the evening. I will have a cold tray also in my study."

"Very good, sir." The maid curtsied again and left.

"Another headache? I must be quite delicate," Vivian teased as soon as they were alone.

"That's one of the things I like best about you, Cousin dear."

With a loud crack of thunder, the skies opened up at last.

"That should cool the Delaneys's ardor if they are still on the road." Vivian laughed as he pulled the window panel shut.

Connal's mouth moved over hers. Hot and hungry and demanding. Both rough and tender. Cascades of hot desire flowed through her. Bethany could think of nowhere she wanted to be more than right where she was.

She wanted Connal Delaney, and his lovemaking, more than anything else. More than *anyone* else, now or in the future. And especially more than anyone in the past. Certainty echoed into the deepest recesses of her soul. Fear and trembling hovered far away in the distance. This wasn't just lust or a desire for comfort, although they were there in the mix. The feelings swelling so near to bursting inside her were so much more.

"Connal." She breathed out his name when he released her mouth long enough to allow her breath.

"I brought you here seeking shelter, to protect you from the storm. But, God help me, it would seem you need protection from me." His breathing was as ragged as her own, his dark eyes intent on hers.

"Perhaps it is you who needs protection from me, Connal Delaney." The crackle of the fire and the sound of the rain competed with the drumming of her heartbeat. There was no right or wrong, no rhyme or reason to the need swelling urgently between them.

Outside in the rain, responsibilities waited, uncertainties lurked. Past mistakes, regrets, all the pain and fear they usually carried would claim them both when they went out there. In here there was only the need to be together, to blot out all the loneliness and sorrows, if only for a few moments.

"God help us both."

His mouth was on hers again as he pulled her to him. She reveled in the hot, urgent kisses they shared. Nothing mattered but his lips on hers, and the demand for more raging hotly to life inside her. This man, this time, were hers and hers alone and she would not give them up. And she would be his just as completely.

"I want to—"

"—make love to me." She finished the demand for him.

A growl of agreement came from deep in his throat. His mouth moved to her cheek, her chin, her throat. The pressure of his lips beneath her ear, the warmth of his breath on her skin, the feel of his hands moving over her, intoxicated her.

Laces came free, followed by buttons and ties. Her outer skirt and petticoats sighed to the floor in eager surrender. His jacket and waistcoat, his cravat, flung free. She was all but naked in his arms. It should not feel so right to be with a man not her husband. But it did. Being held by Connal, caressed by Connal, felt right in ways her married life with

Finn never even approached. Like the difference between running free and being shackled in a prison.

What was it Connal said the other day? Something about kissing her being the right thing to do even though it should not be.

"You are so very beautiful." He leaned down to press a line of kisses across the tops of her breasts. The heat of his breath on her skin was tantalizing. She wanted nothing more than to be naked in his arms, to seek and find the same kind of completion she had known last night.

His fingers worked her laces and he soon stripped her out of her corset, leaving her in naught but pantalettes and stockings.

There was something indescribably sensuous about having his gaze feasting on her bared flesh. She was caught between wanting to stand still and enjoy his admiration, and at the same time, help him remove his own clothes as quickly as she could.

His mouth pressed against the full curve of one breast. Heat streaked through her, liquid with anticipation as he kissed and licked and nibbled across her skin until at last his mouth closed over her nipple, sucking it into his mouth.

She flung back her head as her knees trembled and pleasure shot through her. "Connal, oh, oh . . ."

She could not string even the barest sentence together as his mouth tugged and suckled at her. His hands swept her back, holding her secure as the sensations he delivered rippled through her and weakened her still further. She gripped his shoulders as shudders rippled through her, long and silvery and undulating.

She collapsed against his shoulder, still trembling in the wake as he held her to him. She could hear the rapid thudding of his heartbeat through his shirt, feel the rasp of his breath against her hair.

"You . . . You have a habit of doing that to me, sir." Her voice trembled. "I am not quite sure how . . ."

"Indeed." He held her tighter and brushed his mouth against her neck. He sought her lips again for a long and languid kiss as his hands molded her to him from breast to belly. The hard heat of his arousal throbbed against her. Her toes tightened and flexed. Dear God, surely *this* was heaven and she didn't deserve it. She'd never felt so wonderful, so willing. Certainly Finn had never . . .

She cut off the thought, unwilling to follow that dark path. Not now. Not now in Connal's arms. Finn did not belong here. But she couldn't shake her memories as she pushed out of Connal's arms.

"I cannot . . . I need . . ." She fumbled for words as the pain inside her, the pain she had held back so successfully for so long, came rushing up like a black floodtide through a levy.

"Bethany." Concern filled Connal's eyes as he tried to draw her back into his arms. "What is it?"

"I . . . I . . ." She hugged her arms around her middle and backed away from him. Being naked before him no longer seemed glorious, she felt vulnerable, foolish and inadequate.

"What is it? Did I hurt you?" Connal followed her

as she backed away. One step, two. But it was Finn who pursued her, tormented her.

Tears dripped onto her cheeks and she couldn't stem them. How very embarrassing. Trying to stop them only made them come harder.

"Tell me what is wrong." Connal's voice was hoarse. He cupped her shoulder. She forced herself not to pull away, even as her tears continued to flow. "What have I done? How have I hurt you?"

She read self-loathing in his eyes. He blamed himself for her sudden outburst. Blamed The Wicked One. She couldn't let him believe he had done anything to hurt her.

"No, Connal, it is not you. It is *not* you."

His dark gaze met hers and she could see the barriers rising in his mind. See the hurt and self-doubt she was inflicting on him.

"Then what? Who?" A flat tone marked his voice.

"Finn." The name fell like a stone between them.

Connal's features narrowed. He said nothing.

"I . . . Finn . . ." She took a breath and stopped trying to stem the tide of tears determined to pour like the rainstorm beyond the cavern opening. "Finn . . . was not gentle . . . he . . ."

She couldn't finish the sentence as her throat tightened over the memories. She swallowed and tried again, finding the courage in his eyes. "There was no pleasure between my husband and me. Until last night, I never knew . . . I did not realize . . . things could be like that . . . for a woman."

"Pleasure." He shook his head, saying the word as though he had trouble deciphering it.

"Yes." Pain tightened her throat again. "Finn was

not gentle or considerate in his demands. My marriage held only . . . pain . . . pain and duty."

The intensity of Connal's gaze on her reminded her of the first time she met him, as if he was trying to look into her very soul. "He hurt you?"

"Yes."

He raked a hand through his hair. His brows drew together. "He *hurt* you?"

"I was not appreciative . . . cooperative enough . . . not responsive enough . . . I could never do or be enough." All the old doubts and fears threatened to smother her. "He did not want Ross, I did. He did not like many of the same things I did. But he did like making sure I knew exactly how I failed him as a wife."

She could not let the cold and lonely existence she had lived with Finn steal any more of her life. Any more happiness. She took a step closer to Connal. "Being with you . . . last night . . . and here—"

"I am so very sorry." Connal bent to pick up her discarded clothing. "I had no idea. Please know I have no wish to hurt you in any way."

"Oh, no." She stepped closer to him and closed her hand over his atop her petticoats. "No, no, please. You don't understand."

"I understand that I will not make you cry, Bethany." He dipped his head and brushed his mouth across her forehead. "I am selfish, wanting you without any thought to your wants."

Fresh tears flowed, but the pain seemed to be easing away. "Connal Delaney, you have never hurt me." She leaned up to him and pressed her mouth to his. "I want *you,* Connal."

She slid her fingers to the fastenings of his shirt, undoing the buttons one by one.

"I want *you.*" She spread the fabric and slid her hands over the taut, warm muscle beneath. She slid her hands lower, down over his flat stomach and to the opening of his trousers.

"Bethany." There was both warning and plea in the sound of her name.

"Aye?" She tipped her head to look up at him as she undid the buttons and slid her hand beyond the edges of the fabric until her hand brushed his firm, velvety heat.

He sucked in a breath at the contact.

She smiled as pure feminine power washed over her. She curved her fingers over him and stroked him slowly, feeling the length of him, the heat, the power. "I want you. Us. This."

"Dear God." He gritted his teeth. "You do not know what you do to me."

"True." She leaned up to kiss the underside of his jaw. "But I am very willing to find out."

"Bethany." His hand covered hers, stilling her questing fingers. "If you are afraid . . . if you do not . . . tell me now. I want you too much not to take you."

She kissed him again and tightened her fingers around him, getting her reward as he groaned against her mouth. "I want to take you."

"But . . . Finn . . ."

"You needed to know what I needed to tell. The past is gone."

"And now?"

"And now . . . You make love to me as you promised to do."

He grinned down at her, a flash of white teeth in the darkened confines of the cavern. "I made no such promise."

"Oh, aye, ye did," she told him, doing her best to mimic Jack and Bridget's brogue. "Ye promised everything with the heat of yer body, the touch of yer hands and the feel of yer mouth on mine."

"Aye, I see ye have the right of it there." He fell in with the game and kissed her fully, his member straining against her palm.

His tongue delved into her mouth and laved her own in slow, teasing strokes that mirrored the motion of her hand against his heated flesh as she explored him. He was so hot and so full and so mesmerizingly smooth.

She gripped the edge of his trousers in her other hand and tugged downward. He sighed into her mouth as the fabric eased over his hips and down to the ground. She spread her hands over his chest and trailed her fingers over his ribs, his belly and farther down as she knelt to ease the trousers over his feet and off.

Eye level now with the object of her fascination, she curved her fingers around his length once more and stroked it back and forth, back and forth. He groaned. She bent forward, wondering just what he would . . .

"Saints in heaven." He groaned as she placed her mouth on him. A string of unintelligible Gaelic followed as she took his heat into her mouth and flicked her tongue against him. His fingers slid into her hair as she continued, back and forth, back and forth, enjoying each groan wrung from him and each little tremor.

"You will be the death of me." He pulled away from her, breathing hard as he collected himself for a moment.

He drew her up against him. *"Ta tu go h-aileann, mo chroi."*

"I wish I knew what you were saying."

"I want you more than words—" His mouth covered hers once more and stilled any further questions about ancient Irish phrases. She understood the feel of his body and the needs raging between them, and that was all that mattered.

He tugged his greatcoat from its nook by the fire and stretched it out along the ground, then he turned and pulled her against him for a long kiss that threatened to draw her very soul from her body. He knelt and pulled her down with him, lying on the coat as he pulled her atop him.

Heat drenched her head to foot as she lay prone atop his hard length. Her legs slid to either side of his hips as he kissed her and kissed her and kissed her some more.

His hands guided her until the very tip of him was teasing her so close and yet not quite close enough. She wriggled her hips experimentally and was rewarded with a groan as his length dipped the tiniest bit inside her.

"Yes." She couldn't stand the wait any longer, relief was so very close.

"Connal." She shifted her weight downward even

as he surged up to meet her. Twin groans split the air around them.

"You are mine." He claimed her, meaning every word. She was lovely and wonderful, totally and completely his in this one moment in time. Hell and be damned to the consequences.

"Connal."

She completed him, completed his very soul in ways he couldn't name, let alone describe.

"Mine," he managed again as he began to move inside the sweet heat of her silken body. "What happened in the past or what happens in the future does not matter."

He pressed kisses to her face, her neck, her mouth as she rocked back and forth on top of him. "Right now . . . *You are mine.* That is all that matters."

"Yes, oh, yes. Oh, Connal."

Her mouth was on his and he couldn't get enough of her as he quickened the pace of his thrusts. In, out, in, out. She was heaven in his arms, heaven against his body, he couldn't think beyond his overwhelming need for her. She met him thrust for thrust, as much caught in the rhythm of their mating as he. Caught in their needs as instinct took over and rational thought flew away.

Heat and passion, friction and thrust, sweet, sweet feeling. Her legs tightened at his hips and she squirmed atop him. "Oh, oh, oh."

He was so deep inside her that he could feel each quiver, each shudder that shook through her as she cried out, tremors shivering through her in rapid succession.

His satisfaction notched all the higher. He followed her into the abyss, awash in naught but quicksilver sensations, the need to never let her go and the willingness to protect her no matter the cost.

In the aftermath there was nothing but the echo of their breathing and the distant sound of the rain. For long moments they lay clasped in each other's arms. Connal was stunned at the depth of satisfaction he knew in making love to Bethany. Never in all his travels, and his attempts to live up to the moniker Finn left him, had he ever known the feelings she unloosed in him so easily.

Finn. He was . . . not gentle . . .

The hesitant way she let out those words echoed back to him. She hardly seemed aware of the strength she possessed, first for having lived with Finn, then having confessed his brutality—and now being able to look at him with her blue-eyed gaze so untouched as she declared she wanted to make love.

"Bethany." He stroked her back. "I am sorry for . . . everything . . . Finn ever did to you."

"Finn is gone."

Connal cupped her face in his hands and met her gaze, needing her to understand that he meant every word he said. "Were there some way for me to make amends, to have him pay the price, I would see it done."

Her gaze was soft blue, ashine with tears. She smiled down at him. "I think he has already paid whatever price there is possible for him. But thank you for your offer."

He kissed her very softly, enjoying just the tender

pressure of lip to lip and shared breaths. Just holding her, just touching her, was satisfying in some deeply indefinable way. Even without lust or the explosive wonders inherent in lovemaking, holding this woman provided him satisfaction at its most basic level.

Imagine that.

Their kisses drifted, slow and easy, slow and soft until the pleasure of holding became the anticipation of having her all over again. The cavern echoed then with the sound and fury of their loving. They drifted to sleep in each other's arms, content to let the world stay very far away.

He woke to silence and the immeasurable peace of having Bethany nestled against him. The rain had stopped, he had no idea how much time had passed since they entered the cave to await the end of the storm. It could be hours. It could be days. He smiled the tiniest bit. It didn't matter at the moment how long they had been here, only that staying much longer would not be a viable option.

She stirred against him and stretched. "Oh." Color canted over her cheeks and then she smiled. "Hello."

"Hello." He kissed her.

"I . . . we . . ." Her glance went to the opening of the cave. And the shadows gathering outside. "Ross—"

"Aye." He stroked a lock of hair behind her left ear. "It is time to return to Glenmeade."

She nodded, but made no move.

He felt the weight of his responsibilities descend on him again. There was much to do in the coming weeks. The work he had spent most of his life on. And all hanging now by the slimmest of possible threads. Holding Bethany, loving her, did not change the circumstances surrounding them. She had come to Ireland looking for family, a home for her son. An opportunity to start again after the wreck Finn made of their lives in America.

And now . . . Now she faced the possibility, albeit unknowingly, of losing everything again. The thought galled him more than anything else he had considered.

He released her and pushed to his feet, taking a moment to gather her things and offer them to her before reaching for his own.

She accepted his help to get to her feet. Despite his best intentions he pulled her to him for one last kiss. He did not deserve any of her attentions. But he could not keep himself from wanting her.

The gig's seat was still damp, but the horse had managed not to get herself lost while she waited out the storm in the outcropping near the cavern. The skies were nearly cleared, but it was almost dark. The last colors of sunset glowed behind the deep green hills. Their family would be worried. The re-alization startled a laugh from him. Bethany may have come here looking for family but he was the one who had found one. Jack, Bridget, Bethany and even little Ross, his family.

With Bethany beside him, tucked under his greatcoat, he headed the mare back to Glenmeade.

Thoughts he'd managed to hold off while they were in the cavern came back with a vengeance.

He glanced at her, next to him. A light breeze stirred her hair. The gaze she turned up to him was open and honest and as blue as the morning sky. She needed the security she had come here seeking. He would do whatever he could to provide it for her, for her son, for his family. He'd called her *mó chroí* in the throes of passion, his heart. He needed to protect her no matter the cost

"Are you all right?" She leaned closer to him, her hand on his arm.

The light touch caught at him somewhere beneath his ribs and he longed to turn the carriage back and steal more time for just the two of them. "I was just thinking that I never enjoyed a rainstorm more."

Color suffused her cheeks, making her eyes all the more vivid a blue. "I do believe I agree with you. But . . . You were frowning."

"We have much to do to ready ourselves for success in Curragh."

Chapter Fifteen

James eased his arm out from under Vivian and stole from the bed. He settled the coverlet over her shoulders before opening the window so he could enjoy his cheroot without leaving any telltale odor lingering in the room to rouse his staff's suspicions.

Not that many of them could possibly still be fooled by Vivian's pose as his *cousin*, but since appearance was what mattered most in maintaining respectability and reputation, he tried to do as much as he could to maintain the illusion.

For their sake.

He should have gone downstairs to his study to smoke. Or gone to his own suite of rooms down the hall, but he liked watching Vivian sleep. Watching her had become one of his primary occupations in the wee hours after he had sated their more urgent needs.

The storm's fury passed just before sunset, scrubbing the night sky clean and polishing the stars so they shone clear and bright. The wind had softened to a whisper. From his perch on the windowsill he blew a cloud of smoke and watched it wisp away into the darkness.

Melancholy burdened his days in a way he'd never before experienced. Not when his parents died from the ague within a week of each other, not even when he returned home to the dreadful news almost a month after Rosleen's death. He'd been alone since then, alone with his regrets and his anger.

He'd expected to feel triumphant at this point, exultant even. His years of slow, meticulous planning and clandestine interference were about to culminate in the final decimation of the Delaneys. A decade-long project brought to careful fruition. Isn't that what he had wanted all this time ? The very core of what he had promised Rosleen?

He shook his head and took a long pull on the cheroot before blowing out the smoke in a thin stream. Instead of elation, he felt empty.

Except when he was with Vivian.

Here in this room, in her bed, in her body, he found a certain . . . completeness . . . he'd never known before. That notion was as unsettling as it was foreign. He blew a final smoky cloud and flicked the stub off into the night, a tiny flare of light disappearing over the gardens.

He certainly was not ready to let Vivian go, not yet. She filled any room she occupied. She was outrageous, flirtatious, sensual and utterly beautiful. And that was when she was dressed. Out of her clothes she was the most responsive, inventive and intuitive woman he had ever known. Making love with her ran the gamut from soft and sweet to saucy, imaginative games.

The excitement of just being together, infrequent and clandestine, had always been a part of the interludes they snatched while he was in America over these past years. He found it amazing that his enjoyment of her, his enthusiasm for her companionship, had not diminished even after weeks of having her available to him on a daily basis.

If anything, his passion for her increased each day.

But the thing he had not expected, would never have anticipated, was this time in the night, when the sight of her asleep and vulnerable slid into parts of him he'd thought long dead. No woman had ever made him feel the need to watch over her as she slept. This protectiveness was not just something he would never have envisioned. It loomed as an inconvenience in relation to his current plans. The only aspect relating to Vivian that did not meld with his decisions.

He had every confidence, however, that he would be able to overcome any impediment this attachment might prove. When it became necessary.

Until then he would enjoy these few stolen moments, and her, to the utmost. Perhaps when this was over he would marry her, if only to spend more nights like this.

He glanced back toward the bed, only to find it empty. Vivian's arm slid along his shoulder down along his chest. She pressed her sleep-warmed softness against his back and giggled. "I was hoping to catch you unawares, my love."

The husky notes in her voice rippled through him, leaving the niggling idea that she had indeed caught him unawares but in a completely different manner and far more vulnerable than she intended or realized.

He closed his eyes, accepting her comfort, enjoying her warmth for just a minute in silence. He could barely acknowledge the truth to himself, let alone grant her the power over him such truth would bring. He was not about to tell her that somewhere in all the plotting and all the games, he might have fallen just the tiniest bit in love with her.

He pulled himself out of her embrace and stood. "Go back to bed, Vivian."

"Not without you." The candles burning low on the mantel provided enough light for him to see the concern in her eyes. "You slip away every night, brooding in the dark. Then you leave me. Stay this time."

So she knew. At least . . . She knew he liked to watch her sleep even if she did not know the rest of his thoughts. He had no intention of sharing anything with her that might tip the balance of power between them. He needed her to finish what she had started with Connal.

He pulled her to him and kissed her, his hands on her shoulders. Her mouth opened beneath his and he mated their tongues together, slow and soft. Then he pulled back and met her gaze.

"You know I cannot." Padding across the bedchamber, he walked out into her small sitting room to retrieve his clothes and retire to his own room. The remains of her late-afternoon bath glistened darkly in the low light cast from the room's wall sconces. "Go back to bed, it is cold."

"James." She stood in the doorway, a crimson satin wrapper thrown around her shoulders. Her ebony hair flowed around her in disarray. "There has to be more. I need there to be more."

"More what?" He dropped his trousers back onto the chair where he'd found them and paced over to her. He cupped her cheek in his palm, then slid down to her neck so his thumb could bat the sapphire earrings she still wore. The diamonds surrounding the deep blue gems sparkled in the lamplight.

"More what, Vivian?"

She drew in a shaky breath. "As soon as Sherman . . . died . . . well, as soon as was practical, I came here to you."

"And I welcomed you. Without hesitation. I took you into my home, and my bed." He batted the earring again.

She nodded. "Just as I have always complied with your requests." Her gaze was steady on his. "I became Finn Delaney's lover, fed him the information you wanted him to know. My part in his . . . destruction . . . destroyed my life." Her eyes glistened.

"I know that." He ignored the twinge of guilt that went with the admission. "What more do you want from me?"

"I want to know what the profit is."

"Profit? Money?" He could hardly believe his ears. After he'd been up in the middle of the nights acting the moon-calf and toying with ideas of permanency. He fought hard to keep from closing his hands around her throat and strangling her on the spot. "You want to negotiate your price for assisting me?"

She stepped back the tiniest bit, but anger flashed darkly in her eyes.

"Do not dare such words again." Her tone was

low and heated. "I have paid a dear price for your vengeance, James. And I have asked nothing of you in return. I did not come all this way looking for your money. I came here for you."

She might as well have been screaming at him. The words hit with the same force. No one since Rosleen had called him to task so succinctly. And no one had ever dared such a feat while he stood stark naked before them. He was more than a little taken aback.

She drew a shaky breath, closed her eyes and blew it out very slowly. "Sherman always said to look for the profit, to find out what the other party really wants from a deal and let them think they are going to get it."

Her dark gaze fixed on him once more. "So I want to know what you get out of destroying the Delaneys. This is too personal to be just another set of business transactions."

"Satisfaction." He grabbed the discarded trousers, pulled them on and fastened them.

"Satisfaction for what?" Vivian followed him, tossing her ebony hair over her shoulders. "For who?"

"For my sister's death. For their seduction. Their betrayal. I vowed the Delaneys would all reap the loneliness, the despair of dreams destroyed, their very lives shattered, and their reputations in utter ruins, I vowed they would all know just exactly how Rosleen felt.

"My sweet little sister." He closed his eyes for a minute, picturing her laughing as they rode the meadows and hills of Kildare as children; how she'd looked the day she'd agreed to marry Connal, her eyes sparkling with happiness; but suddenly all he could see was the image that had haunted him for a decade, the sight he had seen only in his nightmares: Rose being dragged from the river, water streaming from her gown, from her hair.

He picked up his shirt and shouldered his way into it. "She was far more delicate than any of us realized. She needed better care than a maiden aunt and an absent brother provided. She deserved a man who would give her a full measure of trust and care. Instead, she was driven to suicide by the Delaneys. Both of them. Finn *and* Connal."

Despite his intention to deliver the information impartially his voice shook as anger swelled his chest. He bit back the tirade building inside him and struggled for control. "Vengeance *is* the profit, Vivian. It is the only thing that matters. The last thing I vowed to see through for her."

He met Vivian's shocked gaze without caring that she looked pale and dismayed. Dismay was a luxury he could not afford.

"Get dressed," he told her. "I will give you the details in any degree of solidity you require. But I am going to fetch a decanter of whiskey first."

He quit the room before she could say anything further and returned after grabbing the whiskey and two tumblers from his study. He didn't really want to relive the sad story of Rosleen. But the story had made the rounds of Kildare on a regular basis since Rosleen's death. He'd even discreetly fanned the flames a time or two himself, to keep public sentiment roused against Connal whenever the dolt had done one of his altruistic acts that seemed to be turning sentiments in his favor.

He found Vivian pacing the length of her sitting

room. The red robe still swirled about her long legs as her bare feet traversed the carpet.

She turned at his entry. "James—"

"Aye, Vivian." He kicked the door closed behind him. "I probably should have told you this several years ago. I let you go on thinking I was after Finn for business reasons because I thought it would make it easier on you. Taking you away from him was to be his final punishment. But our . . . relationship . . . has changed somewhat and you deserve to know it all."

He set down the decanter and glasses on the mahogany table by the bathtub and poured two fingers' full into each glass.

She accepted his revelation in silence. He was not surprised. She knew as well as he did that their affair was far more than it had been previously. That she had more at stake in his plans than before.

He handed one tumbler to her and toasted her silently before tossing the contents back in one swallow. Familiar fire burned its way down his gullet. She sipped hers with more decorum before tracing her fingertip around the glass's edge.

"Tell me of your sister."

He poured himself one more finger of whiskey and stoppered the decanter with a soft crystal chink. "She was lovely, my sister. Young, trusting, with dreams of happiness and a family. She had long pale hair and big dark eyes. She was the light of my parents' lives, well loved by everyone who knew her. Her death would have killed them, if they had not already been carried off. I suppose that is one relief available in the whole sorry story.

They did not live to see her in such ruin or to know she . . ."

Vivian's hand touched his shoulder. He met her gaze. Mingled sympathy and understanding lay there, waiting for him. He turned away.

"We had known the Delaneys all of our lives. I grew up with Finn and Connal. They were as much brothers as cousins and they might as well have been related to me as well. We were inseparable at one time. I knew Glenmeade as well as Oak Bend and vice versa. Who would have known how all of that would change?"

He laughed without humor and raked a hand through his hair. The whiskey's burn in his stomach did little to assuage the pain writhing there as well.

"She fell in love with Connal sometime over the first winter I was away, studying in Edinburgh. We thought it some schoolgirl crush at first. I can remember Finn and me laughing about it. But it was not just a simple crush. A year later Connal asked for her hand. I could hardly believe it, but I was relieved she had chosen Connal, not Finn. Married. My little sister and one of my best friends. It seemed a good match. She was young, but he would care for her, protect her, cherish her as she deserved. I trusted him."

He took a sip of his drink to burn away the bitter taste of those last words. "I gave her over into Connal's care right before I left for Edinburgh for the last time. When I returned she was gone."

"What happened?" Vivian voiced the question so softly she almost didn't hear her. Not that it mattered. He needed no prompting to finish this.

"Finn seduced her. He and Connal had always

made a competition of everything in their lives. School, horses, work . . . why not women? Rosleen was just one more conquest, one more test of manhood. He lay with her, heedless of her youth and vulnerability, not even concerned that he ruined her life in search of his victory over his cousin."

"Oh, James."

He held up a hand to still her sympathies. "Let me finish, Vivian. You need to know the whole of this. When she found out she was pregnant she went to Finn first. He cared nothing for her, or the child he had begotten. He wished her good luck in explaining it to Connal. That much she put in the note she left behind."

Vivian sucked in her breath but held her peace, if peace was possible to hold at this point in the telling of the tragedy.

"Although she said nothing directly about Connal in her letter, I surmise she went to him next, confessing everything to him. Finn's seduction and rejection. The child. I picture her begging him to forgive her. To accept her. To understand. He turned her away, that much I do know, as though she had never been anything to him. She had nowhere to turn after that. No one to help her. I was still in Scotland. She was all alone with her shame. She took her own life."

Silence held when he finished, with only the echo of Rosleen's pain shivering in the air around them. He drained the dregs from his glass.

Vivian's body pressed to his side as she looped her arms around him. "I am so sorry."

"I am long past sorrow." He tipped up her chin so he could see her face. Tears shimmered along her pale cheeks. "You have no idea how hard it has been to hold back my rage. To mete out their punishments and extract the maximum suffering. Two of them managed to escape their full measure. Brennan, the man who raised those devil's spawns, was easily lured into debt, almost to the point of ruin. His stroke ended his penalty, although the debt has continued to ensnare Glenmeade. And Finn, well . . . You know of Finn's untimely escape."

White-faced, all Vivian could do was nod. She too had suffered because of Finn.

"Connal cannot be so lucky. He must be made to suffer all the more. Not only because of his failure, his rejection of my sister, but because I have had to swallow his meager apologies, his excuses and be his friend all these years."

He put his hands on Vivian's shoulders. She did not shrink from his touch. "So, you understand that I must finish this?"

"I . . ." She hesitated, then nodded. "Yes, I understand your need to avenge your sister's death."

"And you will help me." That wasn't really a question.

"Yes." She answered anyway. "Yes, I will help you find peace for Rosleen in any way I can."

"Thank you." He pulled her into his arms and kissed her. Gratitude welled hot and salty in his chest. She was a boon in his arms. Salve to the pain of dredging his sister's story so freshly into the present. He could drown in Vivian's welcoming embrace and he would do so without protest.

"Come back to bed with me, James." Sultry and low. "Leave the rest to later. Let me make everything go away for you, for just a little while longer."

"Aye." He scooped her into his arms and moved back toward the bedroom. He still needed to tell her the rest of his plans for bringing the final Delaney down and taking the Stables for his own. But he could tell her that in the morning.

There were a few hours yet until dawn.

"If that is your wish." Vivian's irritation was as clear as the morning sky over them when she continued. "But how can you expect me to marry him? How can you plan—"

"I do not expect there to be a real marriage, Vivian." How could she question him now that he had spread his plans before her?

"Then what?" She paced away from him, her red velvet riding habit whispering with anxiety. "Do you expect it to be a sham? Do you really think a man like Connal Delaney would accept such a thing? I do not."

She turned back to face him, one brow arched. "Besides, there is his fascination with his little cousin-in-law to consider. I have done all but offer myself to him on a gilded platter already and he is immune. He may not yet realize it, but the man is in love with her."

"Love?" That would tighten the stakes still further on their trip to Curragh. "Are you sure?"

"Yes." Vivian's mouth held a tight line of displeasure. "I have had enough experience with men to know when a man's mind is fixed elsewhere. He could have had his pleasure with me in the parlor while you were taking dear little Beth on her tour. The possibility clearly never entered his mind."

"Be that as it may, darling, aside from your pout over that slight, his desires matter very little." He crossed to her side. "You will not actually marry Connal, you need only appear to be interested in the marriage. I will see to it the proposal is made. You agree and I will see to the rest."

"And what of Bethany?"

"What of her?"

"How do you plan to keep her out of the fray?"

He looked into her eyes and realized he could not tell her that part of the plan. Vivian, for all her willingness to help him, would not agree to go forward if he revealed his intentions for Finn's widow. Her understanding would stretch only so far.

"Leave pretty little Bethany Delaney to me. I will make quite sure she does not create an impediment to Connal's proposal to you."

He brushed his fingers along Vivian's jawline, enjoying the sudden droop of her eyelids as he tipped her lovely chin up toward his and kissed her with languid thoroughness.

"Trust me to deal with the Widow Delaney appropriately. She must accept her share in the destruction after all. She married Finn of her own choice. Gave him a son. If she has to pay with a little heartache, so be it."

"As you wish, James." The words he'd been waiting to hear. "I trust everything to you." With that Vivian fell silent.

"Thank you, my dear." And the guilt that twinged deep inside him would just have to subside into silence also. After all these years he was not about to set aside his plans to avenge Rosleen's death.

Not for Connal.

Not for Vivian.

And not even for himself.

"Will these be the last of them, lass?" Jack cast such a wary eye at the pile of suitcases and boxes collecting by the foot of the stairs that Bethany nearly laughed.

"Now, don't ye even think about giving us a hard time about what we should or should not be taking with us, Jack Branigan," Aunt Bridget scolded him from the landing. "Ye know right well we all have ta go about looking our finest else people will think Glenmeade is full of pinch-pennies who haven't got enough ta spend on the horses if they aren't willing ta take care of their own needs. Besides, ye'll appreciate our efforts when ye see them."

"I'd appreciate a few less boxes to try to pile on the cart," Jack said, but in a slightly lower tone.

"What was that, love?" Bridget reached the bottom of the steps. She slipped her arm around his waist. "Did ye say ye could hardly wait ta show me just how much ye appreciate all our preparations?"

The lines of exhaustion around Jack's mouth disappeared as he smiled down into Bridget's eyes. "Something like that."

"You don't mean to kiss her again do you, Mr. Black-Jack?"

Try as she might, Bethany could not persuade Ross that Jack's name was anything other than Black-Jack. Her son already had his nose wrinkled at what was sure to be a most unseemly display, in his estimation. Ross was positive his great-aunt was in love with a pirate, which was almost enough to make their romance acceptable.

"Aye, lad, I'm afraid that's exactly what I mean to do. Every day from now on." Jack winked at the boy who had just helped bring the last of the boxes downstairs. He proceeded to prove true to his word by giving Bridget a very chaste peck on the cheek.

"I intend ta hold ye ta that. Ye're my witness, Ross." Bridget pushed Jack away, but she was smiling and her cheeks were decidedly pink.

"Why would I want to witness that every day? Once is more than enough." Ross was so serious, and he looked very vexed when they all burst into laughter.

"C'mon lad, ye can give me a hand with these." Jack's eyes were twinkling with pleasure.

They looked so happy. Bethany was thrilled her aunt had this second chance at love even as a tiny part of her couldn't help being jealous. Since the day she and Connal returned from Oak Bend, they had all been busy with preparations for the trip, but where Jack seemed able to take short breaks or come back to the Manor for the occasional meal, Connal was barely in the house at all.

She tried to console herself with the knowledge that he needed to oversee the preparations for this trip to Curragh. They were going to a horse fair, after all.

But the knot in her stomach, which seemed to grow a little heavier each day, told her he was deliberately avoiding her and she couldn't stop the buzz of doubts and questions swarming in her thoughts from drowning out more rational explanations for his being careful to never be alone with her. The few snippets of conversation that they had exchanged all dealt with the arrangements leading up to their departure today, and even then he had seemed so remote, as if there was an invisible barrier between them. Was it the fact that she was Finn's widow, or what she had confessed about the marriage itself? Or, did he think her a wanton?

"I would be glad to take some of these, too." She offered to help transfer their baggage outside to the waiting cart. Anything to distract herself from her current course of thinking, she'd lain awake too many nights traveling these now-familiar paths. And missing Connal's arms around her.

A few minutes later they had everything outside and Ross was helping Jack figure out how he was going to shift things around on the cart to fit their baggage in with the mountain of stable gear already loaded on it.

"While the gentlemen finish here, we should go to the kitchen and see how Jenna O'Toole is faring with the lunch basket, *isean*," Bridget suggested.

Bethany nodded. "This looks like it will certainly take a while."

"I only hope they remember they have ta leave room fer us." Bridget chuckled as they crossed the portico. They no sooner gained the foyer when they spotted a small carpet bag that had been overlooked.

"It's the one I packed with our shoes."

Bethany scooped it up. "I can run this outside and join you in the kitchen in a minute."

"I'll see if Jenna can spare us a couple of mugs of tea, shall I?"

They headed off in opposite directions. Bethany

cleared the front door, satchel in hand, to find her
son deep in conversation with Jack.

"You won't be too busy will you, Mr. Black-Jack?
You'll remember?"

"I'll keep my eyes out for just the thing, lad. I
promise."

"Promise what?" she asked, causing them both to
start and turn to her with twin looks of guilt.

Ross swallowed hard, hesitating.

"Well—" Jack began.

"No," Ross interrupted. "I'll tell her, Mr. Black-
Jack. Mama thinks I'm still a baby, but I'm not. A
man takes respons . . . responsibility, that's what my
cousin says."

"He's right, lad. Even when it's the hardest thing
to do, a man takes responsibility." Jack took a step
back.

"Tell me what, Ross?"

"I asked him to keep an eye out for a pony for
me. Don't make that face, Mama. I didn't ask him
to buy the pony, just find a good one so you could
see how gentle they were. Not too big or too fast."

Ross gulped some air. "I thought if Mr. Black-Jack
or Cousin Connal showed you, you would at least
think about it harder. Because so far, your thinking
about it hasn't gotten me any closer to getting my
pony."

Right at that moment he looked so serious, and
so sincere, he did look older to her. Perhaps even
old enough for a pony. She just hated the thought
of giving him such a longed-for treasure, only to
have to take it away again if they left here once the
estate questions were settled.

A prospect that seemed more than likely, given

the way things were looking. She couldn't stay here with Connal if she was not really with him. Not even for Ross and a pony he had yet to possess.

"If Mr. Branigan can at least show me what to look for in a good pony, I promise to think very hard. But there will not be a pony coming home with us this trip. Understand?"

"Yes, Mama." He looked as if he wasn't sure whether he'd gained any ground in the argument or not, but he squared his shoulders and reached for the carpet bag in her hand. "I'll take that. We're almost finished."

"Thank you, Ross."

It was Bethany's turn to be startled as Connal spoke from only a foot or so behind her. He must have walked up from the stables. This was the closest she'd been to him in days and her heart ached when she saw how tired and careworn he looked. She suppressed the urge to reach out and smooth the hair that was falling across his brow. But even Ross had grown too big for such fussing from her.

"I want to make sure I have all the paperwork in order, then we should be ready to set off. Lochie has the horses ready," he said to Jack, then turned his attention to her. "Bethany, could you come with me to my study for a minute?"

"Certainly." She looked over at her son. "Stay close by, Ross, so we can say our good-byes."

"Yes, Mama."

She followed Connal into the house and down to his study. She had no sooner stepped inside when he turned and pulled her into his arms. His gaze raked her face for the span of several heartbeats. She was too stunned to think, to react, to breathe.

All she knew was that he was holding her and, as unhappy as she had been, it wasn't until now that she knew just how much she had ached for this moment.

He cupped her cheek with one hand, then drew her into a soul-shattering kiss that tore away any barriers that had been built between them. He poured a desperate, yearning desire onto her lips, demanding all of her pent-up passion and longing from hers. She clung to him, utterly lost to the maelstrom he loosed within her.

He pulled back from her, panting but keeping a firm grip on both her arms to balance her when she would have stumbled, so swept up had she been in his embrace.

"Bethany." He looked so distressed. "God, I missed you."

"I was here the whole time."

"Aye. Staying away was the hardest thing I have ever done." He looked even sadder, if that was possible. "Preparations notwithstanding, if I had not, I do not think I could . . . I . . . just wanted you . . . I need you to remember that anything I did . . . I do . . . is to protect you . . . protect Ross . . . Glenmeade . . . the future you deserve."

He looked deep into her eyes, as if trying to see into her very soul. "Promise me you understand. Promise me you will remember that when you think about this down the road. No matter what happens or what anyone might tell you to the contrary. Promise me you will always know that this was what mattered most to me."

Her thoughts whirled together. Nothing he had said made any sense. She was more confused now than she had been in the days when she hadn't seen him at all.

For a moment, the questions hovering inside her hammered for release. But she looked into his eyes and realized she could not ask them. Not right now. He had enough of a load believing he carried Glenmeade's future on his shoulders.

For now, the feel of his arms around her and the wonderful kiss they had shared would have to be enough. Right now, even though she didn't really understand, he desperately needed to believe that she did. "I promise, Connal. I will remember."

He took a deep breath and let it out slowly. "Good."

He bent over and grazed her lips with his, a soft, gentle salute. "Now, go fetch your coat and bonnet. We have buyers to impress."

Chapter Sixteen

"Yer room is at the top of the stairs, Mr. Delaney. Second door on the right. The rest of yer party settled down fer the night. The necessary is down the backstairs."

His elderly guide carried the smell of chamomile and elder flowers as she gestured with the single candlestick she held. Flickering light from its flame chased shadows up the tall casement.

Connal shifted the small satchel, containing his shaving gear and change of shirt for the morning, into his left hand as he grasped the banister in the other. It squeeked in protest beneath his fingers. The hour was late and he was weary beyond words, but he forced himself to do more than just nod and start up what looked to be a narrow mountain of stairs in this equally slender town home. He was too tired to reach for cordial, but he could be polite to his ancient hostess. "Thank you, Miss Douglas."

"Will ye be needing a candle ta light the way?" She squinted at him through thick glasses, her eyes almost bigger than her face. "I don't like giving candles ta guests if I can help it, not since two summers ago when some drunk fool set the O'Neill's house aflame over on Milk Street, but I'll give ye one if ye like. If ye think ye're going to need it."

"No, I am sure I will be fine. Second door to the left?"

"My sister will have the coffee and biscuits on before dawn since ye need an early start fer the fairgrounds." That was all the reply he got as the tiny woman headed down the darkened hallway, taking the small glow of candlelight with her as she headed toward the home's kitchen, leaving him completely in the dark.

"Second door to the left it is." He hoped he actually managed to sleep a few hours. More was riding on his actions and reactions tomorrow than he had ever thought possible. And knowing that Bethany was sleeping nearby could only lead to further frustration.

He'd assumed he and Jack would be bunking together and been surprised when the wizened-faced woman who greeted him when he arrived informed him they were each in separate rooms, quite a luxury under the circumstances. Unless the gesture was necessitated by the rooms being as narrow as these stairs, he amended, picturing small beds jammed up against one wall and barely enough room to turn around without knocking a shin or an elbow.

Especially in the pitch-black.

True to his word, as always, James had secured not only their entrance and exhibit space on the fairgrounds, but these lodgings as well. Because the demand for rooms increased on occasions such as the races and horse fairs sponsored by the Irish Turf Club, the townsfolk in Curragh regularly opened their homes to visitors. They were not luxury accommodations, but most visitors just wanted a place to lay their heads and change their clothes. And the host households benefited from the extra coins here and there.

He eased his way down the narrow hall, navigating the darkness using his fingertips and hoping the Douglas sisters did not have any furniture lining their second-story hall. He eased open the door and stepped inside. Giving himself a minute, his eyes adjusted somewhat to what little light filtered in the lone window. Dark shapes coalesced from the gloom. The largest directly across from him must be the bed. He moved his hand to the side and contacted the back of a chair by the wall right next to the door. Beside that a washstand. Good.

He quickly stripped out of his jacket and vest, dropping them on the chair, and washed away the dust of travel and the grit left from feeding and settling his stock in for the night down on the fairgrounds. Lochie and his two oldest boys would see to them overnight.

Sitting on the edge of the bed to pull off his boots, he was rewarded with a loud creak that bounced off the walls in the narrow chamber.

"Who's there?" The whisper edged through the night air from the far side of the mattress.

"Is there somebody here?"

The voice was husky with sleep and alarm, a voice that sounded familiar, dear. Hints of cinnamon, vanilla and his heart's deepest desire hung in the air.

"Bethany?"

"Yes."

"It's me, Connal." Had bad fortune or the Douglas sisters somehow conspired to give him his fondest wish and his greatest torment by putting her in his bed, or had she come here seeking him on her own?

"What are you doing here?"

The bedding shifted beneath him and the mattress ropes groaned their creaky protest as she sat up, another dark shape taking form in the dimness.

"Miss Douglas sent me up. Second door from the left, she said." *Had* she said left? Was he mistaken? He obviously was mistaken.

"That is where you are, all right. But your clothes are all unpacked and waiting for you across the hall."

"Oh."

"Oh, indeed."

The smile in her voice suffused him with warmth. He should get up and back right out the door. Quickly, before anyone else realized his blunder. But like this morning in his study, once he had her near he could not help himself. He wanted to tarry for far longer than a few stolen moments. He wanted to crawl under the bed coverings and stay there with her the whole night.

"I should apologize for my error. For disturbing you."

"Don't."

"I should leave—"

"Stay."

He reached for her blindly and pulled her into his arms, choosing not to question the whys or hows for a moment, just holding her sleep-warmed

softness to him. He had never felt anything so
wonderful in his life.

"Connal."

She said his name on a sigh that tore away any lingering claim he had on self-control.

Her fingers sought his face and pulled him down
until their lips met. There was no other place he
wanted to be, could even consider being at this
moment, in this lifetime, than here with this
woman.

"Connal," she repeated, the longing in her voice
and the warmth of her breath fanned his cheeks
and sent cascades of desire showering through him.
He held her tight and kissed her, long and deep.

He'd tried to warn her for two weeks. To tell her
all that was at stake and what his choices were. What
their choices were, but every time he was in a room
with her, every time he caught even a fleeting
glimpse of her, his desire for her threatened to
overcome all logic, to defy reality.

If he was successful tomorrow, if he could garner
enough interest in Glenmeade Stables that he
could pay off the loans and secure their future, he
would ask Bethany to marry him. It was such a big
if he didn't know how he dared to even dream it,
except through the strength he drew from her.

He teased her lips open with the tip of his tongue
and then edged inside to touch hers. She shivered
in his embrace, not from the cold, but surely from
the same sensations she pulled from him. Their
tongues played with one another, flicking and circling. She melted deeper into his arms.

I know what kind of man you are . . . Isn't that what
she'd said the night she'd sought him out in the

new stables? *You are an honorable man.* He'd been overcome with wonder at the simplicity of that statement, the honesty. Imagine, The Wicked One an honorable man in her eyes.

Her fingers laced through his hair as she drew him closer still while she drank deeply from his lips. He wanted to be an honorable man for her. He wanted to be the kind of man who could make her happy. Make her safe. But what if he could not make Bethany safe and have her with him at the same time? What if he failed tomorrow and he could not make enough connections to stave off the creditors?

Reality hit him hard, here, perched on her bed, holding her, kissing her, wanting so much more. He was anything but an honorable man.

Vivian can be the key to your salvation . . . You could do far worse . . . James's words echoed back to him along with the dead-weight feeling in his stomach such a plan engendered.

If he failed tomorrow, if he was forced to follow James's scheme to wed Vivian Brown in order to save the Stables, taking advantage of Bethany like this not only proved her wrong, it proved he was indeed the type of man who fit his reputation. In her eyes he would be worse than wicked. And he would be repeating past mistakes all too easily.

It would hardly be fair to tell her now, especially not here in the intimacy of darkness and the warmth of her all-too-tempting embrace. To tell her and leave her to pick up the pieces and go on in the morning. To have her anxiously waiting, judging him, judging herself, in the background.

Frustration ground through him.

He should have told her the full story of his

indebtedness long ago. She and Ross deserved better than the state he had them all in at the moment—years of the debt he had scrimped and saved to repay, only to use the money to buy his prized Cleveland Bays on a gamble that he would turn enough profit to make up for his initial outlay. Her arrival with Ross had forced the investors to call the loan early. Could he even tell her . . . any of that . . . without having her fix the blame on herself? Would she look at him in the same way when she realized he had very nearly ruined her in the same manner as Finn had?

The questions poured icy water over his ardor and settled in his stomach in a frozen block.

He pushed himself back from her tantalizing lips, the tempting softness of her breasts as they grazed his chest. Oh so slowly, he eased away, holding her panting in the dark for a moment. He could not let her blame herself for his lapses in judgment. Uncle Brennan's gambling got the Stables into the mess initially. His own gamble might cause them to lose the Stables once and for all. Her arrival might have brought matters to a head, but she was blameless and she deserved better.

"Sweet as this is, I must seek some rest tonight. Tomorrow is too important. You should rest, too. I am sorry for intruding, for scaring you."

He grabbed his clothing from the chair and opened the door to the even darker hallway and the empty bedroom across the hall.

"Good night, Connal."

She sounded so sad, so lost, he nearly turned around.

"Good night, Bethany."

* * *

"I really cannot get used to the width of these crinolines, Aunt Bridget." Bethany twisted and looked down at the hem of her jonquil Kerseymere day dress. "I'm not sure I will make it down those narrow steps these are so wide."

Bridget gave the triple-flounced skirt a thorough inspection. "Aye, if they hadn't been featured in that volume the draper provided I'd hardly credit them as real. Ye look pretty as can be, *isean*. It's good ta see ye dressing as ye should. It's been a long time."

Connal had insisted on providing the funds they spent at the draper's for fabric and with Betsey's help both Bridget and she refurbished and made whatever they needed for this trip. True to her word, surprisingly, Vivian sent over a lovely ball gown.

"Well, you look very fetching today, too, Aunt Bridget. That shade of blue is especially becoming. But I think happiness is what really brought the sparkle to your eyes."

Bridget blushed. On the trip to Curragh, Jack rode along the side cart, telling tales of the Fian of old and spinning the stories about a host of other Irish heroes through the ages.

Connal spent his time deep in conversation with Lochie Tavis, his stable master. He carefully avoided her even when they stopped to share the hamper of food Jenna had packed for them. Every once in awhile she'd felt the heat of his gaze on her, but if she glanced over at him he would quickly look away. His behavior baffled her to the point of madness.

A soft rapping on the door found one of the Miss Douglases waiting outside to deliver a note. The elderly sisters looked very much alike. For the life of her, Bethany could not tell one from the other, although one sister seemed to have charge of the kitchen and the other took care of the guests and answering the door.

"This just came fer ye, Mrs. Delaney. The girl what brought it has already left," the woman said as she stepped inside and handed a note to Bridget, who glanced at it, rolled her eyes and handed it on to Bethany.

"And yer husband left ye a message as well," Miss Douglas spoke up.

"My husband?" That startled Bethany as she glanced at the note from Vivian.

"Aye, he was up by dawn on his way down ta the fairgrounds. He said ta tell ye he'd see ye there."

She meant Connal, of course. "Mr. Delaney is my cousin, Miss Douglas. My husband's cousin."

"Well, that explains the request for separate rooms." Miss Douglas's wizened face lit up. "My sister thought perhaps ye was in the family way and he was being considerate of yer delicate condition. I guessed that ye'd had a spat, him being who he is. And banned him from yer bed."

Bethany had no idea what the polite response would be to these speculations. "How interesting. It makes the truth so boring. But we are just related through marriage. Nothing more."

No matter how much more she had wanted there to be last night, or all the other nights since their return from Oak Bend.

"Pity." Miss Douglas bobbed her gray head. "The

truth usually is much more boring than what is told. We were so excited at the prospect of having The Wicked One under our roof. We were certain ta have a few good tales fer the sewing circle, but yer husband's cousin turns out ta be a hard-working man, just worried about his horses, like most of the exhibitors. Not a lick of scandalous behavior last night, although my sister is holding out hope fer after tonight's ball."

Just as her hostess was finishing up, Bethany's gaze fell on a scrap of cloth on the floor between Bridget's feet and the washstand. She was about to ask Bridget to see what it was when she realized it was Connal's vest. Scandal fodder for certain. Bethany clutched the note.

"Oh, my, I just realized Mrs. Brown's note says we should meet her in a quarter hour, Aunt Bridget. Are you ready?"

"I'll need ta fetch my bonnet and gloves."

"You do that and I will make sure I have everything and meet you downstairs." Bethany kicked the vest a little farther so it was under the washstand as she ushered the other ladies out of the room. "If you will excuse us, Miss Douglas?"

"Aye. I'll come back ta tidy up yer rooms after midmorning tea with my sister. My sister looks forward ta that mug o'tea every morning, rain or shine. Luckily today is a sunny one fer the fair."

Bethany retrieved the vest. Having dropped it in almost total darkness, he would have been hard-pressed to locate it. It smelled of man and horse and windblown grass. She hastily folded it and stuck it inside one of her bags. Picking up her bonnet and gloves she went to meet Bridget.

The last thing she wanted to do was spend the day with Vivian Brown, strolling the streets of Curragh or the fairgrounds, but since James Carey was sponsoring this trip she could hardly refuse his cousin's invitation.

Dressed to the teeth in a Mexican blue grenadine dress with a peplum jacket and black velvet ribbon trim, Vivian descended the steps at her lodgings after keeping Bethany and Bridget waiting for at least three-quarters of an hour. Bridget passed the time commenting on all the fine accoutrements of this establishment as opposed to theirs. Chief was the generosity in the dimensions in the rooms and the passages.

"Beth, dear, it is too good to see you and your aunt again," Vivian gushed. "But I could have sworn I asked if you would like to meet at eleven."

"It is half-past eleven, Vivian."

She looked surprised. "Well, then we are both late. And we had best be off or the men will be wondering where on earth we are."

Bethany doubted anyone had even noticed they had not yet made an appearance. "I, for one, am hoping they are too busy to have noticed."

"Well, there is that." Vivian pursed her lips. "Maureen, my guests grow impatient. Pray fetch my bonnet and reticule."

"Yes, ma'am." The maid bobbed a deep curtsy.

"She has such a way with hair." Vivian patted her glossy hair, gathered at the back and falling loose in sausage curls. "If you would like, I am sure I can convince her to do something to dress your hair before tonight's festivities."

"That is very kind, but perhaps we should decide after our visit to the fairgrounds."

From the maid Vivian accepted a broad-brimmed hat festooned with ribbons the same shade of blue as her dress and a pair of black kid gloves. After murmuring her thanks she placed the hat on her head, dipping the brim at a jaunty angle. She gave herself a final look in the hall mirror and nodded to Bethany.

"James left us a brochure that will guide us through the fairgrounds. Shall we be off at last?"

They made their way along the streets that led to the clearing where the tents had been set up. Bridget took charge of the guide and ended up several paces ahead of them so all they had to do was keep their eyes on her.

Vivian proved to be an amusing companion, keeping up a flow of conversation mostly centered on the odd mix of fashions being displayed by those also in town for the horse fair.

"What was she thinking when she bought that hat?"

The confection in question had caught Bethany's eye as well.

"I mean, really, there she was at the milliner's in whatever backwater town, and even if she thought that three peacock feathers and pink ruching was just what she needed, did they not at least offer her a mirror?"

"You are too bold, Vivian."

"Why thank you, Beth." Vivian's carefully dulcet tones sounded only casually cordial, but her eyes had that same twinkle Ross got when he was waiting for a promised treat.

Surprised to find just how much she had enjoyed their trek to the fairgrounds, Bethany discreetly pointed to another woman, well past her prime, who wore a bonnet of purple velvet rosettes trimmed with apple green ribbon trim.

"Two words," Vivian dropped her voice. "Violet pot."

Bethany put her hand to her lips to suppress an outright giggle. Vivian had a keen wit, especially for the absurdities of fashion.

They rounded a corner and were confronted by a colorful hodgepodge of tents, banners, booths, wagons and more. The noise was deafening. Noxious odors blended with the steam rising from cauldrons of sausage-and-potato soup, fish stew and other delectable treats.

"Wow" was all Bethany could say.

"Wow, indeed," Aunt Bridget commented.

Even Vivian was silent as they drank it all in.

"Let us see which is the right way ta be heading. I fer one would hate to tramp up and down one section of aisles, only ta find our lads are someone else."

"James wrote a number in the upper corner of that map," Vivian volunteered. "It should be in the area where the tent for Glenmeade is located," she continued, pointing to a hastily scrawled note, "Number 17–8."

Bridget looked over at the congested field and back to the map. She turned the map sidewise. She wrinkled her nose. Then Bethany and Vivian both looked at the map and could not make heads or tails of which way they should head.

"We shall just have to ask," Vivian said at last. "We cannot keep standing here in hopes lightning strikes their tent to show us the way."

"I beg pardon, ladies. I hope you will not think it too forward of me to enquire, but may we be of some assistance?"

A very short, elderly gentleman dressed in an old-fashioned but meticulously tailored frock coat, doffed his hat and bowed. There were two other gentlemen with him, one who looked to be his son and the other a stripling youth. They, too, bowed.

"My name is Clement Sawyer, this is my son, Thaddeus, and my grandson, Anderson." His accent marked him as an American. "If I may be so bold, are you trying to locate one group in particular or just trying to decide on the best route for a general tour?"

"One in particular." Bethany was standing nearest to Mr. Sawyer so she handed him the map. "Glenmeade Stables. It is supposed to be located at this number but we cannot see it listed anywhere."

"Well, that's your problem, my dear. There was a mix-up at the printer's and apparently things are not as they should be on this map. But as luck would have it we know just where the Glenmeade area is. Don't we, boys?"

"Father—" Thaddeus Sawyer had warning in his voice.

"Don't be a fussbudget, Tad. I am just offering our assistance to these fine ladies. I am not out in a hay barn tossing bales around. Just having a conversation."

Thaddeus looked more than a little skeptical.

"We would not wish to discommode you, sirs,"

Vivian spoke up in her most sultry voice. "But any assistance you could offer would be greatly appreciated. Especially since we are all fellow countrymen in a strange land."

"We have just come from a most informative look at the offerings of that very stable. Glenmeade Stables is the talk of the fair, among horse buyers, at least. Such fine stances, meticulous records of the bloodlines. If you would accept our escort, we would be most happy to take you to your destination."

Clement Sawyer fixed his son and grandson with a no-nonsense stare that practically dared either of them to gainsay his offer.

"But the doctor—" his grandson tried manfully.

"Said I should take it easy on our travels, but I will be fine, young man." Clement Sawyer was a match for either of them, and probably most other people who stood in his way, from the few moments Bethany had been able to observe. "I can think of nothing easier than escorting three lovely ladies for a stroll."

"Would you do me the honor, Miss . . ." He held out his arm.

Bethany looked over and saw that Vivian already had her arm tucked into Thaddeus Sawyer's. Bridget nodded and accepted the grandson's arm.

"Mrs. . . . Mrs. Delaney. Thank you, we accept."

"Ahhhh." Mr. Sawyer's face lit up as the small party crossed the street and entered the fairgrounds. "Isn't that the name of the owner of Glenmeade Stables? Is he your husband?"

They spent a very pleasant interval strolling past the exhibits of carriage- and cart-makers, stalls filled with harness and tack for sale, new and used. An exhibition ring in the center bustled with activity. Each of the breeders present had massive tents erected to house their horses and keep them somewhat segregated from the throngs.

Aunt Bridget soon had the grandson out of his sulks, playing pretty much the same game the ladies had played on the way through the streets—attributing the most outrageous stories to some of the characters she picked out.

True to her nature, Vivian Brown had Thaddeus Sawyer wrapped around her finger in no time. She was definitely the kind of woman who thrived in the company of men. Bethany found spending time with her far easier when Connal was not the object of her considerable attentions.

She also learned that Mr. Sawyer was a horse breeder from Maryland who had come to Ireland in hopes of acquiring a stallion or two to take back with him to improve his stock of hunters. And the stud he most wanted to acquire was Connal's white stallion, Teagan.

"I do not think you will be able to persuade Mr. Delaney to part with that particular horse, Mr. Sawyer. The amount of your offer is not the impediment. He has plans for adding to his own bloodlines. Perhaps he might be willing to send you one of his new colts once they are ready."

Mr. Sawyer chuckled and patted her hand as it rested on her arm. "I like you, Mrs. Delaney. You may be a novice, but you have the soul of a true horse trader.

"Yes, ma'am, a real horse trader." He stopped walking. "I'm actually sorry to say that this is the end of the line."

So absorbed had she been in his conversation she

had to blink to focus. Then she saw Connal and Lochie Tavis talking to another man and she understood. They had arrived.

Her heart did a little flip when she saw Connal so relaxed and at ease. He looked every bit the man-in-his-element with his shirtsleeves rolled up and a pencil tucked behind one ear. He glanced over at her before giving the mare Lochie was holding a pat and excusing himself.

"We had about given up on you," he said to her. His smile of pleasure at seeing her was so genuine a part of her melted at the sight.

He turned his attention to Clement Sawyer. "It is a pleasure to see you again, sir," he said as they shook hands. "If you don't mind my asking, what was that about being a horse trader I overheard when you walked up?"

Mr. Sawyer laughed again. "I was talking about this young woman here. Mrs. Delaney. She's trying to interest me in two colts that have yet to be conceived over that fine white stallion I have my heart set on. She must be your partner because she sure knows how to look out for business."

"Not yet . . ."

Had she heard Connal correctly?

"As I told you earlier, Mr. Sawyer, Teagan is not for sale. Not for any price."

Clement Sawyer looked over at his son still deep in conversation with Vivian Brown. "Everything is for sale for the right price. Trick is finding someone gullible enough to pay that price."

"Well, thank you for bringing our ladies to us. I suppose they are victims of the infamous map misprint. I am surprised anyone has found their way to us."

"You are the talk of the show. At least, the only talk worth listening to when it comes to horseflesh. People always have a way of finding quality."

Bethany extracted her arm from her escort's. "Thank you again, Mr. Sawyer. I do not know how else I can repay you for your service."

"Will you be attending the ball tonight?" he asked.

She nodded and he smiled, the kind of smile that showed just how successful he must have been with the ladies when he was a younger man.

"Save a dance for me, why don't you." He glanced up at his son as Thaddeus Sawyer made a small coughing noise. "Or at least sit and have lemonade with me during one."

"I would love to. Whichever dance you prefer."

"As long as you remember you promised the first dance to me, Bethany."

Connal took her arm and her heart flipped again.

Chapter Seventeen

As long as you remember you promised the first dance to me, Bethany.

Bethany reached for the small hand mirror one of the Douglas sisters had managed to unearth. Did she glow as bright on the outside as she felt on the inside? The face that stared back at her from the small glass was far different from the one she had become so familiar with during her marriage. Happiness glowed in the depths of her eyes and tilted the corners of her mouth. Happiness and . . . hope.

She had spent a wonderful afternoon at the horse fair. She never would have guessed such would be the case when she first realized Connal was planning on her attending.

And now she was all but ready to go to a ball.

And dance.

She had not been out to dance anywhere in more than six years. And she had never owned or worn a gown as lovely as this in all the years of her life. She felt like a princess . . . a queen. She smoothed her hands over the lemon-cream satin stomacher of the gown Vivian had sent to her and hoped Connal would be pleased with what he saw—no, rather, would be proud to have her with him at the ball.

Just as she would be proud to be on his arm. It might not be tonight, it might not be next year, but one day the rest of the world would see Connal Delaney the way she did. They would look beyond his reputation and see the man within.

The same soft shade of yellow damask shot with pistachio made up the skirt of the gown. Pistachio Alencon lace created the flounces on the skirt and the lower third of the pagoda sleeves. Because the bodice not only had a stomacher but was whale-boned, she had no need of a corset. The gown's low bodice was off the shoulder and offered her no chance of wearing a chemise. She had never worn anything like it. Although she knew she was covered by the gown, she couldn't help feeling just the tiniest bit . . . decadent . . . to be fully dressed and yet wearing so few layers. At least the bodice was lined so it wouldn't itch against her bare skin.

They returned late from the fair so there was no time for Vivian's maid to do more than give Bethany a few tips. She rather liked her hair swept up on both sides of her head with nosegays of creamy-white Boronia tucked in just over each ear.

A soft knock on the door. Her heart leapt. Was it Connal?

"*Isean*, the carriage is here, but before we go I need yer help."

She opened the door.

"I need ye to pin this brooch right here." Bridget pointed to her bosom. There was a gap between the second and third buttons. "This will fix the problem, but everyone will know."

"Come in for just a minute. I think I can fix you right up." She rummaged in her satchel, pulling the contents out willy-nilly until she found a length of black Chantilly lace. Looping the lace over her aunt's shoulders she crossed it in place, tucked in the ends and placed the brooch in just the right spot to hold it all together.

She passed Bridget the hand mirror. After holding it at various angles to view the full effect, Bridget smiled. "This is just the thing. It looks like this is all part of the dress design. Thank ye."

"You are quite welcome. I am just glad I packed that lace. All those years of having to scrimp and make do have made me very creative and always prepared."

"Indeed?" Bridget's gaze fixed on the items Bethany had emptied from her satchel.

Bethany followed Bridget's gaze to the pile on the bed. On the top was Connal's vest. Heat crept across her cheeks. Even though she had been innocently asleep last night, and he had entered her room by mistake, she would have gladly let him stay.

Bridget's smile as she met Bethany's gaze erased any lingering doubt about how her aunt felt about Connal. "I'm glad ye both seem ta have found yer . . . fresh eyes . . . I believe is how ye put it that night. I wish ye both well."

"The carriage is here." Jack's call from the foot of the stair had them grabbing for their reticules and lace gloves before Bethany had time to comment, but knowing that her aunt supported her meant the world.

The closed carriage James had provided as transportation for the ladies had been quite cramped, what with the width of their skirts and petticoats. The gentlemen had ridden over on horseback. Their conversation in the jostling coach had been limited, given the loud creaking of the equipment and the need to pay attention to keep from squashing their hair against the sides as it swayed from the ruts in the road. Bethany had started to feel positively green from the motion by the time they arrived and sought refuge inside.

"You look . . . quite lovely in that gown, Beth."

Was there a hint of pique in Vivian's tone? The three ladies handed over their wraps to a maid, then proceeded into the retiring room and shook the wrinkles from their gowns.

"Doesn't she just?" Bridget all but gushed with enthusiasm. "Although the seamstress had quite a time with all the excess material provided when it first arrived. Betsey did a fine job taking it all and fitting it to Bethany's more delicate proportions."

As much to save her aunt from becoming a target in return as to save Vivian, Bethany suggested, "Aunt Bridget, would you go ahead and find the gentlemen? We can all meet up by that pot of lilies by the entrance."

"Of course, *isean*. I will see you both outside."

The strains of the orchestra and the hubbub of voices pushed into the room as she opened the door and then closed it behind her. For the moment Vivian and Bethany were alone.

"Eh-sheen?" Vivian asked as Bridget exited.

"Little bird. It is a pet name she has called me since childhood."

"It suits you." Vivian reached out and stroked Bethany's skirts. "As does this dress. I really fell in love with this material, but the color did not show to advantage on me, at least not as advantageous as I liked when I was helping my late husband at these sorts of events. I am sure Connal must be gratified at the impact you will make tonight."

"Thank you, Vivian. For both the compliment and the gown. You certainly look exceptionally lovely tonight. No matter the shade, blues become you."

Bethany could sincerely say that. Tonight, Vivian's sky blue gown with its bared shoulders showed the almost-ethereal white of her skin to perfection. Her ebony hair and the black lace of the gown highlighted her striking coloring.

"I know Connal is grateful to both you and James for everything you have done to make this trip a success. True friends are rare in life. I had hoped to find a quiet moment to add my thanks to his tonight."

The door opened as another group of women came in to shed their outer garments and repair any damage to their costumes or coiffures.

"Enough girl talk." High color rode Vivian's cheekbones as though she did not quite know how to react to Bethany's gratitude. "Let us join the gentlemen, shall we?"

Connal, Jack, Bridget and James were clustered by the entrance next to the large porcelain vase full of lilies. Bethany's heart did that little flip she was rapidly beginning to expect whenever she caught sight of Connal. As he conversed with his friend he looked tall and straight and darkly handsome in a way that distinguished him from any other man in the room.

James Carey's thoughtfulness and generosity in the friendship he extended Connal was truly remarkable. She would have to try harder for Connal's sake to set aside both her misgivings where Vivian Brown was concerned and the niggling doubt that bit her occasionally about James himself. She knew all that he gave to Connal in their friendship, but she had a hard time understanding what it was he got from the connection.

"You look . . . You look . . . amazing," Connal said as he seemed to drink in the sight of her after he and James threaded their way through the throngs of beautifully dressed partygoers to reach Vivian and her.

"I quite agree." James's gaze, however, was fixed on his cousin. For a moment, there was a decidedly uncousin-like light in the depths of his gaze as he looked at Vivian before turning his attention to Bethany. "You are a vision."

"I beg your pardon, gentlemen." Clement and Thaddeus Sawyer's approach forestalled any further greeting. "But these ladies promised us both dances and the orchestra is about to strike a quadrille."

Bethany caught the briefest of exchanges between Vivian and James, before Vivian gave Thaddeus a huge smile in greeting and accepted his arm. "How charming to see you so soon after our arrival," she gushed. "Have you met my cousin, Mr. Carey?"

"Yes, we met earlier in the day. How do you do

again, sir. And Delaney." Thaddeus shook James's hand and offered Connal a nod.

"Pray, take good care of Mrs. Brown. She is quite my favorite connection," James said to Thaddeus and then turned his attention to Vivian. "I will find you after this dance set, Vivian. Enjoy yourself."

Thaddeus and Vivian turned and disappeared into the throng.

"It is a pleasure to see you again, Mrs. Delaney. You look very fetching tonight." Clement Sawyer bowed over her hand. The sincerity in his voice brought heat to her cheeks.

"She does indeed," Connal agreed. "And how are you this evening, sir?"

"Still interested in that stallion of yours," Clement answered honestly.

"Teagan is still not for sale. Not for any price." This exchange had all the earmarks of good-natured ground-testing between competitors, one rife with mutual respect. Or so it seemed to Bethany as the two men shook hands.

"Everything has a price, wouldn't you agree, Mr. Carey?"

James's gaze lingered still on the path Vivian and Thaddeus were taking toward the dance floor in the next room. He seemed to pull himself with effort back to this room. "Yes? Price? Yes, I believe just about anything can be obtained if you strike the right bargain, find the price that makes the loss to the seller bearable."

Was it her, or did James seem a little preoccupied tonight? He certainly held himself tense, as if suppressing energy.

"May I also claim my dance now, my dear?"

She realized Clement was addressing her and turned her attention to him.

"I am afraid Mrs. Delaney promised me the first dance, sir. I promise we will seek you out the moment she is free."

"I will count the minutes," Clement said with a twinkle in his eye. "And I am still anxious to continue our conversation over your breeding scheme, Mr. Delaney. It sounds extraordinarily similar to the results I am looking for myself."

"Well, you are in luck. Mr. Carey is almost as familiar with my plans as I am, wouldn't you say, James?"

"Even more so," James agreed pleasantly enough, any tension no longer in evidence. It must have been her own nerves that made her see them in James. "Perhaps I can be of service while Connal goes off to enjoy himself."

Connal started. "I could always—"

"Nonsense." Both James and Clement spoke as one.

"I was jesting with you. I would like to pursue a conversation with Mr. Sawyer," James said.

"And I am sure there is much to be gained by discussing things from Mr. Carey's vantage and then talking to you later."

"Well, I am glad that is settled." Bethany was torn between amusement and chagrin. After all, she had barely been consulted and had not given voice to her preference even if her preference was to spend a few minutes in Connal's arms.

The three of them had the grace to look startled, either because they really had forgotten she was there or because her agreement had never been an issue to them.

"I would love to accept your gracious invitation to dance, Mr. Delaney."

He took the hint and offered her his arm. "Would you care to dance, Mrs. Delaney?"

"Yes, thank you." She took his elbow with a smile that included both Clement and James and they set off through the crowd, cutting along the edge of the dance floor as the last of the sets were assembling.

Just as they reached a set of outer doors, the orchestra leader struck the warning note that the ball was going to begin.

"Connal, we are going to miss the opening measure."

He pulled her outdoors. "Not if we choose to dance out here."

Relief cascaded through her. For his sake she had been trying to hold her fears at bay over attending such a large event and having to dance in public. He stopped and caught her to him. "Unless you mind being alone out here with me? Would you prefer to go back inside?"

The scent of windblown grass and Connal filled her as she took a deep breath. His eyes sparkled in the light from the lamps hanging from strategically placed poles throughout the grounds. With his hands on her arms and the warmth of his body so close she could think of nowhere she wanted to be more than right here with him.

"I am content to have my dance here." She would be content just to stand here with him, for that matter.

He looked around them. She noticed several

gentlemen enjoying their cigar or cheroot and eyeing them with keen interest.

"Not here." He looked around a little more. "We need a little more privacy, I believe."

"Yes." She hoped there would be a kiss or two involved with the dancing if they could find a discreet location. There were several lamplit paths leading off through the terraced gardens.

"How about that way?" She nodded in the direction of a path with a tall hedge that led toward a pond. A pagoda-style gazebo glittered on the edge of the water.

Connal's gaze lingered on her lips and for a second she thought he meant to kiss her here and now, for all the world to see, with the orchestra playing just feet away and a crush of people to witness. That would do little to separate him from his reputation. She forced herself to step back out of his hands.

"I would love a closer look at the lights reflecting on the water, Mr. Delaney. You may either escort me or not." That might convince anyone who cared that he was merely trying to save her from herself rather than carry her off into the darkness.

She took the path on her own with Connal hard on her heels.

"Thank you." He took her arm again. "You are much better at discretion than I am. I had not thought how it might look to have The Wicked One dragging a woman off into the darkness. All I could think about was a few minutes alone with you."

His thanks warmed her, but his last statement set her on fire. She had ached for moments like this for what seemed an eternity. Now, here he was, his arm linked with hers. Contentment was too tame for what she felt, especially because she always wanted more, but she felt more complete because he was here and that was novel and oh-so satisfying.

They rounded a corner and for a moment the hedges hid them from the view of the partygoers. He pulled her into his arms and pressed a hot, hungry kiss to her lips. With his hands on her bared shoulders and his mouth on hers all thought scattered. She only knew she wanted more, she wanted him closer.

She wanted him.

Footsteps on the path ahead forced them apart. She struggled for breath, for some scrap of conversation to still the raging protest screaming through her at the interruption.

"How did your business go today?" she managed.

"Good. Phenomenally good."

His answer was halting, husky. The fact that he was having a hard time talking pleased her all out of proportion.

"There are a number of men interested enough to be planning to come to Glenmeade over the next months. I have hope for the future. For our future."

A couple strolling up from the pond passed them. The woman had her arm twined intimately with the gentleman's and she seemed absorbed in her own world. The man managed a mumbled "Good evening" as they passed.

Had she heard Connal right? *Our* future? Did he mean that in a general, Glenmeade way, or in a more personal way? He quickened their pace until they reached the pond at last. Folding chairs were grouped at the water's edge, but it was the gazebo that drew her attention.

"I imagine this is going to be a popular spot as the night progresses, but we should have it to ourselves for a while yet," he said as they stepped up onto the platform that held it. "I need to talk to you."

"Just talk?" Bethany tilted her head to one side and looked up at him with a smile.

"For now," he answered with obvious effort as they stepped inside the gazebo.

The slatted shutters had been lowered, leaving the interior completely closed off, especially when Connal shut the solid panel door behind them. Twin lanterns hung from hooks on either side of the small room lined with benches that met the shutters to form the exterior walls. Bethany realized this in the scant seconds before Connal pulled her into his arms for another shattering kiss.

Several minutes later, although, in truth, she lost track of time, Connal pulled away from her. They were both breathing raggedly. Connal drew a deep breath. His eyes searched her face. Did her need for him show in her eyes? If he would just take her back into her arms at this moment, kiss her, make love to her—impossible as that might seem—she swore she could not ask for more. They stood frozen for more than a few seconds.

"We need to talk," he said again finally. "I had hoped to wait until we got home. But I cannot."

"All right." She nodded. Talk was the last thing she wanted from this man right now, throngs of partygoers in the distance be damned. He, here, was all that mattered to her. "Go ahead."

"Do you want to sit?" He gestured toward the benches.

"No. Go ahead." Get to the point, she screamed inside, her nerves rising.

He took a deep breath. His gaze stayed focused on her. "I have not been totally honest with you, Bethany. Not about Glenmeade. About what I did."

This did not sound good. She held her breath, a knot forming in her stomach. No matter where this went she was determined to face it head-on.

"God, you are so beautiful," he said.

The compliment only tightened the knot as he struggled with himself to go on.

"Years ago, after Finn left and I had gone, too, Uncle Brennan fell pretty deeply in debt. Gambling, poor investments. The amount was huge and the pressure probably brought on his stroke. That is when Jack came for me. I had been living pretty wildly in Dublin."

She held her peace, the tension thickening as she waited for him to get to the point. His gaze remained fixed on her face.

"James arranged for a group of investors, speculators, who agreed to hold off collecting the debt until I had raised the money through working the Stables and making them profitable once again. It took years, but I finally had almost the full amount, plus interest."

Connal stopped, closed his eyes and inhaled deeply. When he opened his eyes again and puffed out a breath, his expression was grim. She resisted the urge to reach out and try to smooth some of the furrows from his brow.

"Then I got the news about Finn's death. There was no listing of you, or Ross. Glenmeade was mine alone," he continued. "And James found a notice about the Cleveland Bays up for sale. He knew acquiring even one was my dream to try to breed stronger hunters, a whole herd of mares with a stallion in his prime seemed too good an opportunity to miss. I gambled with what I thought was just my future. The construction, purchasing the Bays, all came out of the nest egg I had set by to pay off the investors. They knew I was assuming a big risk with their money, with my future, but they seemed to agree it was worth it."

He took a step closer. He grasped her elbows. "Are you able to follow all this? I know it is a great deal to take in."

"I understand," she answered as her stomach swirled. "Then we arrived and that changed things for you. Is that why you have been so worried?"

He nodded. "The risk of the new horses, the debts already owed, are mine, but I am only a part-owner of Glenmeade now, and so the risk for the investors is too great and they want their money."

Her stomach swirled again and then tightened into a knot. "Cannot the other owner, could not Ross, accept part of the risk?"

"Not until his inheritance is settled, until a guardian is named officially to oversee his interests. The delay throws the arrangements, the risks I took, into question."

He must hate her. Perhaps not in an active way. But somewhere in his deepest recesses resentment must be brewing for all the troubles her arrival had caused. The ground tilted beneath her feet. "I am so sorry."

"No. Never say that. I will never be sorry you came to Ireland in search of a family. Because you found one. You found me." His grip on her elbows tightened.

"That is why I wanted to talk to you alone. To tell you, to thank you. I think we . . . the Stables . . . have turned the corner. This trip made all the difference for the Stables, just as you have made all the difference to me."

"What?" She wasn't following him.

"Despite the mix-up in the map, this has been a very successful experience. The contacts I made, the deals that are in the offing, bargains struck, should make it possible for me to pay the debts and keep Glenmeade's future intact. I owe it all to you."

"But James—"

"James smoothed the way, but you made it necessary for me to come here, to be successful, and you made it possible for me to believe I could face the awkwardness of all the gossip in order to achieve my dreams. You have made it all worthwhile. Thank you."

Perplexed, she just looked at him. She had caused him all this trouble, all the anxiety, endangered his deepest desire—and he was thanking her?

"Say you will forgive me and make me the happiest of men."

"Why would I forgive you for being successful?" He must be exhausted from all the work. He wasn't thinking straight. Yet he certainly didn't smell like he had been drinking.

"Nay, my love. I need you to forgive me for not being totally honest. For keeping this from you. I did not want you to have to worry about your future. If this had not worked out, James and I had a contingency plan."

"What was that?" She couldn't help asking.

A small shadow crossed his features, immediately making her regret the question. He squared his shoulders. "Proposing marriage to Vivian Brown."

It was a good thing he still held her, she nearly tripped over that revelation. "You would have married Vivian to save Glenmeade?"

As beautiful as Vivian Brown was it was hard to see this plan as a hardship for any man.

"Not so much Glenmeade as your future, Ross's future. You lost everything once because of the mistakes Finn made. I hated the thought of you losing your security again. This time because of my mistakes. Thankfully it will not come to that."

She must be daft because the way it sounded to her, the man she loved had been willing to marry somebody else in order to secure her future. Despite the topsy-turvyness of that possibility she found it to be the most romantic of gestures. Tears welled.

"Marry me, Bethany," he was saying. "Marry me, make my world complete."

"Yes." Her agreement welled from deep inside. This was what she wanted, to spend her days with him, to spend her nights.

He kissed her then, pulling her close. She wrapped her arms around him, welcoming the soft scratch of his wool against the tender skin above her bodice as proof this was not a dream.

He poured all his pent-up passion, his triumph, into this kiss, tasting her lips, teasing her tongue, holding her oh so close.

She moaned against his lips when his hand brushed against the fabric across her breasts. She wanted to feel his hands on her. To have him stroke and tease and caress her body just as his mouth was kissing and nibbling and exploring her mouth.

"Unlace me," she whispered against his temple as he kissed his way along her throat.

He didn't need a second invitation. His fingers fumbled with the ties at the back of her dress for a moment, then her dress slipped away from her skin. He dipped his hand into her bodice and drew her breasts up and out, squeezing and fondling them, one in each hand while his lips claimed her once again.

His attentions made her moan, over and over as his tongue teased hers and his hands kneaded her. She reached down and rubbed the palm of her hand along the length of the erection straining against his trousers, cupping him. He moaned in response.

She tore her mouth away. "Make love to me, Connal. Take me now."

His face searched hers. He looked wildly around the gazebo for a moment. Scooping her into his arms he carried her over to the door. If he meant to carry her off into the darkness with her gown's bodice drooped down to her elbows and her breasts exposed, she was not going to say no. Her need for this man was that overpowering.

He rammed home the bolt on the door and locked them in, then set her down. He stood there, looking at her, his eyes glittering darkly in the lamplight.

"Don't move," he growled. He quickly doused the lights and rejoined her.

"You are mine, Bethany," he said from the darkness.

"And you are mine, Connal," she agreed.

He took her in his arms then, kissing her fiercely. She thought she would expire on the spot if she did not feel him inside her sooner than now.

His hands fondled her breasts again, rolling the nipples in his fingers, caressing their firmness. He released her lips and stooped enough to kiss first one breast, then the other. He drew the sensitive tip of one into his mouth and suckled her vigorously. She pushed against his shoulders for balance as his attentions had her squirming and he backed her against the smooth painted door. The door was so cool while the rest of her was steaming.

"Pull up your skirts." His voice was husky with desire. She knew just how he felt and complied while he released himself. "When I pick you up, wrap your legs around my hips."

In less than a heartbeat he had her under her arms and up in the air. With her back against the door and her legs loosely around him he sought the slit in her pantalettes and guided himself into her.

"Oh, my," she managed as he pushed into her, filling her. She was so ready for him.

His arms wrapped around her waist, hers around his shoulders, and then he began to move with long, deep thrusts.

His lips suckled her breast as he pumped up, up, up. Reaching deep into her as he loved her.

He loved her—Those words pumped through her thoughts, through her heart. Held up in his arms like this as he loved her she felt free, like she was flying. She squeezed her legs tight around his hips and buried her face in his shoulder so his jacket muffled her cries of ecstasy as she floated away and he followed her, filling her as he climaxed.

They stayed locked together panting for some time. How long she had no idea. She just knew she had never been happier.

"God," he said as he finally set her on her feet and they both rested against the door. "I could die today and know I am the luckiest of men."

He looked at her sharply in the gloom of the darkened gazebo. "You did say yes? You will marry me?"

She laughed and stretched up to kiss him. Several minutes later she answered. "Yes, Connal Delaney. I will marry you."

She smoothed her skirts. "Now, please help me tie my laces. We need to get back to the ball before we hand anyone more scandal to chew on. Besides, I believe Mr. Sawyer is still waiting to claim his dance."

Connal caught her to him. "Just a few turns on the dance floor, that's all. No going outdoors with anyone but me."

"Yes, my love."

Chapter Eighteen

James paced the confines of the small gazebo he had adopted as his meeting place for the evening. Now that the time had finally come—the culmination of his plans—excitement and dread tore at his gut.

There has to be more, James.

Vivian's warning filtered through his mind. In fact he could not seem to forget the look on her face as she had spoken to him. In that one moment, she looked like the same Vivian he had always known and yet . . . And yet in some way he was seeing both the sleeping woman he longed to protect and the vivacious vixen he longed to bed.

His gut twisted tighter. His hands fisted at his side. Damnation. Now was not the time for anything to occupy his thoughts other than the destruction of the Delaneys. Not even a distraction as delectable as Vivian.

There has to be more. Her words echoed.

Perhaps it was this *more* she was seeking through her sudden friendship with Thaddeus Sawyer, the

American horse breeder he had practically had to pry off her a few moments ago. Did she have some intuition about his intentions, some thought that she might need a new nest to fly to soon? He should be grateful, but the thought of her . . . of her . . . Jealousy was an unwelcome distraction at the best of times. Tonight it was but another obstacle he would easily overcome to gain his vengeance. Pity, remorse, forgiveness, regret . . . all were obstacles he had already conquered. He would manage this one as well.

He thudded his fist against the gazebo's latticed wall. The shutters remained closed to gain some privacy from all but the most curious of eyes. Located at the far end of the lake from the ball, there was little chance anyone would disturb him tonight. The frivolities and the champagne flowed too heavily back at the house. He could not allow rampant emotionalism to hold sway in his thoughts. Friendship and history were tools to be used. No doubt or scruple would prevent him from putting the final nail in Connal's proverbial coffin, now that the time had actually come.

And if a wayward celebrant discovered The Wicked One receiving a measure of well-deserved humiliation, so much the better.

Footsteps sounded on the path behind him. Vivian opened the door for Bethany Delaney.

A wave of calm washed over him. He could do this. He *would* do this, for Rosleen, as he had planned. The punch he would deliver was a different one than he had planned, but much more painful. He watched Bethany's face as she realized who was waiting for her.

Finn's diminutive wife, Connal's lover. His wife-to-be. All in one delectable package perfectly designed to be the weapon of his enemy's coup de grace.

Who would have known she would become the key through which he would achieve his final revenge? Worry marked her brow and twisted her hands together as she made her way toward him, leaving Vivian behind in the doorway.

"What is it, James? What has happened?" Her hand touched his arm. "Is it Connal?"

It was all there in her wide blue eyes, plain for the world to see. She loved Connal Delaney, as she had demonstrated all-too eagerly only a little while earlier. The sounds of the two of them locked in an embrace, their bodies moving together, heedless of their surroundings or any who might be listening, echoed in the back of his mind. Grimly he hoped Connal had enjoyed the act, because it was the last time he would have the chance with this woman.

James covered her hand with his and drew her farther away from the door Vivian guarded. Vivian frowned at him, but he ignored her displeasure. He wished he could have taken the time to convince her of the rightness of his plan. He could, and would, make many things up to her later. Now was not the time.

"Please, James, tell me what has happened."

"Oh, sweet Bethany. You are so correct in your fears. Connal is in trouble."

"What kind of trouble?"

This was it, right here, the culmination of his long road to bring the Delaney family up to the table to pay their debt.

He stepped with her to the far wall of the gazebo. The frown on Vivian's face tightened; she held herself as still as Bethany. There was nothing he could do to protect Vivian from the blow he was about to deliver. In time she would come to terms with what he was about to do, and eventually understand he had no choices left.

"Glenmeade Stables, Connal, is deeply in debt."

Bethany's brow furrowed. "Yes, yes, I was aware of that. Connal told me——"

"He cannot have told you the whole of it, my dear."

"What do you mean?"

"Even Connal is not aware of the true state of his indebtedness. Only that there is a debt and it has come due."

"Please, James, speak plainly. I do not understand you."

"I will tell you the whole of it." He took Bethany's bared shoulders in his hands, appreciating her softness despite the tense, unhappy look on Vivian's lovely features. "Brennan Delaney gambled his way into the debt hanging over Glenmeade Stables. Connal believes the debt is owed to a group of rather . . . patient . . . investors. Men once willing to wait for their investment to prosper, to see his business expand until such time as he is able to pay them for their largesse. In truth, such is not the case."

"What do you mean?"

"There is no investor's group. Connal owes his financial debt to one man."

"You?" She was every bit as quick as Vivian had said.

He snatched a glance in Vivian's direction, and enjoyed the brief satisfaction of her raised eyebrow, before turning his gaze back to Bethany.

"Aye."

"But . . . You are his friend. Did you not assume Brennan's debt to aid—"

"I have been Connal's good friend all these years, through all the trials life offered us. But he betrayed that trust a long time ago, that betrayal made him my enemy. He has much to answer for, much to pay for, as did your husband. It has taken me a very long time to work this through to its conclusion. But here we are."

"Betrayal . . . conclusion?" Confusion and then dismay flitted over Bethany's features. " . . . Rosleen . . ."

"Aye." He nodded, pleased she had so easily fit the pieces together. If even Connal's beloved could place him at fault for Rosleen, how could there be any question of why his punishment needed to be extensive?

"You?"

"Do not fret about the details, my dear. Suffice it to say that you are right. Connal, and Finn before him, owed a debt to my sister. To my entire family. Rather than exact payment in kind in a large amount, I have dogged their lives. Turning their efforts to dust, destroying their dreams. But the time has come for the final redemption for Connal."

He felt her tremble beneath his fingers, but she did not back away from him. "How?"

"That is completely up to you, Bethany. You may choose the final direction of Connal Delaney's punishment."

"And I make this choice in what way?"

"Why Finn thought so little of you is beyond me. You have far more fire and determination than he ever gave you credit for. Your coming to Ireland, so much sooner than I had planned, made things a bit murky at first, but they have smoothed out since then. But I digress, you must choose—Connal can either lose Glenmeade Stables altogether or he can lose you forever. The choice is yours."

"Mine?" Color flared over her cheeks as she shook her head in denial. "But—"

"I know how things are between you. Your . . . time . . . in this very spot earlier this evening was perhaps not the most discrete decision you could have made. But it cemented your worthiness as a cudgel against him."

Fresh color stained her cheeks a deeper shade, heightening the vivid blue of her eyes.

"Ultimately you will either see him lose the Stables through foreclosure or you will see him suffer the loss of yourself. Watch him lose his home, his stables and everything he has worked for—or remove yourself permanently from his care and keeping . . . and marry me."

Vivian's gasp carried across the gazebo to lodge uncomfortably in his middle. Her heated gaze tore at him, rife with pain, and questions he could not answer. In the next moment she was gone into the night with a swish of skirts.

"Marry you?" Bethany broke from his grasp. "I will do no such thing."

"Then you damn Connal Delaney to lose the one thing he has spent his life protecting . . ." He gritted the words out, angered out of all proportion.

"—the Stables." Horror clung to Bethany's tone and paled her lovely skin still further.

"Aye. Glenmeade Stables. Finn lost them when he went running off to America. Connal will lose them when I foreclose." He tamped back the emotions roiling in his middle. He could not give in to any of it. Not now. He was committed. He would complete this. "He can spend the rest of his days with the horses he loves and the nights thinking about you in my bed."

"No."

"The choice is yours, my dear. He loses the Stables or you. Either one works for me."

He stroked the back of his hand along her glistening cheek, trying hard to picture her in Vivian's place and realizing he would be paying a price as well. And Vivian? Vivian was, if nothing else, a survivor.

Connal traversed the ballroom floor for the fifth time in as many minutes. He had lost sight of Bethany after her dance with elderly Clement Sawyer. Now that gentleman was deep in conversation with a dedicated group of Turf Club members and she was nowhere to be seen.

Bridget signaled him. "Have ye seen Bethany? She went ta fetch a glass of punch. Then I saw her leaving with that Mrs. Brown."

Certainly spending extra time with Vivian was not what she needed. Not when she had promised the rest of the night to him. Especially when they had planned on sharing their happy news with Bridget and Jack. "I will find her. Pray, do not fret."

He rounded the floor one last time and spotted

Vivian just beyond a small group of revelers. She looked pale and distracted. He had never seen the vivacious Vivian appear so lost and colorless. He crossed to her side, tension knotting his stomach. Something was very wrong.

"Vivian, are you all right?"

"James . . ." She leaned against Connal's arm. Her cheeks held the sheen of tears.

"Has something happened to James? Where did you leave Bethany?"

She didn't answer.

"*Vivian.*" He enunciated her name very clearly. "Answer me."

Her dazed expression cleared and she locked her gaze with his. "He is back there. With her."

Something in her tone, flat and lifeless, tightened the knot in his stomach still further. "Show me."

"It will do no good. He has waited too long and he wants this more than . . . more than anything else. I thought . . ."

"Vivian, take me to them *now.*"

She looked at him for a moment longer, her light blue eyes scanning his face, and then she nodded. "Very well, come with me."

She led him away from the ballroom and down the path he and Bethany had used earlier, out through the gardens and down to the gazebo by the pond. She paused beside the gazebo. "In here. Be ready. You will not like what you encounter."

He frowned, already reaching for the door latch. It lifted easily beneath his hand. He opened the door. The gazebo was empty. Fear stabbed him.

"No." Vivian's face paled still further.

"Where *are* they?"

"I do not know. They were . . . Oh, Connal . . ."

He gripped her shoulders and held her fast. "You had best start telling me exactly what is going on here and right now."

"I . . . I . . . I am not James's cousin. And he . . . He is not your friend, Connal. At least he is not what you believe him to be."

"What are you talking about? Of course James is my friend."

"He . . . James . . . He holds you responsible for the death of his sister. He always has."

"Rosleen?" Not again. He was not going to lose Bethany to the misery Finn began so long ago. He could not believe James meant her any harm. Vivian must be mistaken or telling some twisted tale.

"James holds you just as responsible as he always held poor Finn."

Something in the way she said his name . . . "You knew Finn?"

She nodded. "Yes, I knew him very well. He was like you in appearance, though you look much younger, the excessive drinking aged him, I think. But he . . . He was a sad man. Leaving Ireland broke him on the inside where no one but he could see."

Her succinct summation of his cousin burned a quick path through Connal's soul. He did not have time to ponder Finn's remorse or what his deeds might have cost him. "Tell me what James is planning. Why take it out on Bethany after all these years?"

She had to be wrong. Jealous. Confused.

"He . . . did not tell me everything, but he plans

to crush you at all costs, to either ruin you by marrying the woman you love—"

"Did you say *marry?* James is planning to marry Bethany?" Like hell.

Fresh tears streamed down Vivian's face. "—or through the loan arrangements for your business. That loan he controls. He made Bethany choose between Glenmeade and you."

Her face was pinched as she said the last.

James made Bethany choose? Oh, God. Ice water sluiced through him. They had made love in this very spot not more than an hour ago. She'd accepted him as her husband and then been forced to take it all back and accept any sacrifice to prove her love, precisely because he had been willing to do exactly the same thing. He knew it to his very core.

He turned away from the memories and pulled Vivian out of the small building with him. He was going to put a stop to this.

"Where are they now?" He'd lost one woman he loved because he did not act quickly enough. He would not lose another.

"I have no idea. They were here only moments before you found me. If they have left already . . ."

"Come with me." He secured Vivian's elbow firmly in his grasp and hurried back up the path.

So James was his banker. The pieces fit together with a solid click. The timing, the offers—all had come through James—and he'd never given it enough thought to wonder why. What a fool. A fool whose eagerness for profit was even now putting the woman he loved in jeopardy.

The path split, one direction continuing on to

the ball, the way they had just traversed without spotting James or Bethany, and the other to the grounds holding the carriages and horses for the guests even now celebrating the successes at today's fair. James and Bethany couldn't be far. They just couldn't.

The night sky seemed dull. The air flat. He raced to the carriages, dragging Vivian with him. He had to get to Bethany. He would not allow James or anyone else to ever again force her into anything she did not want.

He was not . . . gentle. Bethany's pales features as she'd made her confession of Finn's mistreatment echoed through him, making him grit his teeth and quicken his pace. If James had hurt her in any way he would pay. Nothing the man had done to him or to Finn or to Glenmeade would compare to his abusing Bethany.

Vivian panted along at his side, her skirts hiked in her hands.

They broke through the line of birches lining the long, curved drive of the Irish Turf Club to the long row of carriages and gigs. Movement down the row caught his attention. He released Vivian and ran.

"James! Stop!"

"Connal!"

Bethany's scream, hope and fear mingled together, tore at him.

"Go back!"

"Listen to her, Connal. She is coming with me. Her choice. She will be my wife come morning."

"No, she will not."

Vivian caught up to him, passed him by. "James—"

"Be silent, you have done enough already just bringing him here." Anger hissed from James as he faced his *cousin*.

"This is between the two of us," Connal told him. "Bethany has nothing to do with this, with us, with Rosleen."

James took a step closer to the carriage. Light from its lantern flashed dully against the derringer in his hand. Fear tightened Connal's gut. He had a gun. He would shoot Bethany. Dear God!

"Let her go, James, for the love of God."

"No." James pushed her into the carriage and slammed the door. "I am not going to kill her, Connal, so stay your fears. She is going to marry me. I will not mistreat the mother of my children, but if she is unhappy with her choice, that will be fitting payment for what she has done."

Bethany looked out the carriage window, her face pale, but she held her peace. James must have threatened her, scared her into silence.

"What has she done to you? What did she do to Rose?"

"She bore Finn's son. Gave him something he should not have had. Not after what he did to Rose."

Thoughts Connal had echoed himself on more than one occasion. But this . . .

"You know how I felt about Finn and what he did to Rose. To us all." Connal managed the words through gritted teeth.

"Aye, I know only too well how you feel about your dear departed cousin. I was the one who had to listen to your sorrows all these years. Swallow everything you needed to get off your chest and never say anything about what I was planning or how much I hated you for what you did to my sister."

Listening to the pain-filled venom in James's voice tore at Connal. He had been so wrapped up in his own memories, his own torments—over what had happened between Rose and Finn, over the resultant effects on his own life—he had taken everything James had ever told him at face value. And he had been grateful, *grateful* for his friend's understanding. And all the while . . .

What a fool he had been. What a fool he was still.

"I loved her." The wound that had never truly healed broke open again. "She knew that. So did Finn."

"Then you should look at my marriage to Bethany as my means of rescuing her."

"How so?"

"Your love did nothing for Rosleen. When she was at her very lowest ebb, when she needed your help, you turned her away." Pain and anger vibrated through James's words. "Finn abused her body, *you* abused her soul. I left her to your care and you abandoned her like garbage at the side of the road."

The weight of James's words fell like hammer blows.

"No."

"*Aye.*"

"I loved her, James. I loved her. I would have cared for her despite her affair with Finn." Connal straightened his shoulders as the words came out of his mouth. The truth he had kept inside all this time because it would have sounded too self-serving.

But nothing would be too humiliating to say or do at this point, if it would end with him keeping Bethany safe.

"Rose and I argued in the first flush of anger and betrayal. We never had the chance to make any decisions. I would have come to accept the child, to love them both. I needed to see Finn first, to make sure he would leave us alone to find our way when I got the summons to return to Oak Bend."

James's mouth was a grim line. "You have a debt to be paid, my friend, and I swore on Rose's very grave to see it done."

The derringer in his hand leveled toward Connal.

"You know I loved her, James. I have carried her pain all these years."

"Then join her."

"No!" Bethany's voice cracked. She tried to open the carriage door, but James shouldered it shut.

"James, no!" Vivian gasped.

James leveled the gun higher.

Connal calculated the distance between them and his options, given their proximity to the two women. There was nowhere to turn that didn't endanger them further.

"James—"

"Good-bye, Connal. Perhaps we'll meet again on the other side."

"No!!" both women screamed at the same time.

Connal braced himself. A flurry of movement behind him culminated in Vivian's pushing in front of him. Jasmine and cinnamon overwhelmed him as she plastered herself against him. He tried to pry her away, but she would not budge.

"Vivian, get away—" Connal told her.

"Stop, James!" Tears sparkled on her cheeks. "This cannot be what your sister would have wanted from you. For either of you."

"Get out of the way, Vivian."

"No. Do you not see?" She was trembling against Connal, but her grip on him was tighter than a leech. "She loved Connal. She wouldn't want him to be punished like he has been, let alone for you to murder him. Finn betrayed you all, and he has already paid full measure for his misdeeds."

"He died too easily."

Vivian shuddered. "Oh, no, it was not easy. You were not there. You did not see what happened. You did not hear his words or know his regrets. *I* did."

So that was her connection to his cousin, Connal realized. She had been there at his death. How much more twisted up could their lives get?

She gulped in a quick breath. "He lost everything he held dear when he left Ireland. His father, his cousin, the Stables that had been his life. He carried misery and shame with him and they were his constant companions. I never knew why until you told me. But I recognized his pain just the same. He died filled with regret, with Rose's name on his lips and a faraway look in his eyes."

"Get . . . out . . . of . . . the . . . way." James enunciated very slowly, but there was a tremor in the hand holding the gun.

"I love you, James. And they"—her nod encompassed Connal and Bethany—"are in love as well. You will sacrifice our happiness in order to fulfill a bitter revenge of pain and misery that cannot possibly have been the desire of the girl you described to me. Rosleen was loved by all who knew her. That is what you told me. If you truly meant that—"

"Love will not bring my sister back. Connal loves Glenmeade. He loves Bethany. He cannot have both. He should not have either. And he cannot have you, Vivian. Not for a shield, not for an advocate. You need to be at my side—"

He took a step forward and stumbled.

"No!" Bethany lunged from behind James as the gun fired. Pain lanced Connal and knocked him backward as Vivian's scream echoed in his ears. The ground thudded against his back. His mind spun.

"Connal!" The urgent sound of his name came from several sources at once, Bethany, Vivian and . . . James.

In a moment the three of them surrounded him. Bethany's hand grasped his. And James . . .

"Connal, I . . . I . . ." James's throat worked and his face was stricken. "I . . . shot you . . . and I didn't mean to miss."

"Hush now." Vivian kissed his cheek.

Despite the fire throbbing in his left temple Connal struggled to sit upright. Bethany sidled against him to support him with her body. He was going to have one hell of a headache, but he was quite certain he was going to live.

"I never meant to hurt Rosleen." He managed the words steadily. "You know that, have known it for the past ten years. I never lied to you about any of my feelings for her, for Finn or for what happened. You are my friend, James, you always have been. If you still seek vengeance, then leave it between you and me. Leave Bethany and Ross and Vivian out of this whole sorry mess. If the Stables are the pound of flesh you demand, so be it."

"Oh, Connal." Bethany's fingers shook against his neck.

James's face was white with shock. A shudder rippled through him and he hung his head gulping in deep breaths like a man drowning.

At last he looked back at Connal, pain clear in his pale eyes. "No, Connal, Vivian is right. I just did not want to listen to her. I have sought vengeance long I could think of nothing else. My search for vengeance has done nothing but . . . poison my life and . . . the lives of those around me. Perhaps that was the true redemption I was looking for. I have always felt that I failed Rose. Failed her by my absence in her life when she needed me the most. In pursuing vengeance I have been absent from my own life as well. I cannot fix that or any of the past by hurting you more."

"James." Vivian's voice held tears.

Having James finally confront the past lying between them lessened the burden Connal had carried. Beneath it all, James was still James and they had been friends for way too long. He held out his hands and waited. In a moment James's hand took his.

"I will settle the debt on Glenmeade with you at your earliest convenience. I can sell the Bays. And I had a fairly substantial offer for Teagan. Now that I have someone to build a future with I do not need to be in such a hurry. We have time."

"A lifetime."

Bethany agreed so readily it warmed his heart.

"Stop, Connal." James interrupted him, his face tense with some internal struggle. "You can more than settle the debt on Glenmeade if the contacts I made today are true and hold true."

"They will hold true. I have a list of your contacts I would have reworked down the road, but today and where I am concerned, they are solid."

"Settle when you can, Connal. The debt and the purpose it served are pieces of the past I need to leave in the past. We begin anew from here."

"Agreed." They clasped hands once more.

Then James turned his attention to Vivian and drew her to her feet. In moments he had kissed her in a way that left no doubts about her ever having been his cousin.

"You are a very wise woman," he told her. "And if you will have me, I would humbly offer myself as your husband."

"Accepted," she told him softly before turning her gaze toward Bethany.

He felt Bethany's fingers tighten at his shoulders. She had heard everything Vivian had said to James just as clearly as he had. She knew.

"Bethany Delaney, I wronged you in your marriage," Vivian said from the shelter of James's arms. "That I did not know you is my only excuse. I cannot repay—"

"You did nothing that had not been done before, Vivian."

Bethany's tone was strong. Connal's chest swelled with pride despite the pain throbbing in his skull.

"I . . . I thank you for answering questions about his death I have not been able to discover on my own."

Vivian nodded.

James nodded once more to Connal and then turned away with Vivian at his side.

"I knew." Bethany's voice was softer at his ear. "I knew there was something . . . odd . . . about her story. Her husband was the man who shot Finn after finding him in her bed."

"Aye." He turned to face her.

"Oh." Her face crumpled at the sight of his wound.

"I am sure this looks far worse than it is. James never was a very good shot."

"Do not jest." Tears sparkled in her eyes. "I was afraid I would lose you before . . . before . . ."

"You did not." He caught her chin in his hand and tipped her face up to his. "And I did not lose you. I love you, Bethany Doyle Delaney. More than I thought it possible to love anyone. I want you in my arms and in my life for the rest of my days."

"Oh, yes." She sighed against his mouth as he kissed her and tasted the wealth of love and passion dwelling within her petite frame.

"And James?" She took his handkerchief and dabbed carefully at the wound on his temple.

He hissed in a breath. "James has nursed his wounds for a very long time. He did not possess the strength you have."

"Strength?"

"Aye, my love. You have more strength in you than you know. You survived Finn's mistreatment and managed to love me despite our similarities. You have already forgiven Vivian for her trespass in your life and you are willing to forgive James. I can see that in your eyes."

She smiled at him. "They have both had their share of pain. I know what it is to have Finn Delaney in your life. He gave many people pain. Rose, you, his father, Vivian and James, Ross, we have all been victimized by a man who lost his life so miserably there at the end. We can choose to harbor those pains and resentments or we can move on. I simply chose the latter."

He kissed her again, marveling deep in his soul that she had become his.

It was sometime later that Jack and Bridget found them.

After a quick flurry of explanations, Jack laughed as he helped Connal up onto the cart. "So that is how The Wicked One finished the night the first time he goes out to a social event in a decade, getting shot."

"Oh." Bethany smiled. "The Douglas sisters will be so pleased."

He looked at her. "What?"

"Seems they were counting on a scandalous tale or two to share with their friends after hosting The Wicked One."

"By all means let us help them raise their stature with their friends. Marry me as quickly as we can arrange it," he whispered.

"With unseemly haste?" She laughed.

"Aye, I have been The Wicked One for so long, it will surprise no one and only help me live up to my reputation."

"I will marry you at any time, in any church you can arrange. I love you, Connal Delaney."

Her words rang in his ears as he pulled her closer. What more could a man ask for?

Epilogue

Glenmeade Stables
County Kildare, Ireland
Spring 1860

"She says they will not be back until he has shown her every inch of Rome." With a sparkle in her eyes Bethany looked up from the letter she was reading.

Connal leaned down, unable to resist stealing a kiss as warmth spread through his chest. Sometimes it still awed and amazed him to have this woman at his side and to know she would be there with him no matter what the future might bring.

He spread his hands down over the swell of her belly. Another new Delaney grew within her, ready to bring even more light and love into his life.

"They will need to return soon."

"Yes." She laughed against his mouth.

He couldn't help smiling back. If anyone had ever told him he would find the laugh of a pregnant woman erotic, he would have offered the poor, misguided soul another drink and a ride home after.

"She also volunteered that Jack already told her they would need to be home before the next Delaney lad comes calling." Her hand linked with his across her stomach. "I wonder why he assumes the next will be a boy."

Laughter rolled toward them from the general direction of the stable yard. Four boys raced past in varying sizes from Ross down to Christian and disappeared around the corner.

"And what else could our babe be?" he asked. "Careys have girls, my love. You and I?" He kissed her again. "We make boys."

"Someday, Connal Delaney, those Carey girls may lead our Delaney lads on a merry chase."

"Aye." He shook his head, enjoying the soft feel of her hair beneath his chin as he held her. "Vivian and James's eldest is already eyeing young Matthew and both of them are barely out of the nursery."

"If she has her mother's vivacious nature and her father's cool head for planning, Matt will have a need for caution. But I think we have a few years yet." She leaned up and kissed his cheek. "Bridget says she and Jack should return within the next few weeks. They'll be here in plenty of time."

"Good . . . I never thought to have this."

"What?"

"Children, a family, a woman to share my life, I never thought to have you."

She turned up to him and looped her arms fully around his. Cinnamon and vanilla, her scent, flowed around him as she kissed him, slow and satisfying.

"I told you, you were not The Wicked One. You deserve everything you have and more."

"Mmmmm, perhaps you could show me this . . . more you speak of."

"Are you asking me to dance, sir? I thought I danced the legs right out from under you just last night."

"Oh, I believe I could use another lesson. I am not sure I got the steps just right."

"Come with me, sir, and I will show you any step you could possibly want. We'll just keep practicing until you get it right."

He pulled her close as his heart swelled. He was already there. But he would tell her that later and spend the rest of his life loving her with everything he had to give.

"I love you, Bethany Doyle Delaney."

Her eyes sparkled at him, soft and glowing, and all for him.

"I know." She told him.

About the Author

Elizabeth Keys is the pseudonym for Mary Lou Frank and Susan C. Stevenson—lifelong friends and award-winning writing partners. They both grew up in southern New Jersey and continue to live there with their families.

Susan is vice president of a bank and Mary Lou works as a grant-writing consultant for local non-profit agencies. Between them they have two husbands, seven children, and assorted dogs and cats, who fill their lives with love and laughter. They create the kind of stories they love best: stories about achieving your heart's desire through love's special magic.

They are members of New Jersey Romance Writers and Romance Writers of America. Nominees for RWA's prestigious RITA Award, they have also been honored by *Affaire de Coeur* magazine for Best Up and Coming Author, Best Foreign Historical, and Best Historical Works.

Look for information on upcoming releases on their website, www.elizabethkeys.com.